Enamored with a Scarred Duke

HISTORICAL REGENCY ROMANCE NOVEL

Sally Forbes

Copyright © 2024 by Sally Forbes
All Rights Reserved.
This book may not be reproduced or transmitted in any form without the written permission of the publisher. In no way is it legal to reproduce, duplicate, or transmit any part of this document in either electronic means or in printed format. Recording of this publication is strictly prohibited and any storage of this document is not allowed unless with written permission from the publisher.

Table of Contents

Prologue 3
Chapter One 12
Chapter Two 20
Chapter Three 27
Chapter Four 34
Chapter Five 42
Chapter Six 50
Chapter Seven 56
Chapter Eight 64
Chapter Nine 73
Chapter Ten 80
Chapter Eleven 87
Chapter Twelve 94
Chapter Thirteen 101
Chapter Fourteen 108
Chapter Fifteen 114
Chapter Sixteen 120
Chapter Seventeen 126
Chapter Eighteen 133
Chapter Nineteen 140
Chapter Twenty 147
Chapter Twenty-One 151
Chapter Twenty-Two 158
Chapter Twenty-Three 165
Chapter Twenty-Four 169
Chapter Twenty-Five 174
Epilogue 182
Extended Epilogue 185

Prologue

The SS Seraphine, off the coast of Greece

"I say, Edmund, have a care! Have a care, you fool!"

Laughing, Edmund hopped down from the side of the ship, landing nimbly on the deck.

"You worry entirely too much, Charles."

Charles rolled his eyes and shook his head. "And you, my friend, don't worry at all. What if you'd fallen over the side?"

"I wouldn't." he replied confidently. "I have excellent balance, I can swim well, and besides, the sea is flat as a pancake. Look at it – not a ripple to be seen."

Charles was quite used to his position as the resident pessimist and pointed immediately to the gathering of iron-grey clouds on the horizon. "What do you call that, then?"

Edmund waved dismissively. "The captain isn't worried. Perhaps a storm would be an adventure. One last jaunt, before we set foot on English soil once again, and resume our dull, boring lives."

There was a brief pause, and Edmund grimaced, shooting an apologetic look at Charles.

"Forgive me, I forgot about your father. That was a careless thing to say. I know you have a tragic reason for cutting short our Grand Tour."

Charles forced a quick smile, then averted his gaze, staring at the horizon. The sea and sky were so blue that it was hard to tell when one ended and the other began. It was true, they'd seen the most remarkable sights during their travels, and part of him ached at the thought of never travelling again.

Still, he hoped against hope to make it home before it was too late. His younger brother and his new sister-in-law were there, as was his mother, but the idea of never seeing his father again made Charles feel sick.

Or perhaps that was just the motion of the boat.

"Mother has high hopes that Father can hold on until I return." Charles said. It felt strange to talk about his father in that way. He shifted his position, resting his elbows on the side of the ship where Edmund had so recently been balancing. The wind was getting up, making the rigging slap against the masts.

Edmund leaned on the side next to him, nudging his shoulder.

"Your father adores you; you know. It will be good to return to such an adoring family. I myself will only be greeted by my cousin; I think. She was thrilled to hear that I was returning early."

Charles sighed, biting his lip. "Whether Father recovers or not, one thing is certain – he can't run the estates for much longer. I'll need to become Lord Northwood, in reality if not in name. It's a great deal of responsibility. Mother will worry – you know how she is – and of course there'll be William, hanging over my shoulder, convinced that he could do better than me." Charles snorted. "Sometimes I do wish he'd been born the older son. After all, he's the one settling down, with a nice wife and a pleasant home."

"You can't think like that." Edmund said firmly. "You simply can't. There will always be petty jealousies and small issues in even the most loving family. William cares for you, I know he does, even if he does envy your position. Trust him a little more, why don't you?"

Charles ran a hand through his hair, the black curls disarranged from the sea breeze. He wasn't even wearing a cravat. Society would be shocked to see him now. He grinned at his companion, and Edmund grinned back, nudging his shoulder against Charles'.

They hadn't been friends for more than a year or two, but Edmund had a habit of diving deep into a friendship. Charles felt as if they'd known each other all their lives. It was pleasant to have a companion to travel with, and it was nice to have Edmund to himself. When they returned, they would be expected to seek out wives. Edmund, as the more handsome of the two – glossy chestnut locks, bright green eyes, and a square, well-featured face – would be immediately snapped by some eager heiress and her mamma.

Charles, on the other hand, often felt out of place in London Society. Oh, it wasn't that he was not well liked – he was often complimented on his wit, and he was good-looking enough to catch the eye of most young ladies – but he lacked the charm and sincerity which seemed to come so easily to Edmund. He had it on good authority that at least three young ladies had all but broken their hearts upon learning that Edmund was leaving on a Grand Tour.

They made a remarkable pair – tall, athletic, well-favoured, and handsome in a way that did not contradict the other. Charles had large blue eyes to Edmund's green ones, and a pale, oval face. Charles had often been described in various scandal sheets as having a 'Puckish expression', whatever that meant.

"I don't want to go home." Charles found himself saying. Edmund laid a comforting hand on his shoulder.

"I know, I know. But once all is settled back home, if your father isn't on the cusp of death after all, perhaps we can travel again? Not so extensively, I suppose, but still."

"Perhaps." Charles said, not really believing it. A fresh gust of wind swept across the deck, making him blink. The air stung with salt, and the breeze was icy now where it had been warm before. Glancing up, he saw that the iron-grey clouds were creeping across the sky towards them, and the sea had lost its idyllic blue tint.

Sailors were dashing to and fro over the deck with growing urgency, and a feeling of dread began to pool in Charles' gut.

"I think we should go below." He said, just as the captain strode past them. The man faltered, seeming to see them for the first time.

"Good day, young gentlemen." He said, sounding breathless and distracted. "Looks like we're in for a patch of bad weather. Why not go below and return to your cabin? Might be best, I think."

Charles swallowed, feeling light-headed with panic. On their travels, they'd been remarkably lucky – no real storms. Even the light tossing of the sea had made him sick at first, and he didn't dare imagine what it would be like to experience a real storm.

Edmund, however, seemed almost gleeful. He nudged Charles in the side, beaming.

"A bit of luck at last, eh? A proper storm."

Charles glared at him. "Are you mad? Do you actually think you're going to enjoy this?"

"Oh, no, of course not. It's going to be truly awful. However, think of the stories we'll have to tell when we return. We'll be heroes."

"We'll be seasick!"

"Oh, stuff." Edmund said firmly, leading the way towards the hatches which led below deck. "It'll be an adventure."

***

It was not an adventure.

Charles' stomach heaved in tandem with the heaving of their cabin room. He could swear at times the room was almost on its side.

The cabin was designed for storms, and everything was more or less bolted down and set firmly in place. Everything except Charles and Edmund, of course.

Charles had tried to lie down in his narrow bunk, but that only made the sickness worse. He desperately wanted a breath of fresh air, but that was impossible, of course. There was a bucket set by in case he vomited, but Charles very much did not want to be sick. He suspected that the bucket would overturn with the heaving of the ship, and that would only make things worse.

Edmund, who also looked rather green, perched on the edge of his bunk, bracing his fists on his knees, and watched Charles anxiously.

"You don't look well. Do you want me to take you to the doctor?"

"And what would he do? There isn't a great deal you can do for seasickness."

"He might give you a sedative."

Charles considered this. There was something pleasant in the idea of going to sleep and waking up when the sea was calm again.

"Alright." He conceded. "Let's go carefully, though."

The two men staggered around the lower decks as if they were drunk. The ship lurched and rolled from side to side, plunging into deep troughs of waves and then climbing just as steeply up the other side. It all combined to make it impossible to walk in a straight line, or to stay upright for very long at all.

They passed one of the hatches which led up onto the deck, and Edmund paused.

"Don't you want to have a peek?" he whispered.

Charles glowered at him. "No, I do not! It's dangerous!"

"It's dangerous to go up there, certainly. But just taking a peek won't do much, will it? Imagine how powerful a storm might be, out here on the open sea. We are truly at the mercy of nature, aren't we?"

Charles groaned. "Is that meant to be reassuring?"

"Not particularly. Look, you can stay down here, but I'm just going to poke my head up and have a look."

There was no point arguing. Charles sighed and shrugged, bracing himself on the ladder-steps while Edmund climbed up. They were forced to pause and duck their heads as some salt-water came pouring in, then Edmund continued on his climb. As promised, he barely poked his head above the hatch, and Charles heard him suck in a breath.

Abruptly, he darted back down, face white and eyes wide.

"Jonny McCurtain is about to be washed overboard!" he gasped.

Charles felt sicker than ever. Jonny McCurtain was a young sailor, one who'd come aboard at the same time they had – albeit to work instead of paying for his passage – and they'd struck up a sort of friendship.

Before he knew what he was doing, Charles was climbing the ladder beside Edmund, boots slipping on the slick wooden steps. He peered above the hatch entrance, and his breath was immediately taken away by the wind.

The deck sloshed with water, and more waves were splashing over the sides at every moment. The ship rocked and heaved, and the grey sea seemed to rise up on all sides.

Then he saw Jonny, where he seemed to have fallen from the rigging. He was clinging onto the side of the ship, only his arms, head, and shoulders visible. His face was bone-white, his hair plastered to his head, and his mouth was moving. Shouting for help, no doubt, cries that no one could hear. With another great wave, he'd be swept off into the sea.

Charles cupped his hands to his mouth and bellowed for help, until his throat was sore.

No answer.

"We have to go up there and help him." Edmund shouted, pitching his voice above the roar of the sea. "There's no time to lose."

Fear and dread coiled in Charles' stomach. "Can't we fetch help?"

"There's no time! Look, you can stay below if you like, but I'm going to try and help him."

Without waiting for an answer, Edmund propelled himself up the final few steps and onto the deck. Cursing to himself, Charles followed.

It was a thousand times worse on deck. The wind nearly pushed him off his feet, forcing him to bow his head against the driving rain, and he was soaked to the skin in seconds. The deck was slick, and he lost his footing more than once.

Edmund was just ahead, forcing his way on towards the side of the ship. Jonny had seen them approaching, and a spark of hope lit itself in his eyes.

Beyond him, Charles saw a huge trough of water opening up, and the prow of the ship dipped horribly.

We'll never do it, he thought, bile rising in his throat. *We'll never haul him back to safety and get back below deck before that wave hits.*

They reached the side, and Jonny grabbed feebly at them with numb, ice-cold hands. Charles hauled on one arm and Edmund the other, and together, inch by slow inch, they lifted him up over the side. The three men collapsed onto the deck, gasping for air, salt-laced water stinging their eyes. Then Charles looked up and saw the wave hovering above them and heard shouts of alarm and shrieks from the men up on masts, still hanging onto the rigging.

"Hold on!" Charles heard himself scream, grabbing for a pile of half-torn rigging left on the deck.

Then the wave crashed down on them.

The seconds stretched into hours. Charles could have sworn that he was underwater, that the ship was scuppered for good, and they were all dead. If it hadn't been for his hand tangling in the rigging, a knot tightening hard enough around his wrist to cut off the feeling in the limb, he would have been swept overboard.

Then, just as abruptly as it had come, the water receded, the ship bounced up out of the sea like something irrepressible, and Charles gasped for breath. He found himself sprawled on the deck, tangled in the ropes, and Jonny was nearby, hanging onto something, eyes closed, shivering.

They'd been spotted, and a few sailors came running towards them.

The feeling of dread in Charles' stomach sickened to acid.

"Edmund? Edmund!" he screamed, wrenching his hand free of the rigging, not caring how the rough rope grated against his skin. "*Edmund!*"

The storm was not over, not by a long shot. When Charles leaned over the side of the ship and peered into the roiling grey waves, the ship all but dropped out from underneath him.

He saw Edmund at once.

He'd been washed overboard and was being carried further away with every passing moment. Somebody screamed, *Man Overboard*. And Charles was only faintly surprised to realize that it was him.

The captain was at his side in a second, soaked to the skin.

"He's lost." He said, his voice hoarse. "We can't turn the ship around."

"Let me go." Charles burst out desperately.

"You'll drown."

"I can swim!"

"In this water, it doesn't matter. We haven't seen the last of those huge waves, my lad."

Charles reached out, grabbing his shoulders. "Please, let me go."

"I'll not lose you both, lad."

"Tie a rope around my waist. I'll dive in and get him, and you can haul him back in."

The captain deliberated for a second.

"Very well." He said at last. "But on your head be it."

They produced a long length of rope, tying it around Charles' waist tightly enough to pinch the skin. He stripped down to his breeches and shirt, leaving his fine coat and expensive boots crumpled carelessly on the deck. Waves still struck the sides of the ship, making the whole structure shudder, but the waves were not crashing over the deck anymore.

Not yet, at least.

Climbing up on the side, Charles gave himself no time to think. He dived in, the icy coldness of the water hitting him like a physical pain.

The captain had been right about the sea. Charles considered himself a strong swimmer, but he was no match for the sea. Not at all.

He managed to keep himself mostly afloat, pulling himself through the water in a desperate front crawl, the rope around his waist heavy and reassuring at the same time.

He saw Edmund in a trough of waves, just a glittering chestnut head above the waves. Charles shouted his name, and Edmund, clearly at the end of his strength, tried to pull himself towards him.

Just a little closer, Charles thought, a flicker of hope starting up inside him for the first time.

The two men got close enough to see each other, and Charles saw Edmund flash that quick, easy smile that charmed so many people.

"Take my hand, Edmund!" Charles shouted. "They'll pull us both in!"

Edmund stretched out his arm. He was breathing raggedly and shaking with cold, eyes red and sore from the salt water. The waves were peaking around them again, the water roiling around them as if it were angry that they were there. Charles reached out for his friend, feeling their cold-numbed fingers touch.

"I've got you, Ed." Charles rasped.

Then a wave came crashing down on their heads, so heavy it felt like a house falling on them. Charles was pushed deep under the water, and Edmund's hand was torn away from him, he turned somersaults, helpless against the currents and roiling waves, and was sure that he was going to drown.

The rope around his waist tightened, hauling him backward through the water. Charles shouted under the water, swallowing mouthfuls of salt water.

No, no, no, he screamed in his head. *It's too soon! I don't have Edmund!*

He flailed, tugging at the rope. If he could have undone the knot, he would have done so, and plunged back into the freezing waters and swam back out to find Edmund. He was out there; he was out there.

But the knot was too tight, tied by experienced sailors, and Charles was pulled through the water, helpless.

His back scraped against the side of the ship, and Charles was hauled above the water. It was slow and uncomfortable, as he hung like a dead-weight on the end of the rope, the knot cutting into his stomach. Another wave shook the ship, and Charles found himself thrown out into empty space, the grey skies above and the roiling grey waves underneath. He banged back against the ship, his body too numb to feel the impact.

He hit his head against something, which made his vision blur and his head pound immediately. The only sign that he'd been hurt was the hot blood trickling down the side of his face, leaving almost enjoyable trails of warmth. Charles wanted to lift a hand to his face to assess the damage, but his limbs wouldn't obey him anymore.

He couldn't breathe. The rope was too tight, his entire weight swinging from it. He could vaguely hear men above, chanting and heaving, hauling him up from certain death. Perhaps they thought they were pulling two men up on the end of the line, rather than just the one who'd gone in to try and save the first one.

Edmund. Oh, Edmund, I'm sorry.

He choked and spluttered, gasping for breath, grimacing against the pain. Slowly but surely, he was lifted above the surface of the water, until he was high enough for the sailors to grab him and haul him back to safety.

One of them was Jonny McCurtain, who looked deathly pale and truly miserable.

"Let me go, let me go!" Charles shouted, struggling. "I had him. I had him! I need to go back in. I need to save Edmund!"

The captain crouched before him, gripping Charles' upper arms hard enough for his fingers to dig in.

"It's too late, lad!" he shouted, above the din of the wind and roaring sea. "I saw it all. I saw him go under, and he didn't come up. I'm sorry."

"No, you don't understand! Let me go back, please!"

The captain's face crumpled. "I'm sorry, lad. He's gone. He's gone."

Chapter One

Two Years Later, The English Countryside

"Are you going to mope about here all day, or are you going to come outside? I'd rather like to have a snowball fight."

Lydia, who was currently sprawled on her back in the window seat in a most unladylike fashion, lifted her head to glare at her friend.

"No, Clara, I am not. I'm quite happy here. Don't you know what today is?"

Clara folded her arms and leaned against the library doorway. "I certainly do. I might not have known Edmund as well as you did, but I know that he wouldn't have wanted you to sit here and mourn for him like this. He'd want you to get up and *do* something."

Lydia propped herself up on her elbows, shading her eyes against the light streaming in through the window.

"Edmund loved to be the centre of attention. I think he'd rather like the idea of us all mourning him so intensely."

Her friend did not smile. "That is not amusing Lydia. Make some space, for I intend to take a seat."

Lydia obeyed, shuffling up to make room for Clara beside her.

The library was a large, well-favoured room, full of light and cheer. And, of course, full of books. There had been a remarkable collection of books when her father had inherited the title of Lord Pemshire as well as the Waverly estate, and they had at least doubled the collection. Lord and Lady Pemshire, as well as Lydia, their only daughter, were great readers and loved to collect books.

Clara picked up the book on the window seat, in which Lydia had carefully marked her place. She eyed the title and lifted her eyebrows.

"Mrs Radcliffe? Really?"

"I enjoy her stories." Lydia replied defensively. "I don't hold with all this anti-novel nonsense. Books are meant to be enjoyed."

"Well, far be it from me to say otherwise. Now, Lydia, we really must talk. The Season is starting next month."

"Not really." Lydia sighed. "Nobody will be in London until the end of February or the beginning of March at the earliest. Besides, I don't much fancy the Season. It'll be my second."

Clara pursed her lips, tossing back carefully arranged golden-brown ringlets. Clara's parents were tremendously rich, although they were simply Mr and Mrs Brown. *She* didn't care about that, but it was apparent that her parents hoped she would marry a titled gentleman. To that end, they dressed her in the finest, latest fashion, and did all they could to enhance her natural beauty.

Clara *was* a pretty young woman, although her freckles were the bane of her life. Lydia thought they were rather sweet. She was currently wearing a pink ruffled dress that looked horribly expensive, and a pair of fine silk pink slippers which were, by all accounts, pinching her toes.

She arranged herself and her voluminous skirts on the window seat, and tilted her head in a way which always proceeded a lengthy lecture.

"You can't go on like this, Lydia." Clara said at last. "Your last Season was a disaster."

Lydia sank back against the wall.

"I don't think it went *terribly*."

"You offended Lord Yates by refusing to dance with him and pretending to have a twisted ankle for the rest of the night. You spilled punch on Miss Travis' gown…"

"Not *deliberately*. Nobody can prove it was deliberate."

"… you said and did so many shocking things that you appeared in nearly every issue of the scandal sheets, including running through the gardens of Elmer House in the middle of the night to get to your carriage."

"I was trying to get away from a troublesome gentleman, you see."

Clara groaned. "That doesn't matter. Don't you *see*? You had so many proposals and suitors that you could still have been a success. But you never accepted any of them, and now you're starting your second Season with a cloud over your head. This isn't good, Lydia."

Lydia closed her eyes.

She'd been looking forward to her Season for years. She enjoyed parties, and dancing, and talking, and meeting new people. She knew she was lucky in that respect. Some ladies – Clara, for instance – were troubled with anxiety and shyness, and found the crowded balls and complex social mores to be nerve-wracking, more of an ordeal than anything else. For her part, Lydia enjoyed it. Every social situation was a puzzle, and she prided herself on always finding the answer.

But back then, she'd always imagined Edmund by her side. Lydia was an only child, and Edmund had always been her older brother in all but name, and he'd promised he would stay with her for her whole Season. They were going to open the first dance of her first ball together, and he would help her pick out dresses and jewels and suitors, and they would spend hours gossiping together.

If she hadn't made a single friend or a single conquest for the whole Season, Lydia wouldn't have minded, because she would have had her beloved Edmund.

But Edmund was at the bottom of the ocean. Dead. He'd promised to be with her for her first Season, and then he went ahead and died a year before she came of age. And her Season had been long and empty and dull, full of false people and parties that were so entirely pointless it was all Lydia could do not to scream and scream at the top of her voice.

"I was only eighteen then." Lydia said, as if being at the advanced age of nineteen years old would make such a big difference. "This year will be different, I'm sure."

Clara did not seem convinced, not in the slightest.

"You aren't happy." She said, and Lydia flinched.

"Not happy? Not *happy*? Look at my lovely house, with our fine gardens and extensive library. I'm young, pretty, and I have my whole life ahead of me. Why would I not be happy?"

That was something Lydia had said to herself, over and over again at all hours of the day and night.

Why am I not happy?

Her life was perfect. She knew she was lucky. She knew she was loved. She had plenty of Society acquaintances, but she had real friends too – Clara, for one, as well as Arabella, even though *she* was a married woman now and probably had no time for friends anymore, to say nothing of the rift developing swiftly between them.

There was no reason for Lydia to feel so lethargic and miserable, no reason at all.

If she could only convince herself that her life was a good one, perhaps the pressing sadness that crushed her into her bed every morning and evening would finally ease up, and she could go back to being the jaunty, talkative, cheerful Lydia Waverly.

Except, that was not quite true. She was rather good at *pretending* to be the old Lydia Waverly, and so far, people seemed content with the masquerade. Perhaps she was too good of an actor.

"I know you, Lydia." Clara said quietly. "I know you, and I know that you are finding life... *difficult* at the moment. The Season can be fun, but if you're already in low spirits..."

"I am *not* in low spirits!" Lydia snapped, a little too loudly.

There was a clearing of a throat by the doorway, and she felt colour rush to her cheeks.

The butler, a somber gentleman by the name of Turner, was standing in the doorway, his face polite and smooth. He was far too well-bred to display any change of emotion, anything to hint that he had overheard anything.

He would have done, of course. Turner seemed to know everything that went on in the house.

"What is it, Turner?" Lydia asked, rubbing her eyes. She was so tired. She slept badly these days. Lately, she'd found herself thinking about Edmund more than ever, wondering what it would feel like to drown. Had he been afraid, or frustrated, or simply resigned? They didn't even know what had happened, besides the fact that he had been swept overboard during a storm, and their efforts to rescue him had failed.

Turner looked almost sympathetic, and that grated on Lydia. She hated sympathy. Sympathy and pity were so terribly patronizing.

"Her Ladyship wishes to see you, Miss Waverly." Turner responded smoothly. "She is in the morning-room."

"Thank you, Turner. I'll be there in a moment."

Turner bowed in acknowledgement, and slipped out of the room, noiseless as always.

Lydia got to her feet, shaking out her skirts. Clara was watching her, an infuriating expression of sympathy in her eyes.

"Are you in trouble?"

"I doubt it." Lydia admitted. "I rarely am. You're staying for supper, aren't you, Clara?"

"I'll stay overnight, if you'll have me."

"Of course." Lydia hesitated, then darted down, wrapping an arm around Clara's shoulders and giving her a tight hug. "You know I love you, don't you? You're so very patient with your prickly friend."

Clara rolled her eyes, unsuccessfully hiding a smile. "Flattery will get you nowhere, you wretch. Go see what Lady Pemshire wants, and I'll wait here. I shall endeavour to engage with Mrs Radcliffe's literary works, I believe."

Lydia chuckled, flashing a smile. She hurried out of the library, glancing back over her shoulder to see Clara pick up the Radcliffe novel, opening it up to the first page.

There was a mirror outside in the hallway, just outside the morning-room, and Lydia gave her appearance a quick inspection. Lady Pemshire had once been a renowned beauty, and was still regal and beautiful despite her age, and she still placed a high value on beauty.

Lydia *was* beautiful, if a person cared much for that sort of thing. She had a perfect oval face, like her mother, with a pixie-like nose and delicate chin. She had green eyes and chestnut-brown curls, like Edmund. In fact, they had looked more like brother and sister than cousins.

Of late, however, Lydia's olive complexion was growing sallow, and there were dark circles under her eyes. She hoped that her mother would not notice.

As if she would be so lucky.

Sighing to herself, Lydia shook out her skirts one last time – blue silk, a little too fine for wearing around the house, but she *had* wanted an opportunity to wear this gown – and tapped on the door.

"Mama? It's me."

"Come in, dearest." Lady Pemshire responded.

Lydia stepped inside, blinking in the glare.

The morning room was the brightest room in the house. The huge windows looked out onto the front lawn, which was currently blanketed in snow, glittering vivid white.

It was a room designed for comfort rather than fashion, with a large writing desk in the corner, alongside another bookcase.

The Waverlys did love their books.

Lady Pemshire herself sat at the desk, resplendent in ochre satin, hair dressed as if she were leaving for a ball at any moment. She was exactly fifty-two years old, as Lydia had been born remarkably late in a very happy marriage. Her hair was black, streaked with grey, and she had the same large green eyes Lydia saw in her own face. She smiled at her daughter, gaze flicking up and down her form. The smile faded to a pursing of the lips.

"You seem tired, dearest. Are you sleeping well?"

"Quite well, Mama."

"Humph. You don't look like you've been sleeping well. Would you like a different mattress? More pillows? Fewer pillows? Sleep is very important, you know. As is eating enough. I don't hold with this latest fad of stick-thin beauties, not at all. I hope you're not trying to fit into one of those foolishly small corsets. Tiny waists are not *healthy*, darling."

Lydia threw herself into an armchair. "I know, Mama. I am eating well, don't worry."

Lady Pemshire did not look convinced. "I just want you to be in good looks for your Season, you know."

Lydia swallowed past a lump in her throat. "I'm not looking forward to my Season."

Lady Pemshire got to her feet, moving to perch on the arm of the chair.

"Why not, dearest?"

Lydia didn't look at her, preferring instead to pick at her fingernails. "It's not what I thought it would be. Not without Edmund."

Her mother flinched at his name. "Oh, my poor girl. You still miss him?"

Lydia glanced up at the huge, gilt-framed portrait on the wall, set high above the fireplace.

It was of Lord and Lady Pemshire, with Edmund and Lydia standing for all the world like the son and daughter of the house. It had been done years ago, when Lydia was only fifteen. She could hardly bring herself to look at her own face, bright and happy and full of promise, holding Edmund's hand like he was her brother.

She couldn't bring herself to look at Edmund at all.

"Of course I miss him." Lydia managed, swallowing hard. "I just need time, that's all. A little more time, I think."

Lady Pemshire nodded slowly; lips pursed. "Well, I have the very thing. I received a letter from Lady Fernwood only this morning."

Lydia flinched, sitting upright. "Arabella wrote? She wrote to *you*? Why not to me?" She gave herself a little shake. It would do no good to spiral into annoyance and jealousy. Arabella had wanted so desperately to get married; they all knew that. The three of them – Clara, Arabella, and Lydia – had all embarked on their first Season together, at eighteen years old, and they had all had very different goals.

Lydia had hoped to console herself after the loss of Edmund. Clara had hoped to find love and discover a little more confidence in herself.

Arabella had hoped to be married, to get away from her nagging parents and her bleak home life.

Out of the three of them, only Arabella had succeeded.

If it could be described as success, of course.

"What does she say, then?" Lydia made herself say, drawing in deep breaths.

"Well, as you know, her new husband – oh, what is his name? Lord Fernwood... ah, yes, Henry Fitzwilliam, that's it – has a home in Bath. Arabella writes to invite you to stay with her for a while. The Season isn't starting proper for months, so you have time. Here, read it."

She handed over the letter, and Lydia all but snatched it out of her mother's hand. Sure enough, it was addressed to Lady Pemshire, not to Lydia, and that was another little slight.

Arabella has decided that I am still a child, Lydia thought, with a thrill of anger. *She writes to my mother to ask permission for me to stay, as if I can't be trusted to make my own decisions. How dare she? We're the same age!*

It was the first *real* emotion she'd felt in quite a while.

"I don't want to see Arabella." Lydia responded sharply, thrusting back the letter.

Lady Pemshire blinked. "I thought you two were such friends. Clara has been invited – or, at least, I thought we could take her. We have a home in Bath, you know, although we seldom use it. I thought we could all go, so you don't have to stay with Arabella if you'd rather not. Although it would be rather rude to turn down an invitation. She hasn't been married for very long, and the first year can be... well, the less said about that, the better. I thought that Bath would be a little less overwhelming than London."

"I suppose I have to choose one or the other."

Lady Pemshire tilted her head, narrowing her eyes. "You are not at all yourself, Lydia. You haven't been for quite a while. I've been worried about you, you know. Nothing seems to give you joy. The matter at hand, my dearest, is that Edmund shall not return. Not ever."

Lydia flinched away, swallowing hard. "Mama..."

"I know it's awful to hear, and I know that you already know it, but knowing it is different from accepting it. You're letting your friends slip away, darling. Do you know why Arabella wrote to me, and not you? She said it in the letter. It's because you aren't responding to her correspondence. She's trying, darling, just like Clara is trying. You need more opportunities, and new scenery. Bath can do that for us, don't you see?"

Lydia swallowed again, wondering why her throat was suddenly so dry.

Perhaps her mother was right. There wasn't an inch of this house that wasn't full of memories of Edmund and her. The two of them playing hide and seek, reading books together in companionable silence, or even, more recently, planning Edmund's Grand Tour.

He'd been so excited, and Lydia was excited for him, even though her chest clenched at the thought of seeing him go.

"You should travel, Lyddie. You'd love travelling."

His voice echoed in her head, and she squeezed her eyes closed.

"Very well." Lydia said. "I'll go to Bath."

Chapter Two

Northwood Manor, Bath

Lord Northwood stood on a hill and looked over his estate. The crops were doing well this year, although of course it was too cold and the ground too hard to farm much. What they had planted, though, was promising.

Odd to think how long he'd spent dodging responsibility.

See what came of that.

Unconsciously, he lifted his hand to his face, where a scar ran from the corner of his right eye almost to the corner of his mouth. It was a nasty, jagged thing, vivid pink, the scar tissue raised and streaked with silver. The injury had been done on a wood splinter, the ship's surgeon had said, and he was lucky not to have been hurt much more. Lucky not to have lost an eye, or to have had half of his face carved away.

He didn't remember the pain of the injury happening, but he remembered the pain of it afterwards, as his flesh tried to heal itself.

And, of course, there was the pain of having failed.

"Charles?"

Charles flinched, glancing over his shoulder.

A young man stood there, a little portly, with a round, good-natured face, and the same black hair and blue eyes Charles had himself. He was around twenty-three, two years younger than his older brother.

"You're up early, William." Charles said. "It's barely dawn."

William shifted from foot to foot. "Well, Anne slept badly last night, so I got up early to give her a few hours of peace. You know how restless my sleep can be. I happened to see you walking out of the house, so I..." he trailed off, coughing awkwardly. "So I followed you."

Charles smiled mirthlessly. "And here you are. Well, I was just doing my rounds. I don't sleep well these days, so I've taken to getting up early and looking through the estate."

William nodded slowly. "Father used to do that; you know."

Charles swallowed hard. "I didn't know that, actually. I suppose I wouldn't, since I was never at home."

At one time, perhaps, William would have taken the opportunity to make a point here, lecturing Charles about his duty and various failings, and how he should be working harder to make their father's life easier.

Perhaps he was right, but it was too late now. He was grateful that William didn't feel the need to talk about that anymore. The past was the past, and couldn't be changed, no more than he could have swum any harder through the seas to reach his friend.

You should have done it. You failed.

William clapped Charles on the shoulder, making him jump. His younger brother cleared his throat awkwardly, fidgeting.

"I'm glad you're home, Charles. I know it... I know it has been a long road since you returned, and I know there's... I know there's been difficulties, but I'm glad that you are home."

He swallowed hard, trying to force down the lump in his throat.

"Thank you, Will. I know I haven't exactly been the best of older brothers, but I'm glad to be home. I'm glad I saw Father before he died. I honestly thought I wasn't going to have the chance to say goodbye."

There was a long silence between them after that. Charles opened his mouth to speak, but he felt as if he'd lost the motivation to do so. Words had once come easily to him, but no more.

The sun was rising above the horizon, streaking the sky in coils of pink, gold, and orange. It was beautiful. Snow lay ankle-deep, cleared away from the paths and other crucial areas, and it glittered in the oncoming dawn. Beautiful, really. Clean and crisp. A new day.

"Anne and I are having a child." William said, blurting it out.

Charles sucked in a breath and glanced sharply at him.

"Anne and you? Really?"

He lifted an eyebrow. "You seem surprised. We've been married for just over two years now."

"No, I just... well, congratulations. I'm glad for you, truly I am. I'm going to be an uncle. I can't believe it."

He forced a smile, draping an arm around William's shoulders. William beamed, seeming almost relieved.

"You're the first person we've told." He admitted. "We're telling Mother tonight, that's why we travelled down to stay tonight. I must say, I'm terrified. A child, at last."

"What are you hoping for? A boy or a girl?"

William pulled a face. "Frankly, I don't much care, so long as the birth goes smoothly and both Anne and the baby are well. I suppose I should want a boy, since then we'll have an heir. Of course, I'm sure you're going to get married soon and produce heirs of your own."

Charles grimaced. "You too, eh? As if it's not enough to have Mother nagging me about marriage constantly."

William pursed his lips. "She has a point, don't you think? You're Lord Northwood. You're twenty-five years old."

"I'm hardly ancient."

"No, of course not, but you really should be marrying soon. You've been home for two years, and never attended a single Season. You really should."

"I'm a little tired of hearing what I should be doing, William."

William backed away, lifting up his hands in surrender.

"I've learned not to tell you what to do, Charles. Believe me when I say I don't mean to nag you. I know that you know all this. But time is ticking by. You can't... can't live in the past forever."

"If you're trying to tell me to forget everything and forget Edmund, you're wasting your time." Charles said, a little more sharply than he'd intended.

At one time, William would have taken offence to his tone, and gone stalking off in a huff. Marriage and impending fatherhood had changed him, it seemed. He only smiled wryly, shaking his head as if Charles was a somewhat troublesome child.

He *felt* like a somewhat troublesome child, not the Duke of Northwood at all.

Before he could articulate any of these thoughts – if he ever *was* going to articulate them – William spoke up.

"Good Lord, it's freezing out here. I take it you're coming home for breakfast?"

"Well, I..."

"We'd better get going, then. Come on, let's go."

William slung an arm around Charles' shoulders and steered him away from the marvellous sunrise and towards the house.

"Let's go home." William whispered, and Charles wasn't sure who it was aimed at.

***

Northwood Manor was a fine house, a delight of architecture. There was something faintly Gothic about the place, with its swooping, cavernous ceilings, beautiful carvings, and highly polished marble floors.

It was still early in the morning, the sun scarcely above the horizon, and Charles knew that the servants would still be going about their business, getting the house ready for the day. His valet would likely still be eating his breakfast, so Charles decided to dress himself.

It seemed ridiculous to him, hiring a man to dress him like a doll. His valet, Robert, of course did much more than dress Charles. He managed his clothes, kept everything neat and organized, and so on. But when Charles and Edmund had travelled around the world, they'd left all servants and valets behind.

It had been freeing – so freeing.

But all good things came to an end, and Charles was back in his home, albeit as the master of the house rather than the eldest son.

He'd kept the same room, though. He let himself in, closing the door quietly so as not to disturb anyone. He pulled off his crumpled clothes absently, leaving them crumpled on the ground.

Robert was making him lazy. The tiny cabin Edmund and he had shared on that last, fateful journey was so small that they couldn't afford any untidiness at all.

He pulled out the pocket watch last of all.

It was a simple, silver design, heavy and sturdy, and reliable. On the inside was etched a message:

To Charles. Thank you for adventuring with me. Your Friend, Edmund.

There was a brief note attached, indicating that Edmund bought the watch as a gift for Charles upon their return from their Tour.

He'd found the watch in Edmund's things afterwards.

It felt oddly like thievery to take it, since it hadn't been given to him. Not yet at least. But neither could he put it back, since it was his friend's last gift to him. He was never without the watch, but oddly enough, he rarely used it to ascertain the time.

He sank down onto the edge of his bed, perfectly made and inviting since he hadn't slept that night. Dreams again.

He found himself back in the sea most nights, the bitter cold freezing him to the bone, his strength leeching out into the water.

There was nothing like a storm to make a man feel small. Small, helpless, and infinitely useless.

Closing his eyes, Charles let himself sag backwards onto the bed, enjoying the plush softness of the bed beneath him. It was still early. He might have a short nap before he went down to breakfast.

He wasn't very hungry, anyway.

***

"Are you busy, dearest?"

Charles, who was very busy, set down his pen and glanced up at the doorway, where his mother was hovering.

Her Grace, Josephine Everard, was the Dowager Duchess of Northwood, affectionately nicknamed The Dowager amongst her friends, was a petite, nervy sort of woman. She had often been overshadowed by her big, bluff husband, and without him, she seemed… well, diminished.

She wore black silk, fringed with lace and decorated with pearls, and tended to slip around the house in a rustle of taffeta and petticoats. Charles was vaguely aware that he should be a better son to his mother, more supportive, more thoughtful, and so on, but the lack of motivation which had overshadowed the past two years had extended to his mother, too.

"Of course not, Mother." Charles lied. "Do come in."

Josephine beamed and came shuffling into his study.

The study Charles used was not the one his father had used, which was a large, ornate room, impossible to heat but undeniably beautiful. Charles found it more practical to do his work near to the accounts room, a small room filled with ledgers and paperwork and all manner of dull information and was usually occupied by the estate steward. The room Charles had chosen was small, painted a dull shade of green and paneled with dark wood, and was large enough for a small sofa, a chair beside a coffee table, a small hearth, a bookcase, and a desk.

He was vaguely aware that his mother disagreed with this sort of modest room for the lord of the manor, but she hadn't voiced this opinion, so he was happy to live on in ignorant bliss.

He got uncertainly to his feet while Josephine decided where to sit. In the end, she chose the sofa, and delicately arranged her skirts. Charles sank back down into his own seat.

"What did you want to talk to me about, Mother?" Charles asked, as politely as he could.

Josephine pursed her lips, seeming to collect her thoughts.

"It's nice to have your brother and dear Anne here, isn't it?" she said abruptly. "It was a pity you couldn't join us for breakfast."

Charles flushed. "I must have gone back to sleep. I am sorry."

"Well, no matter. There's always luncheon. Charles, I have been thinking long and hard about something I need to speak to you about, and now seems like as good a time as ever."

She drew in a breath, straightening her spine. Charles laced his fingers together on the desk and waited patiently. He knew exactly what was coming.

"You must marry, Charles." Josephine said finally.

He sighed. "Mother, we've been through this. I am twenty-five years old. It's not as if I am past my prime by any measure. It isn't as if time is running out. Besides, there is William."

He was careful not to mention the baby. Relations between his brother and himself were already somewhat strained, and accidentally letting slip some important news would not help at all.

Josephine pressed her lips together in a white line.

"You are the heir, Charles. No, not the heir, what am I saying? You are the Duke of *Northwood*. It's your responsibility to marry and produce children. You are lucky that William is so duty-minded, marrying as young as he did. Perhaps if you had applied yourself to your duty earlier, he would have been able to enjoy his youth a little more. Perhaps he could have travelled, too. I'm sure he wanted to."

Charles flinched. This was not the first time that his mother had alluded to his failings. Even before he had left, there had been tensions. William was their mother's favourite child, and Charles was their father's. The favoritism had always been harmless, barely something to consider.

Until the old Duke fell ill, and it became clear that Charles would succeed him as Lord Northwood, and there was nothing anyone could do about that. Suddenly, his failings seemed even more glaring to his mother, and therefore to William. William's marriage was a mark in his favour, and Charles' refusal to marry quickly became a bone of contention in the family.

"I will marry one day, I'm sure, Mother." Charles responded, as calmly as he could. "In the meantime, perhaps William and Anne will have children."

"Yes, well, we can only hope. But *your* children are the ones who must succeed, Charles. Is the line of succession nothing to you? Oh, I'm not explaining this well. Your father would have been able to explain it very nicely, I'm sure."

Charles bit his lip, trying to compose his thoughts.

"I... I find it difficult to move in Society these days, Mother. The company of others tends to grate on me. The fault is my own, I'm sure, but the idea of crowded ballrooms and that endless, inane small talk... he trailed off, shuddering. "I can't face it, Mother. I just can't."

His tone had turned almost pleading, and Charles hated himself for sounding so weak. Where was the confident, charming young man he had once been? Where was the wit that Society had praised so highly?

His mother was unmoved. Josephine sniffed, fidgeting with the lace on her cuffs.

"The Season is not meant to be enjoyable, Charles." She said, her voice sharp. "It's designed to bring eligible ladies and gentlemen together and allow people to make necessary connections and acquaintances. Really, Charles, I think your attitude is the problem here. A little self-control, some determination, and you could manage quite nicely. I can function perfectly well in Society, you know. Your brother can manage it."

Charles was aware that his hands were clenching into fists, knuckles standing out white. He made himself relax his hands, composing himself before he replied.

"I appreciate your advice, Mother, as always. But I shan't be joining the Season this year, and I'm afraid that is the end of it."

Josephine's mouth tightened.

"I see. Well, I cannot *compel* you to do anything, Charles. But I am your mother, and I would like you to seriously contemplate marriage." She got to her feet, shaking out her skirts. The conversation was clearly drawing to a close.

"You are somewhat reclusive of late, Charles. Isolation does not make a man happy, and you may soon have cause to regret your decisions."

Without waiting for a response, she swept out of the room, closing the door behind her. That left Charles alone, a state he should be used to by now.

Alone, he thought grimly. *I'm going to be alone forever, aren't I?*

Chapter Three

One Week Later

"Wake up, Miss, we're nearly there."

Lydia jerked away, her forehead cold and sore from where it was pressing against the window of the carriage. She didn't remember falling asleep, but the shadows had lengthened since she last looked, and her neck ached terribly from the uncomfortable position she'd let herself sink into.

Her maid, Susan, was sitting opposite, hands folded neatly in her lap. She was a new hire, taken on especially to wait on Lydia when her Season began. Of course, Lydia had been far too languid and miserable after Edmund's death to get to know her new maid. She was embarrassed to admit that beyond Susan's name and age – twenty-five – she knew little to nothing about her.

The maid in question smiled kindly at her, tucking a stray strand of dull brown hair back under her old-fashioned mob cap.

"You must have needed your sleep, Miss." She remarked. "Look, you can see the house up on the hill there. It's very fine, if I may say so myself."

Stretching out cramped limbs, Lydia peered out of the window.

She'd never seen Arabella's new home before.

As promised, it was a remarkable sight. Fitzwilliam House – or Manor, or Lodge, or something like that – was set carefully on the peak of a hill with a steep drive wending its way up to it. The lush fields and hills of Bath spread out around it, some of them carefully manicured gardens, some fields, some left to run wild.

It was, of course, a large house. Arabella had excitedly described it to Lydia many times, in the heady, rushed weeks before the wedding. Her first letter, after the honeymoon had been completed, was full of descriptions of the house, how beautiful it was, how well arranged, how *opulent*.

The descriptions petered out sharply after that.

The carriage took a turn, the ground under the wheels turning from hard-packed dirt to well-raked gravel, and they began to climb. Already, the wind was buffeting the carriage, making it shake from side to side.

"Is it my imagination," Lydia remarked, "or is it getting colder?"

Susan shivered, drawing her shawl tighter around herself. "I think so, Miss. But this is a high hill."

Lydia smiled to herself, glad that the Fitzwilliam residence didn't look *Gothic* in any way. Perhaps a steady diet of Mrs Radcliffe's novels would fuel her imagination a little too much. She didn't want to spend the next few weeks jumping at every shadow and seeing menace around every corner.

She hadn't corresponded with Arabella since she accepted the invitation. Lydia had been very firm that *she* would write to her friend and accept, and not have her mother write on her behalf. Besides, Lady Pemshire was busy preparing to remove to their Bath home. Clara was coming soon.

Not soon enough, Lydia thought with a pang. She missed her friend. Who knew how Arabella might have changed?

The carriage began to slow, and Lydia started fidgeting with her skirts and shawl. It had been a long trip, and she was uncomfortably aware that she would look travel-stained and crumpled. Snatching up her bonnet – which she'd removed and discarded very early on in the journey – she just had time to tie it on firmly before the carriage rolled to a stop altogether.

They were in a large, circular, raked-gravel courtyard, in front of a set of smooth white marble steps, well-scrubbed. A pair of austere looking footmen in rather old-fashioned wigs and blue-and-gold livery came forward, opening the door.

Taking a deep breath, Lydia climbed out.

Remember, this is a fresh start, she told herself fiercely. *Edmund wouldn't want you to spend the rest of your life grieving for him.*

She had expected to see Arabella on the steps, but there was only a grim-looking butler, carefully overseeing things. Lydia stepped down onto the gravel, and Susan after her. The maid hastily melted away, busying herself with Lydia's bags and trunks which were lashed to the roof.

Lydia forced a smile at the butler. "Where is Ara – where is Lady Fernwood, if you please?"

"The Countess is in the drawing room, Miss Waverly. Would you like to change first?"

It wasn't really a question, more of a statement. Still, the unfortunate man shouldn't have phrased it as a question.

Lydia smiled serenely, handing over her bonnet and shawl.

"No, thank you. Tell me, which way to the drawing room?"

There was no time to pinch colour into her cheeks or arrange her hair, as the disapproving butler went ahead of her, pushing open the drawing room and blandly announcing her. There was nothing else but to go in after him.

She stepped into a cavernous room, far too large and cold to be a comfortable drawing room. It was immaculately decorated, expensively so, but the sofas looked overstuffed and uncomfortable, and the priceless antiques and art only made Lydia feel more stiff, terrified that she would break something.

In the middle of it all sat a familiar figure, glossy black hair pulled back in a simple and austere style that covered her ears, wearing grey silk with froths of lace at the cuffs.

Arabella glanced up at the sound of the door opening, and her eyes widened at the sight of Lydia. She leapt to her feet with a squeal.

"Oh, Lydia, *Lydia*!"

She flew across the room, and Lydia found herself wrapped tightly in her friend's arms, expensive lace tickling her cheek.

"I have missed you more than I can say." Arabella said, her voice muffled against Lydia's shoulder. "I was afraid you wouldn't accept my invitation. I thought you wouldn't come."

A lump rose to Lydia's throat. Had she truly been such a bad friend, that her dearest friend thought she no longer cared about her? She wrapped her arms around Arabella and squeezed tightly.

"Of course I was coming." She responded, voice a little wobbly. "I didn't stop to change, I came straight to see you."

Arabella pulled back, and her eyes were a little misty. "Well, I'm glad of it. Perkins, fetch tea, please, and see that Miss Waverly's things are settled in her room."

The butler, emanating disapproval, made a tight bow and disappeared, closing the door after him. Arabella sank back onto the overstuffed sofa and gestured for Lydia to sit beside her.

With the great expanse of Arabella's skirts, it was no easy task.

"So, tell me everything." Arabella said firmly. "What have I missed? Has the Season started?"

"Barely. Aren't you joining this year?"

Arabella pursed her lips. "No, Henry hates the Season. He has too much work to do, he says."

There was something tense about Arabella's tone when she mentioned her husband, and Lydia wisely decided not to press the issue.

"What do you think of this room?" she asked, before Lydia could come up with another subject matter.

Lydia swallowed hard, wondering how to be polite. She scanned the walls, thick with dark and unpleasant artwork, the blank eyes of countless sculptures staring down at them. There was a fire lit in the hearth, a large one, but the flames barely seemed to heat the room. Arabella's seat was close to the fire, and the only one that could feel the warmth, it seemed.

"It is very large." Lydia managed lamely. "Wouldn't you prefer a smaller room, just for yourself to sit in? Something cosier?"

Again, this seemed to be the wrong question.

"Henry's mother – the Dowager Countess Fernwood – always used this room as a drawing room. He won't have it changed." She responded curtly. "Truly, although the woman lives miles away in another house, sometimes it feels as though she is still here with us, watching everything I do."

Arabella bit her lip and looked away after this outburst, and Lydia dropped her gaze to her lap, twisting her fingers together.

Arabella had, according to the scandal sheets and other people's opinions, been the prettiest out of the three. They were remarked upon as pretty girls, but Arabella was a Society Beauty, whereas Lydia and Clara were merely pretty.

Arabella had glossy, jet-black hair that she used to painstakingly arrange into curls. She had the face of a doll, heart-shaped, with big blue eyes, long black lashes, perfect bow-shaped pink lips, and a strawberries-and-cream complexion.

She had had plenty of suitors, but the new Earl of Fernwood was by far the best match. So, she had accepted him. Arabella's excitement as the wedding drew closer left no room for worry – Lydia had never thought of them as ill-matched or marrying for more mercenary concerns other than affection.

So why did her friend look so pale and drawn? Why had the colour gone from her cheeks? Why, despite her shockingly expensive gown and jewels, did she look so miserable and dull?

"I... I take it you are not fond of your mother-in-law?" Lydia managed, and Arabella shot a quick, malicious smile.

"She's dreadful, and Henry *always* takes her side. But you haven't travelled all this way to talk about *her*. I have so much planned for us to do, starting with a ball tomorrow night! When is Clara coming? I long to see her, too."

Before Lydia could answer, the door creaked open, and a gentleman sidled in.

Lord Henry Fitzwilliam, Earl of Fernwood, was not generally considered a handsome man.

Or, as some matrons had said, his wealth and position had become his beauty, whatever that meant.

He was of average height, of a nervous disposition, and wore wire-rimmed spectacles over owlish grey eyes. He was about twenty-five years old and had the air of somebody constantly on the brink of a nervous collapse.

Lydia dreaded to think how he was coping with his newfound responsibilities as the Earl of Fernwood. His father had died a mere six months before the start of Lydia and her friends' first Season, and the brand-new earl had burst onto the social scene, keen to find a wife as quickly as possible.

And he had found Arabella. It had seemed like such a good match at the time.

"Miss Waverly, what a pleasure." Lord Fernwood said politely. "I trust you had a pleasant journey?"

"Yes, very pleasant. It is good to see you again, Lord Fernwood."

He twitched his nose nervously. "I'm sure you can call me Henry, seeing as you are to stay here as my wife's guest. Arabella was so tremendously excited about your visit. She has talked of nothing else."

There was a definite edge in his voice in the final sentence. Arabella's eyes snapped up.

"Well, perhaps I would not have been *quite* so excited if we ever entertained, Henry." She responded sweetly. Henry visibly stiffened, pressing his lips together.

Lydia, who had risen to her feet to greet Henry, froze, not sure where to look. Surely they weren't about to have a disagreement right here and now, in the middle of the drawing room, with a guest right there.

"I had better go and change." Lydia said brightly, keen to go before the butler returned with the tea tray and she was obliged to stay a little longer. "I will be down as soon as I can."

Arabella pouted. "Well, don't be long. I might come up and see you, to make sure everything is well in your room. I've assigned some of the maids to help you unpack."

Lydia bobbed a quick curtsey, receiving a stiff, awkward bow from Henry in return, and made her escape. As she closed the door behind her, she could hear Arabella's voice, shrill and angry:

"I do hope you're not going to spend the week scaring off my friend, Henry! Honestly, have you no manners at all?"

"I am trying my best, Arabella!" came Henry's harsh, angry voice. "What would you have me do?"

Lydia had no inclination to hear more and scuttled away towards the grand thickly carpeted staircase.

***

Sure enough, Arabella really had assigned half a dozen maids to help Lydia unpack. Poor Susan stood useless in the middle of the room, baffled and a little uncomfortable, while the maids whirled around her. It was really unnecessary – Susan could have achieved it all herself, with less muffled arguing over which item should go in which drawer.

"They were already here when I arrived, Miss." Susan said, spreading out her hands helplessly.

Lydia sighed, raking a hand through her hair, which was in great need of unpinning and redoing.

"I see that. Well, there's a dressing room, so if we can herd some of them out of there, I can get changed at the very least."

When Lydia emerged from the dressing room, wearing a fresh, pale blue muslin gown, her hair redone, Arabella was wandering around the room, watching the maids closely.

"Have a care with those." She said waspishly to a young woman smoothing out silk petticoats in a drawer. The maid flushed, ducking her head, and Lydia came to her rescue.

"She's doing a fine job, Arabella, don't snap." Lydia said mildly, and Arabella flinched.

"Oh, there you are. There are so many servants in this wretched house, and should I not closely monitor their actions at all times, they shall surely endeavour to take shortcuts without restraint."

Lydia saw a couple of the maids flinch, pressing their lips together. Beside her, Susan – who Lydia knew took great pride in her work – looked away.

"They're doing very well, I think." Lydia responded. "In fact, I think they can all get back to their regular chores, and let Susan finish the rest."

"If you like." Arabella said unhappily.

Glad to be released, the maids scuttled out, and Susan scooped up an armful of clothes and retreated into the dressing room.

Arabella smiled weakly. "I'm in a rather unpleasant mood today, I'm so sorry. I apologise for Henry."

Lydia swallowed. "Why? He did nothing wrong."

"Oh, he's so painfully awkward. He can't stand to go anywhere; I must practically drag him. I can't bear being in the house, and he can't bear leaving it. It was endearing when we were courting, but I suppose I thought he would grow up a little once we were married."

Lydia wisely kept her opinions to herself. Arabella gave herself a little shake, and turned on a wide, beaming grin.

"Well, what do you think of the room, then? I have put you in the nicest bedroom. The Blue Room."

She glanced around, taking in the bright wall-papers, the plush furnishings, thick carpeting, and high, canopied bed. It was a far cry from her room back home, crammed with books.

"It's beautiful." Lydia said honestly. "Really, it is."

Arabella beamed, as if the praise was for her. "It *is* a beautiful house, and the lands are so very extensive. I'll give you a grand tour, once you've settled in. I am thrilled for the ball – I'm determined that you will dance every dance. There are a great many suitable gentlemen here in Bath."

Lydia chuckled, shaking her head. "I'll dance myself to death at this rate. I am not so preoccupied with marriage, Arabella. Truly, I'm just glad to spend some time with you."

"Nonsense." Arabella responded brusquely. "This is what married women do – they are good at matchmaking their friends, until they have daughters to marry off. I have a great itinerary planned for us. With you here, I don't need to have Henry escort me everywhere. Not that he would, of course."

Lydia cleared her throat, looking away. Tensions between Henry and Arabella were already palpable. It was going to be a long stay.

"Did you say something about a tour?" she asked weakly.

Chapter Four

Is it too late to feign a megrim? Charles thought.

Yes, he thought so. His mother would be so upset if he didn't attend, and he'd promised William. Their relationship was improving, he thought, and he didn't much want to do anything to endanger it.

Anne was coming too. They had broken the news to Josephine about the baby, and the mood in their home was high and happy.

No, I can't possibly ruin all this by backing out of the Fitzwilliam ball. It's not like Henry often entertains, anyway.

Charles' valet made some final adjustments to his cravat – *Cravate en Cascade*, it was called, whatever that meant – and stepped back with a smile.

"Perfect, your Grace."

Charles eyed his own reflection, unconvinced. He *had* been handsome, but in the Society world of satin and silk and perfect complexions, his scar seemed uglier than ever. The scar was a vivid pink, the tissue around it raised, and it stood out staunchly against his pale skin.

He hated it.

Tearing his eyes away from the scar, Charles looked at the clothes his valet – Robert – had selected for him. The man had impeccable taste.

He found himself wearing a dark evening suit, very respectable and plain, but underneath was a wild, oriental-styled waistcoat. It was silk, of course, with blue and pink and gold embroidery, thickly done, the colours delightfully vibrant. He wore hessians – not the ideal choice for a ball, but Charles knew that he would not be dancing much – and they were polished to a high, glossy style.

His hair was arranged in some simple style Robert had seen in a magazine, likely to get disheveled soon when he thoughtlessly ran his fingers through it. His cravat was flawless, and a large sapphire cravat pin glimmered in the centre of it.

All in all, he looked like a fine, handsome, wealthy gentleman, looking forward to an evening of elegant and refined enjoyment.

Assuming, of course, that one did not look at his scar.

"It looks fine, Robert, thank you. No need to wait up for me, I shall undress myself once I get home."

Robert made a bow. "Thank you, your Grace."

He began to tidy up the dressing room, leaving Charles to contemplate his reflection.

Already, his gut was clenching at the thought of all those people, all looking at him. At one time, the idea of a room full of people would be like a challenge to him – how many could he charm? How many new acquaintances would he make?

Back then, it was almost a given that they would like him. And now, Charles knew he only had curious, sympathetic glances to look forward to. Drawing somebody into conversation would mean averted gazes and uncomfortable small talk. It was infuriating and miserable, and the evening would stretch out forever.

Nonetheless, necessity compels.

Somebody tapped on the door.

"Charles?" came William's muffled voice. "Are you ready?"

Charles sighed, straightening his waistcoat. "As ready as I'll ever be, Will."

***

The Fitzwilliam home was a hive of activity. Carriages and fine chaises crawled up the steep drive, their occupants well wrapped up against the nighttime chill. Gentlemen and ladies in bright, expensive fabrics climbed gingerly up the marble stairs towards the doorway, a square of warm, buttery light.

Charles shivered in his thin evening coat and looked forward to the warmth within. He knew from experience that the fine halls would be well lit and warm, with tables for refreshment everywhere you looked.

Not, of course, that Henry entertained often. They'd all laughed about how many parties he would have to throw once he married Arabella, who was said to be quite a socialite. There had been no parties, and that sat poorly with Charles.

"What a fine house." Josephine murmured, leaning forward in her seat to peer out of the window. "That girl he married did well. Miss Gabs, wasn't it?"

"Miss Green, Mother." William chimed in. He sat beside a well wrapped-up Anne, their arms wound around each other. "She was Miss Arabella Green, but of course we'll call her Lady Fernwood now."

Josephine clucked disapprovingly. "I can't say I approve of calling a girl like that *Lady Fernwood*. I daresay poor Evelyn isn't happy, giving up her position to a chit like that and being forced to move into a widow's lodgings."

"Why haven't we met Lord and Lady Fernwood before?" Anne piped up, resting her cheek against her husband's shoulder. "I would have thought they would entertain more."

Charles cleared his throat, glad that they were nearly there, and this line of conversation wouldn't go on much longer.

"I think Henry does not like company." Charles responded blandly.

The truth, as both Charles, William, and certainly their mother knew, was a little worse than that. Ill-matched couples were easily found in Society, but it was sad to see such a young couple disliking each other. Charles had not done the Season with Henry, although they were firm friends. He remembered reading Henry's letters, full of adoration at a beautiful, charming young woman he had met, who had *so much* to say, and was so fascinating, and it didn't *matter in the slightest* that his mother disliked her.

For her part, Charles had heard that Miss Green had had an eye on Henry's home, land, and titles, and was almost certainly drawn to his quiet, mild manner.

A pity, he thought, with a pang of sympathy. *A real pity.*

They were, of course, greeted at the door by their hosts. Henry looked much the same as ever, struggling to look his guests in the eye and twisting his fingers together whenever his nerves got the better of him. He certainly looked the part of a wealthy earl, of course, and his eye kept straying to the resplendent countess beside him.

"Lady Fernwood, it's a great pleasure to see you." Charles said, bowing over her silk-gloved hand. Lady Fernwood was indeed a beauty. Her black hair glittered in the candlelight, and her eyes sparkled. She was wearing a pale pink silk gown that rustled and shimmered whenever she moved, and fine diamonds dripped from her hands, ears, and neck.

She smiled at him, her eyes skipping over the scar, and something around her eyes tightened.

Pity. That was what it was, and Charles hated to see it. He hated to be pitied. Didn't everyone. He forced himself not to react.

"Your Grace," she said, inclining her head. "How wonderful to see you."

Charles straightened. "Indeed, "your Grace" does sound excessively formal. Henceforth, I beseech you to address me as Charles. Henry does, and we have known each other for years."

"It's true." Henry chimed in, then seemed to wish he hadn't spoken, pinching at his already loose cravat.

Lady Fernwood glanced briefly at her husband. "Well, I do love the new fashions of informality. Then please, call me Arabella. I have a guest here tonight, an old friend of mine. I simply must introduce you. Now if you'll just wait... oh, I see that Lord and Lady Worthington are coming up next. I must just greet them, if you'll excuse me."

Charles bowed and shuffled on past. Once the guests were all here and Henry and Arabella free to mingle, he would try and speak to Henry a little.

Not that Henry would be so disloyal as to discuss any issues within his marriage, but really, everyone could see. Charles had known him since they were children. If he couldn't speak up, then who could?

A few acquaintances nodded and smiled to Charles, but nobody stopped to talk to him. William and Anne had melted away immediately, and of course Josephine had taken up her place of honour among the matrons and distinguished dowagers, seated along the wall to observe the dancing. Charles wondered if Henry and Arabella would allow the infamous waltz to be danced here. Most places were allowing it now. Of course, at Almack's, one could only dance the waltz with one's spouse or betrothed, but attitudes were changing.

"Charles! Well, I never! It's his Grace, the Duke of Northwood!"

Charles froze at the sound of an unpleasantly familiar voice. He pasted a smile on his face and turned to face his fate.

He was being grinned at by a tall, handsome gentleman with brown hair, brown eyes, and a shocking combination of a mint-green evening suit and a pink and purple waistcoat.

It was something of an assault on the eyes, but then, of course, Sir Gregory Simms was a Dandy with a capital D.

A tall woman stood beside him, rather too thin, with circles of what seemed shockingly like rouge of her cheeks. She wore a canary-yellow ruffled gown that was in fact quite pretty but looked like an abomination between Sir Gregory's green-and-pink affair.

"Sir Gregory, what a pleasure." Charles lied. "How have you been?"

"Quite well, quite well, you *Grace*. Oh, this is Mrs Habit, by the way. I'm sure you've read about her in the papers. Married to Captain

Habit, who died so tragically abroad. Still, dear Matilda here is quite ready to throw off her mourning clothes and begin to live again."

Charles swallowed. "So I see." He responded coolly, resisting the urge to stare at her vivid yellow skirts and her arm, wound around Sir Gregory's in a most possessive manner.

Sir Gregory's eyes glinted, and Charles steeled himself. Despite the man's familiar greeting, they were not friends. They had never been friends. They had attended school together, where Sir Gregory had cheerfully bullied Charles to distraction, ensuring that he left school without a single friend beyond Henry.

However, Charles had, in a way, gotten the final laugh. After all, he was a wealthy duke, whereas Sir Gregory was a mere knight, and a penniless one at that. Sir Gregory had never quite forgiven him for that.

Sir Gregory's gaze zeroed in on the scar, which seemed even more vivid in the heat of the room.

"Good gracious, that thing gets worse every time I look at it. Don't you think it's shocking, Mrs Habit? One can't help but stare, old boy, I'm sure you're not offended."

Mrs Habit giggled uncertainly. "I think scars can be rather rakish. Very handsome, you know, if they are... are the correct kind of scar."

Charles didn't bother whether his scar was *the correct kind*, as he fancied he already knew the answer. He glanced around for an escape, but none was coming. Sir Gregory was not tremendously popular, and not likely to be hauled away by adoring friends anytime soon.

"Tell me, how did you come by that scar?" Mrs Habit pressed. She was clearly already somewhat tipsy, and the taut atmosphere between Charles and Sir Gregory was making her nervous.

Charles swallowed. "There's not much of a story. There was a storm at sea, and I came about this scar then."

Sir Gregory gave a hoot of laughter. "Goodness, that's not at all the story *I* heard! Now, *I* heard that Charles and his addle-brained friend were standing on deck in the middle of a storm, priceless fools that they are, and were swept overboard. The long-suffered sailors hauled them back again, and Charles scraped his face on the side of the ship as he went."

Mrs Habit blinked. "Oh. That is rather..."

"Although, I seem to recall that the companion did not survive. Is that so, Charles?"

Charles did not reply.

Mrs Habit glanced between them, looking more and more uncomfortable by the minute.

"Tell me, Charles, who was it that chose to stand on the deck?" Sir Gregory murmured. "I do hope it wasn't your idea. What a thing to live with on your conscience!"

"I don't wish to discuss it." Charles rapped out.

Unfazed, Sir Gregory chuckled, taking a long sip of his wine. "As you like, as you like. Still, it's unfortunate."

"What is?" Charles' back teeth were clenched. He was longing for the conversation to end, but it was as if his feet were rooted to the floor, just as they had when they were small boys and Sir Gregory was mocking him then.

Sir Gregory gestured vaguely to Charles' face. "*That*. You would never believe it now, Mrs Habit, but our Lord Northwood was a remarkably handsome man before *that* happened. Pity, isn't it? I daresay it'll only get worse now, with puckering around the scar and all sorts of discolouration."

He gave a theatrical shudder, and Mrs Habit giggled uncertainly. It was clear that she did not exactly approve of what Sir Gregory was saying, but neither did she have any intention to speak up for him.

"Come, come, your Grace, what say you?" Sir Gregory laughed, his wine sloshing over the side of his cup. "Do you wake up and look in the mirror each day and curse your fate? Or do you even own a mirror?"

"A fine question." Came an unfamiliar voice from around Charles' elbow. "I think that could be nicely levelled at you, sir."

All three of them flinched, turning sharply around.

Charles did not recognize the woman who had spoken. She was young, not even twenty by his estimation, and had brown ringlets done up in a simple style. She had olive skin and wore a shimmering yellow-green silk that would have drained any other woman but managed to make her simply glow. She was smiling gently, but the smile did not reach her eyes, and she was looking at Sir Gregory.

Sir Gregory recognized her, it seemed – they had probably been introduced earlier in the evening – but he muttered to himself, not deigning to introduce Charles.

"What on earth do you mean?" he asked, rather rudely. Mrs Habit tilted up her chin, inspecting the stranger with narrowed eyes.

The woman smiled charmingly. "Well, I heard your very loud comments – it's quite a feat, is it not, to be heard over the noise of a ballroom – and I simply had to come and see this gentleman who you claimed was so horribly scarred. Imagine my shock when I saw a man, not permanently marred in a horrific way, but with a small line on his cheek. A rather dramatic reaction, don't you think?"

She glanced up at Charles, briefly. He stiffened as her gaze raked over him. Her eyes landed on his scar, dispassionately so, then moved away. There was no pity, no shock in her gaze, nothing. It was rather refreshing.

"It was a joke." Sir Gregory snapped. "We're old acquaintances. Do you make a habit of barging into private conversations?"

"Do you make a habit of dressing like a marzipan?" she retorted, and Sir Gregory blanched.

"I'll have you know this coat was remarkably expensive and was put together by the finest tailor in London!"

She winced, letting her eye drift pointedly and disapprovingly down Sir Gregory's frame.

"Oh. Oh, dear. I do hope it wasn't *frightfully* expensive. It looks like the sort of thing I would make for my doll as a child, from fabric scraps."

"Did you come over here to insult me, madam?"

She shrugged lightly. "No, but it seems you came over here to insult this gentleman. Perhaps before you pass comments on the physical appearance of others, you should look to yourself a little more. A seam at your shoulder is coming away – I noticed it from across the room. Perhaps you might return to that tailor."

With that, she turned on her heel and glided back into the crowd. She had never spoken a word to Charles, or even to Mrs Habit – she'd saved her barbs solely for Sir Gregory.

Charles blinked, losing her in the crowd. He wished he'd gotten her name. He glanced over at Sir Gregory, who was trying to look over his own shoulder to find the loose seam, while Mrs Habit tried to make him stay still, as movement was only loosening it more.

Suppressing a smile, Charles turned to leave. He was grateful to the mystery woman, not just for standing up for him, but for doing such a neat job of showing Sir Gregory up for what he really was – a ridiculous fool, with a coat too bright for a ball, and a woman hanging on his arm who was almost fool enough to let him marry her and take her fortune.

Shaking his head, Charles picked up another glass of champagne. He drained it quickly – too quickly, really. He didn't want to make a fool of himself for ending up in his cups early on in the evening. Or at all, really.

In the ballroom, the dancing had not yet begun, although the musicians were in place, tuning their instruments.

Charles felt a pang of disappointment. He would not have the opportunity to dance much this evening, he knew that. He could ask ladies to dance, and they couldn't very well refuse, but he could never stomach that. Who wanted a person to be *forced* to dance with them?

No, he would keep his dignity, and stay seated.

It was for the best, really, in the end.

Chapter Five

Charles spotted Henry across the ballroom and felt a rush of relief. He shouldered his way as politely as he could through the crowd, heading to Henry's quiet corner.

Henry had a glass of whiskey in his hand – heavy liquor for this early on in the evening, but Charles kept his judgements to himself – and watched Charles approach.

"It's a fabulous ball, Henry." Charles remarked, finally freeing himself from the crush.

Any social occasion worth attending was always packed to the rafters, everyone knew that. If one could walk across the room with ease, it normally meant that nobody important was there, and the party's existence would not even grace the covers of the scandal sheets.

Even more so here in Bath, especially when the Season was just picking up its feet in London.

"Yes, it is, rather." Henry answered absently. "Of course, I wouldn't know. I had very little to do with it. Arabella managed all of this."

"She is an excellent hostess." Charles agreed. This praise didn't seem to please Henry. He chewed his lip, looking down.

"She thinks we don't entertain enough." He said at last. "What do you think?"

Charles shifted uncomfortably, not wanting to be drawn into a domestic dispute.

"I can't say. You don't much enjoy socialising, do you? But I believe that Lady Fernwood does."

Henry stared into the amber depths of his whiskey. "She does, very much. Always has. I used to admire how she would move around a room, so assured and confident, making new friends in a few moments. Silly of me to think that her character would change once we married."

"Do you *want* her character to change?" Charles asked quietly.

"No, no, of course not. It's just that I thought…" Henry ended the sentence as sharply as if he had bitten his tongue. He glanced over at Charles, and a shutter came down over his face. He would say no more, Charles knew. That was fine, of course. Entirely natural not to want to air out his domestic issues, even in front of an old friend.

Henry's unhappiness, however, was starting to be noticed by more people. Charles wasn't entirely sure what to do.

"I noticed Sir Gregory speaking to you earlier." Henry said abruptly. Charles did not comment on the change of subject. "What did he want?"

"The usual. He wanted to laugh at me and make a joke of me to his new lady friend."

"Mrs Habit? Yes, she is fabulously wealthy, I believe. I didn't want to invite him, but not inviting him would have looked too singular. I don't want him going all over town telling everybody that I am bitter and jealous of him."

Charles snorted, shaking his head. Yet, it was a realistic scenario. Gregory had a knack for twisting the truth, for making himself seem like the victim. It was remarkable, really.

For a moment, the two men stood side by side, sipping their drinks and watching the party go on without them.

"I'm glad you're here." Henry said, after a few moments. "I know you likely entertained hopes of a last-minute illness to keep you at home. But I'm glad to see you, at least."

Charles bit his lip. "I'd like to say I'm glad to be here, but I'm rather tired of being stared at. Tired of being asked, the politest of terms, how on earth I happened to have such a horrid scar on my face."

Henry winced, glancing up at him. "It's not *that* bad."

"No, but Society likes perfect faces, does it not? And mine does not meet the requisite standards anymore."

That, in Charles' opinion, was the worst part of it all. *Anymore.* If he'd been an ordinary man, with ordinary prospects and an ordinary face, perhaps he wouldn't have minded. It wasn't the scar, of course. He was honest enough to admit that his vanity was wounded, that he no longer liked the face that greeted him in the mirror, but of course it went deeper than that.

Edmund, his dearest friend, was gone, and he could have saved him. If Charles had been half a stroke faster, he would have had a firm enough grip on Edmund's hands, firm enough to drag them both to safety. There was no hope of him having somehow made it to land – they were too far away from shore, and there were no boats in the area that might have saved him.

Charles had been, quite literally, Edmund's only hope.

And I failed him.

"You're getting that maudlin look on your face." Henry remarked, draining his glass. How many drinks had he had? Charles was about to ask, then wisely thought better of it.

"What maudlin look?"

Henry shot him a pointed glance. "You know what I mean. Arabella noticed it too. She said, after you first met her, that you had a kind of melancholy look about you, like there was some heavy sadness weighing on you."

Charles chuckled. "Perhaps I was sad that my oldest friend was marrying and moving on."

"No, that's not it." Henry tilted his head to one side. "It's deeper than Edmund now, isn't it? There's a sort of ache inside you, a chasm that's only getting wider and wider, and you are running out of ideas to fill it. Parties like this..." he gestured wildly at the crowd, "... this will only make you feel more alone."

Charles tried to laugh again, but it came out forced and insincere.

"That's not a particularly helpful thing to say, Henry." He remarked, and the words sent a shudder down his spine.

Henry said nothing. What was there to say? They were both in low spirits, and being surrounded by happy, smiling faces, chatter, laughter, and music only seemed to make it worse.

Charles spotted his brother in the crowd, Anne's arm looped through his. They were talking to a young couple whom he did not recognize, talking and laughing. He was watching as William said something that made all three of them burst out laughing. He saw his brother glow with pride at having said something clever, having made his friends laugh. He saw how William looked at once to Anne, to see if she was laughing, if she was enjoying herself. She was – she was looking up at her husband with a beaming smile, and when their eyes met, something passed between them that made Charles' heart ache.

He glanced over at Henry to see if he had noticed, but Henry was staring off into the crowd. He followed his gaze and saw that he was looking at Lady Fernwood.

Lady Fernwood – Arabella, she'd told him to call her – was in the middle of a cluster of ladies, all talking animatedly. She was the most beautiful and finely dressed one there, and clearly the centre of attention. She talked, gesturing wildly, and threw back her head to laugh at something or other.

She looked so happy.

But when Charles glanced back at his companion, Henry's face looked... well, it looked hollow.

"Henry?" he prompted, not wanting to look at that expression on his friend's face for a minute longer than he had to. But perhaps it would distract him from his own loneliness.

Or perhaps coming to talk to Henry had been a mistake after all. They were simply isolating themselves together, now.

Henry blinked, as if waking up from a reverie, and smiled absently at Charles.

"I beg your pardon. I was a million miles away."

No, you weren't, Charles thought. *You were right here in this ballroom, not very far away. You were over there, with* her.

"Nothing to forgive. Shall we mingle?"

Henry winced. "I think Arabella had somebody she wanted you to meet, seeing as you are a close friend of mine."

"Oh, I think she mentioned it."

"It's Miss Lydia Waverly, she arrived yesterday. I must say, she makes a pleasant houseguest so far. I don't mind her being here at all, and of course Arabella is thrilled."

"Well, I shall be delighted to meet her."

Henry smiled wanly. "We should go and find Arabella then, so that the introductions can be made. Shall we brave the throng?"

Charles glanced over at the crowd. He drank back the last of his drink, setting the empty glass down on the side with a determined *click*. He didn't much fancy the idea of pushing his way through the crowd again, and seeing people shrink back as they glanced up and saw his scar.

Still, it was better than standing here on the sidelines, with Henry, which wasn't particularly good for either of them.

"I'm ready." He said firmly. "Let's go then, shall we?"

***

Lydia was starting to suspect that the whole ball — which Arabella had assured her was thrown in *her* honour — was not, in fact, for her, but for her hostess.

Not that Lydia minded, of course — Arabella loved balls and parties, and she was clearly having a wonderful time. However, she seemed to have forgotten that Lydia did not actually know many people in Bath.

Or anyone, it seemed.

She'd been introduced to a great many people, who were all very pleasant, but they all had their cliques and their own acquaintances. Arabella had a great throng of friends, mostly women of varying ages, and Lydia couldn't have gotten close to her even if she'd tried. For the most part, she wandered around the ballroom, taking in the immaculate décor, watching other guests enjoy themselves, and trying not to think of the incident before the party.

The incident in question had assured Lydia that her friend was not, in fact, happy in her marriage. No solution had yet presented itself.

Arabella had come skipping down the stairs, resplendent in pink silk and diamonds. She looked flushed with excitement, clearly pleased with the way she looked and excited for the evening of entertainment ahead of her.

Lydia was standing in the Great Hall with Henry, who seemed to get more and more nervous as the hour for the ball approached.

"Well, what do you think?" Arabella had trilled, turning in a circle. Lydia had gasped and clapped, praising her gown, but Arabella had barely noticed. Her eyes went straight to Henry, who was fumbling with his pocket watch.

"Henry?" Arabella prompted, smiling hopefully and smoothing down the bodice of her gown. "What do you think?"

He glanced up, but his gaze was absent and distracted. "What? Oh, very pretty. Should we wait by the door now, to greet the guests? I don't want to do anything wrong."

Arabella's expression clouded over.

"No, of course not." She snapped, a little too harshly. She turned on her heel and marched away into the ballroom, leaving Lydia and Henry behind.

"What did I do?" he said, bewildered.

"She... I... I'll talk to her." Lydia had muttered, running after her friend.

In the ballroom, Arabella had cornered a hapless footman, carrying an arrangement of flowers, and was loudly scolding him about something or other.

"What's the matter?" Lydia asked, as calmly as she could.

"This rustic put the roses in the Great Hall, but I *said* that they were to go in the ballroom!"

The footman seemed to be on the brink of tears.

"I'm sure it will be fine." Lydia said firmly, gesturing for the footman to go. He did, edging away with a wary eye on Arabella. She let him go, pouting like a child.

"I don't think it's fair to scold that poor footman." Lydia said quietly. "It's not him you're angry at."

Arabella had the grace to look ashamed. "Henry never notices or cares what I wear. It took me hours to get ready tonight."

"I think Henry is nervous about the ball. It preoccupies him, and he can't think of anything else."

"Nervous? Nonsense. Why would he be? A ball is a fun thing."

Lydia rolled her eyes. "For *you*, maybe. I'm sure he didn't mean anything by it. Perhaps you should tell him how it upset you."

Arabella glanced at Lydia; mouth opened to respond. After a moment, she shook her head.

"You don't know what you're talking about. You're not married. However, I intend to change *that* soon enough."

Back in the crowded ballroom, Lydia smiled a little at the memory. Arabella seemed to have forgotten her as soon as the guests started arriving and was entirely caught up with her friends. Lydia didn't mind, of course. She'd occupied herself, mostly by intervening between that wretched dandy, Sir Gregory something-or-other, and some unfortunate gentleman with a facial scar.

It never ceased to amaze her how cruel people could be to each other.

"*There* you are." Arabella appeared from nowhere, latching onto Lydia's arm and towing her back through the crowd. "Where have you been, you wretch? I have somebody I want you to meet. Well, I can't say I *particularly* wanted you to meet him. No, that sounds cruel. The thing is, he's a dear friend of Henry – and heaven knows that Henry has few enough friends as it is – and he wanted you two to be introduced. Henry seems fond of you, by the way. Perhaps he'll let me have more friends over, now that he knows that you, at least, are quite agreeable."

"Very well." Lydia laughed, allowing herself to be towed away. "I thought you'd quite forgotten about me."

"As if I could. No, I simply had a lot of people to greet. Bath is a fabulously friendly town. I have to be careful; you see – all the old matrons and dowagers are friends of Henry's mother, and they all dislike me. They're all waiting for me to make a mistake, to do something shameful. Sometimes I think that Henry is waiting for that, too."

Lydia swallowed hard, not sure how to respond to that comment. Fortunately, it seemed that no response was needed.

They passed the rows of chairs set against the wall, where the most nervous young ladies sat, along with the matrons, chaperones, and dowagers, and a handful of portly gentlemen whose gouty legs wouldn't support them any longer than was strictly necessary. As Arabella had predicted, a particular cluster of older ladies – almost all of whom were in black gowns and wore pearls – watched Arabella go by with a look of pinched disapproval and whispered among each other when she had gone.

"I entertain differently from how the previous Lady Fernwood used to," Arabella whispered, once they were safely past. "They all keep saying that as if I've made a mistake. Well, if I'm not doing anything wrong, why should I not do it my own way? It's hard enough ignoring all the gossips in this town without Henry pressuring me."

"Henry?"

"Oh, yes. He seems terrified to do anything differently to how his parents did it. I don't know why, they never seemed pleased with him. Not until *I* married him, and then suddenly I was not good enough for him."

Arabella's eyes were glittering, and her cheeks were flushed red – Lydia suspected she'd drank rather too much champagne.

"You should be kinder to Henry." Lydia said, as quietly as she could manage. "I believe he's doing his best."

Arabella pressed her lips together. She did not look round at her friend.

"Well, so am I. Perhaps our best is not good enough. What then, Lydia?"

She didn't have an answer. Fortunately, one was not needed. Arabella elbowed her way into a little circle of space in the middle of the crowd. Lydia spotted Henry at once, stiff and uncomfortable in his fine party clothes. His eyes went, as they always did, to Arabella.

Beside him stood a tall, sturdy-looking gentleman with a shock of black hair. He was taller than Henry, and stood stiffly, as though he were uncomfortable.

"Lydia, let me introduce you to his Grace, Lord Charles Everard, Duke of Northwood. Charles, let me introduce you to Miss Lydia Waverly."

The Duke turned around, and Lydia blinked, surprised.

"I believe we've already met." She said, before she could stop herself.

Sure enough, it was the handsomely scarred gentleman who Sir Gregory was acting so venomously towards. The man's smudgy dark eyebrows lifted at the sight of her, and she knew at once that he recognized her, too.

"You've already met?" Arabella echoed. "How? When did you meet? Nobody introduced you, I'm sure of it."

Lydia laid a hand on her friend's arm, hoping to stop the coming fit of pique.

"It was something of an accident. It's a pleasure to meet you, your Grace."

She extended a hand, and the Duke, after a moment's hesitation, enveloped her gloved hand in his.

"The pleasure is mine, Miss Waverly."

Chapter Six

He was a good-looking man, really, scar or not. Lydia didn't for one minute give credit to Sir Gregory's nonsense about a ship and a falling overboard, but she wasn't about to bombard the poor man with impertinent questions.

"How did you meet?" Arabella pressed, clearly desperate to get to the bottom of it.

"Does it really matter?" Henry asked, with a tinge of irritation in his voice.

"Yes." Arabella responded, barely glancing his way.

Lydia sighed. "Well, I *do* know Sir Gregory and Mrs Habit, and I happened to talk to them while they were talking to his Grace. No introductions were made, though."

Henry pursed his lips. "That's not proper, to speak to someone you aren't introduced to. Sir Gregory ought to have done the honours there, but of course..." he broke off, clearing his throat. "My parents were always very particular about things being done *properly*; you see."

Lydia carefully did not meet her friend's eye.

On stage, the musicians began to play the open themes. A general flutter broke out in the crowd, with young ladies looking about hopefully for a partner and the gentlemen visibly steeling themselves to ask. Everyone had dance cards, of course, neat little square hanging from their wrists with a bit of ribbon. Lydia had one too, but there were precious few names in it.

"Oh, the first dance." Arabella was visibly flustered, patting her hair and smoothing out her skirts. "Henry, shall we?"

He looked terrified. "I didn't realise I'd have to dance, Arabella. You know how terrible I am at dancing."

She pressed her lips together. "We have to open the ball, you and I. I can't possibly stand up with anyone else, and I *must* open it. Really, Henry."

Henry sighed. Obviously, there would be no escape. In an attempt to avoid the awkwardness, Lydia glanced away, and met the Duke's eye.

He lifted an eyebrow. "Would you care to dance, Miss Waverly?"

Ladies with unfashionable skin like Lydia – the fashion was for *fair* beauties at the moment, ladies with skin so white a person could see the veins running underneath – did not blush revealingly. Even so, Lydia felt colour rush to her cheeks. Already, Arabella and Henry were hurrying towards the dance floor, hand in hand, and couples were lining up, ready to start.

"I hope you don't think I was hinting for a dance, your Grace." She said smoothly.

He chuckled. "Why would it matter if you were? I've always thought it unfair that the gentlemen are obliged to ask the ladies to dance. If the ladies were allowed to speak up, I daresay they'd be much more forward and confident than we are. I know plenty of gentlemen who are veritable wallflowers and would much enjoy a talkative lady to ask them to dance."

Lydia had to smile at that. "Would you like me to ask you to dance then, your Grace?"

He pretended to think about it, tapping his finger against his lips.

"Why, yes, I think I would."

"Very well, then. Now, I shan't get right into it, of course. One must demur around the subject."

"Of course."

"Your Grace, I see the dancing is beginning."

Playing along, the Duke glanced over his shoulder and pretended to be surprised at the sight of the couples lined up. "Why, *so* they are."

"Have you a partner for this dance?"

"I do not, Miss Waverly, I am afraid. A waltz, is it not? How shocking."

Lydia glanced back at the dance floor. She hadn't noticed it was going to be a waltz. The dance was mostly accepted in London now, of course, with only the most austere of families forbidding it. She could dance the waltz with the Duke and her reputation would survive, but there was still something a little off-putting about a dance that required the dancers to hold each other in their arms.

She recovered quickly, of course, and continued.

"Do you like to waltz, your Grace?"

"I do." He said, eyes downcast modestly. Lydia wanted to laugh. The urge to giggle bubbled up inside her, but their little charade wasn't finished yet. She extended her hand with a flourish.

"Would you care to stand up with me, then, your Grace?"

The Duke acted as if he were fluttering a fan coyly. "I certainly would, Miss Waverly."

He took her hand for the second time, and Lydia felt a strange jolt at the feeling of his fingers around hers. There was no time to think of it, though – the dance was almost beginning, and they were only just able to take their places before the music began in earnest.

Lydia had practiced the waltz over and over, at her mother's insistence, and she could execute the steps well enough. The Duke seemed somewhat rusty, but he didn't miss out on any steps and didn't tread on her toes, so she was happy enough.

For a moment or two, they simply danced in silence, enjoying the music and the well-practiced movements of the waltz.

Lydia caught a glimpse of Arabella and Henry, at the head of the procession of twirling couples. Arabella was smiling, her gaze turned inward as she focused on the dance. Henry was watching her. To anyone unfamiliar with him, he would have looked blank, maybe even disinterested, but Lydia saw the softness in his gaze.

"He loves her." She said, before she could think of who she was speaking to. Before she could entertain hopes that the Duke had not heard, or perhaps would not understand, he followed her gaze and nodded slowly.

"Neither of them is willing to compromise." He said quietly. "They had a good start, but now... I worry for my friend's happiness. And for Lady Fernwood. She seems like a good woman."

"She is." Lydia said vehemently. "I suppose these are the risks of marriage. Did Lord Fernwood travel at all, your Grace? I understand that you are close friends. I heard that he married before he could embark on a Tour."

"He did not do a Tour, but not for want of opportunity. Henry is... he fears the unknown. We all do, of course, but some more than others."

Almost unconsciously, the Duke lifted his hand as if to run a fingertip down the ridged edge of his scar, but snapped his hand down before he could touch. He smiled uncertainly at her, and the dance picked up enough that they did not have breath to speak.

When it slowed down again, Lydia was ready with a new subject matter.

"Did you take a Tour, your Grace? I love to hear tales of travel."

He blinked rapidly. "I did, yes. Have you not travelled yourself, Miss Waverly?"

She snorted at that. It was a very unladylike gesture, which would have caused great distress to Lady Pemshire if she had heard it. The Duke only smiled and shook his head.

"I have not travelled." Lydia confessed. "I have never even been outside of England. Ladies don't, you know. We can read about marvellous places in books, but we can never see them for ourselves. A few acquaintances of mine had the fortune to marry men who liked to travel, and who were willing to take their wives along with them, but such men are few and far between. Arabella was able to go to France for her honeymoon and says that was enough travelling for her."

"And for you?"

Lydia blinked, glancing up at him. Frankly, she wasn't used to remarks and questions being turned back on her. A great many gentlemen in Society simply weren't interested in the opinion of ladies. One of the most important accomplishments – and a somewhat unspoken one – was to be *fascinating*.

A fascinating woman knew how to draw out a man, how to make him feel special. She knew how to listen intently and intelligently, while of course not being cleverer than the gentleman himself. She knew how to tell an entertaining story, and how to ask intriguing questions that would make a gentleman feel pleased with himself and happy to keep speaking.

Gentlemen were not, of course, expected to be fascinating.

Lydia, too, was not *fascinating*, and had no ambitions to be.

And here was the Duke of Northwood, plainly asking her about herself, and to all appearances, was quite eager to hear the answer.

Lydia swallowed hard, responding before the pause became too awkward.

"I would like to travel." She admitted. "I would like to go to France, and Italy, and Germany. I would see museums and view famous artwork that I have only ever read about in books. The world is full of sights to see, and I've barely seen a tiny portion of them."

"Italy is remarkable for culture and art." The Duke said, expertly twirling Lydia around. "As is the Louvre in France. I can highly recommend all the countries you mentioned."

"You have travelled then?"

"I took a Tour, yes. It was… enlightening."

The Duke's face was carefully guarded, and Lydia wasn't sure what to make of that. She was already thinking of questions to ask him, about his travels mostly, and had no idea which to choose first.

"I am surprised you haven't asked the great question yet." The Duke remarked, after a pause. "Although I think Sir Gregory rather ruined it for you."

She lifted her eyebrows. "What do you mean? What is the great question?"

He pointed wordlessly at his scar, and Lydia winced.

"Well, I rather thought it was none of my business. If you wished me to know the circumstances of your injury, I'm sure you would tell me. What if it was a traumatic incident, that you wished not to recall? Recounting it would only upset you."

He smiled grimly. "There are many that do not share your scruples, let me tell you."

The dance was speeding up, heading towards its crescendo and climax, and then it would be over with a flourish.

Lydia found that she was disappointed. Dances were always entertaining, but if her partner was dull or unpleasant, they seemed to stretch out interminably. Conversation lagged at times, or perhaps her partner was a poor dancer, and she ran the risk of having her toes trodden on.

She was glad that the Duke was a graceful enough dancer, at least – he was wearing sturdy hessians, which would have crushed her poor feet through their delicate, satin dancing slippers.

Lydia realized, with a tingle of surprise, that she wanted to dance with the Duke again. She wanted to talk more about travel, about himself, and try and chip away at that blank, guarded smile. What was he really thinking underneath it all? He was extremely pleasant but guarded.

Of course, Lydia would only be able to have one more dance with him. Any more than two dances with a gentleman she was not engaged to was truly shocking. In fact, even two dances were considered rather pointed. Many gentlemen would ask ladies to dance even if they had no interest in them – their hostess' daughter, for example – and it meant nothing, assuming they did not ask her to dance again. Then, people would start to Notice.

Lydia did not want the Duke to feel as though she were trying to entrap him. It didn't help that the Season was set up for just that – for single ladies to catch themselves a husband, and for the single men to try and escape or to let themselves be caught, whichever they liked.

It was a nightmare to navigate.

"Sir Gregory was right." The Duke said, after a long pause. "It was a sailing accident. A storm. I went overboard, and the crew pulled me back in. On the way, I received an injury to my face. I was lucky it was not worse."

Lydia bit her lip. "I'm sorry. That must have been awful."

She thought he said something like, *you cannot understand just how awful,* but by then the music was rising and the dance speeding up, and any chance at conversation was quite over.

They bowed and curtsied to their partners and clapped the musicians. Lydia glanced back at the Duke, suddenly shy.

Arabella came from nowhere, flushed and smiling.

"I saw you two dancing together! You were very graceful."

Before Lydia or the Duke could say a word, Arabella looped her arm through Lydia's, and began to tug her away.

"Come with me," she said. "I have many people to introduce you to."

Lydia allowed herself to be pulled away. When she glanced back over her shoulder, the Duke of Northwood was gone. Try as she might, she never laid eyes on him again for the rest of the evening.

Chapter Seven

"We should have a game of Pall-Mall. I haven't engaged in that activity for I cannot fathom how long. Do you not reckon it would be suitable for us to partake in a slight game of Pall-Mall, Lydia? Henry? Are the two of you attuned to my words?"

Lydia, whose head was thumping horribly after her late night and too many glasses of champagne, stared dizzily at her friend across the breakfast table.

Arabella seemed as fresh and alert as always, despite the fact that dawn was blooming when she finally retired to bed as the last guests' carriages made their way down the drive. She had certainly drunk more champagne, wine, and punch than Lydia had.

Lydia reminded herself that she was here to build bridges and make a few more opportunities for herself, cleared her throat and smiled.

"I haven't played Pall-Mall for an age, Arabella. I think I'd like that. We should arrange something soon."

"I was thinking this afternoon," Arabella said, off-handedly.

Across the table, where he was bent over a newspaper, Henry's head shot up.

"This afternoon?" he repeated sharply. "You can't be serious. We've only just had a party. Mother would be shocked to hear of something so frivolous."

The temperature at the table dropped a handful of degrees. Lydia cleared her throat and pretended to be entranced by the pattern on the tablecloth.

Arabella shifted to stare at her husband.

"It's an ordinary thing to do. The days of people taking days and days to recover from a social event are quite done, Henry."

"Mother never said so."

"I imagine when she was young, many, *many* decades ago, things were indeed different." Arabella responded tartly, and Henry flushed.

"I really don't like this idea, Arabella. You'll get a reputation as being *fast*."

Lydia winced. She would have loved to absent herself from the table, but it would be too pointed, and would do nothing to prevent the oncoming argument.

Besides, she wanted to see what happened.

"Fast?" Arabella repeated. "*Fast*? I really don't believe that a married woman who invites a few friends around for a companionably game of *Pall-Mall*, of all games, could be unkindly dubbed as fast. Tell me, Henry, are you absolutely decided on locking me up in a tower, away from the world? Why not set a dragon at the base of the town to guard me, to keep me in? Oh, wait, I forgot. There is already a dragon. Your dear Mamma, of course."

It was clear that Henry was running out of words to describe how he felt. Frankly, Lydia pitied him. She'd been lucky enough to have sufficiently pedestrian opinions and enough quick wit on hand to defend them, but Henry seemed to be struggling to put his feelings into polite words.

So, naturally, he dispensed with the politeness.

"How dare you speak of my mother like that? I won't have it, Arabella!"

She shot up onto her feet, leaning forward to glare at him. "I am not your mother, Henry! If you wanted a lady with the manners of a proper, dull old dowager, you ought to have married one. There are widows aplenty in the world, and I wish I had known that you intended to keep me away from Society before we married."

He got to his feet too. "I don't intend to keep you from Society. I wish you would not overreact so, Arabella. Just last night, we had a fine party."

Arabella gave a hoarse laugh. "Indeed, we did. The first party we've thrown since we married, which was almost a year ago, don't you know? I am excessively fatigued by this state of ennui, thoroughly weary of emulating your wretched mother – who, incidentally, seems to hold the belief that you lack the intelligence to navigate your own marital contentment, and thus insists on assuming control over it – and I am tired of it just being you and I, every evening, week after week, month after month, and no doubt year after year if you have your way. I want to see my *friends*, Henry!"

There was a tense silence. Lydia glanced at the door, wondering whether she should make a dash for the exit after all. She decided against it. They'd notice, and then it would just be embarrassing for everyone.

"I thought you enjoyed my company." Henry managed, after a few minutes of uncomfortable quiet. "I wasn't aware that I was so unpleasant to be around."

Arabella flushed red.

Tell him you're sorry, Lydia willed her. *Tell him you didn't mean it. He thinks that you dislike him so intensely that you crave the Society of others.*

The fault, of course, lay pretty heavily on both sides. Henry did not enjoy socializing, and only wanted the company of his wife. However, he believed that she found him boring.

Lydia knew fine well that Arabella did not consider Henry boring. She thought he was intelligent, shockingly clever, always with something interesting to say, always fun to be around. However, Arabella was a social woman, and liked the company of her friends, too. She now thought that Henry thought her silly and trite, and wished to keep her away from her friends out of pure malice.

It would be funny if it were not so tragic.

"You are not unpleasant to be around," Arabella said at last, her voice wavering. "But I want to see my friends. Why must you keep me away from them? It isn't fair."

Henry's lips pressed together in a thin, white line. He glanced sharply at Lydia, who dropped her eyes back to the tablecloth and wished she were invisible.

"Very well," Henry said, and his voice sounded strained and exhausted. "My mother always said that a full day should be taken after a ball. Two full days, in fact. However, as you have so eloquently said, you are not my mother, and as the new Lady Fernwood, you have the right to do as you wish. Of course I would not prevent you from socializing as you like. I am not a tyrant."

Arabella sank back down into her seat, looking simultaneously mollified and deflated.

"I'm glad," she said lightly. "And, you know, Henry, I don't intend to invite a lot of people. Only a handful, you know, for a quiet game of Pall-Mall and a little afternoon tea on the lawn. It'll be ever so pleasant. I daresay the guests will be gone even before dark."

Henry smiled, tight-lipped. "I'm sure. And *I* am sure that you won't expect me to join."

Arabella blinked. "Of course you won't be compelled to..."

"Very good. I'll be in my study, and I think I will dine at the club this evening."

Now Arabella looked shocked. "But you hate your club. You said it was too crowded and noisy."

Not bothering to reply, Henry pushed back his chair and stalked out of the room, head held high. Silence fell over the breakfast-table, and Lydia didn't dare break it.

Arabella shifted in her seat, glancing over her shoulder at the door, as if she expected him to come back.

"Well," she said, when it was clear that Henry really had gone, "I think that was handled as well as it could have been. Don't you think, Lydia?"

Lydia smiled weakly and wisely said nothing.

***

As promised, the guests invited for afternoon tea and a game of Pall-Mall were no more than six. There was Lord William and Lady Anne Everard, along with a pair of young lady sisters – Miss Lucy Bolts and her younger sister, Miss Tabitha Bolts – and their older brother, Maximilian Bolts. Lydia had not had chance to meet the Bolts siblings at the ball, but they seemed enormously likeable, quick to make jokes and put others at their ease, and clearly doting on Arabella.

The sixth guest was the Duke of Northwood, and Lydia was a little embarrassed to admit that her heart started to hammer when she saw him riding up the drive. He was the only guest who arrived on horseback instead of by carriage, and his brother immediately began to berate him in a low voice for such an ungentlemanly choice.

Miss Bolts – who clearly had designs on the Duke – instantly jumped to his defense, while her younger sister, Miss Tabitha, stared at him with large, round eyes.

Lydia tried to swallow back a pang of jealousy. After all, the two ladies had been nothing but kind and friendly to herself. She had always held great pride in being a woman of depth and integrity, never succumbing to the temptation of betraying her fellow women for the sake of a man. Now was the time to make good on that vow.

"Well," Arabella said, when they were all clustered in the parlor. "Now that we're all here, let's have some light refreshment and then go out to the lawn for Pall-Mall. Shall I suggest we play in pairs?"

This idea was met with approval. Lydia, who had chosen a seat a little set back from the group, was in the perfect position to watch the others look around each other for partners.

The Duke – her eyes seemed drawn to him wherever he was, and she tried to convince herself it was because he was taller than the rest, and of course there was that dashing scar – immediately looked to his brother.

But Lord Everard was glancing down at his wife, and the two nodded at each other. One pair, at least, was made then.

The Duke moved over to Lydia, a little hesitant.

"Miss Waverly, I wonder if I could persuade you to pair with me for the game? I'm afraid I'm not much acquainted with the others. I'd rather hoped that William would be here."

Lydia bit her lip. Since Arabella didn't much know the Duke herself, she could assume that he had been invited as a way of coaxing Henry out of his study.

It hadn't worked.

"I should love to partner with you, your Grace. I should warn you that I'm not much good at Pall-Mall."

He winced. "Neither am I. Fortunately, I'm not particularly competitive. Just as well, really."

Lydia looked over to Arabella, who was glancing inquisitively her way. Lord and Lady Everard had just announced their pairing.

"The Duke and I are a pair," Lydia said, feeling a trifle guilty at Miss Bolts' disappointed face.

"Then it is only the Bolts and me to dispose of. Miss Tabitha, how about your pair with your brother, and Miss Bolts and I shall form the final pair. What say you all?"

The plan was met with approval, and they all swigged down their tea with impolite speed and moved out towards the garden.

Lydia tapped her ball with the mallet, and watched it bounce across the lawn and neatly miss the wire hoop set out as a goalpost. She winced and glanced apologetically at her partner.

"I beg your pardon, your Grace. When I said I wasn't much good at Pall-Mall, I wasn't being modest."

He chuckled. "I think we've paired well, in fact. Either of us would have dragged down another pair, as the rest of them are very good at the game."

Lydia had to laugh at that. "It certainly is for the best, then."

The game was a simple enough one. Wire hoops were set all over the lawn, and the aim was to use the mallets to knock balls through the hoops. Mr Bolts had informed them all that in some parts of Society, the game had changed a little and was now being called Croquet. He didn't think it would catch on.

It was now somebody else's turn, and Lydia fell back to stand beside her partner, watching the game.

Her headache was still there, although not so bad as before. Arabella had chosen her guests well – they were pleasant company, and Lydia was enjoying herself. Even the stiff Duke was relaxing a little, although that could be her imagination.

"I had thought Henry would join us," the Duke said, his voice carefully lowered. She wondered briefly if he was trying to make sure that Arabella didn't overhear. Did he know about their marital issues? "Is he well, Miss Waverly?"

"I believe so," she said, matching her tone to his. "I don't think he was pleased at having guests over so quickly after the party."

"Ah, that seems right. Henry has always struggled with social occasions. Some people do, you know."

Lydia nodded. "I'm aware. Our Society doesn't make any allowances for those who'd prefer quiet, solitary pursuits to a ball and conversation."

He glanced at her, curious. There was something about his gaze – intent and almost unblinking – that made Lydia shiver.

I'm just cold. There's a sharp chill out here, and this shawl is not enough, she told herself firmly.

"And which do you prefer, Miss Waverly? Quiet, solitary pursuits, or Society?"

She smiled wryly. "Why must a person choose? I enjoy both, depending on how I feel. I have good friends and acquaintances, and a rich enough family to keep me comfortable. I am remarkably lucky, and I am not so ungrateful as to find ways to be dissatisfied with my own life."

She regretted saying that almost immediately. The Duke flinched, and Lydia cursed herself.

"Not that I am saying that anyone who is unhappy is *ungrateful*," she said hastily.

"Of course not," he murmured, and she couldn't help but think that he didn't quite believe her.

The game went on. Miss Bolts and Arabella were likely to win, and the Duke and Lydia were of course in the last place.

Lydia didn't mind. It was good to see her friend laughing and squealing with delight whenever she hit a good shot. Arabella kept glancing up at the house, as if expecting to see someone at the window, and her face fell just a little when there was no one there.

She hastily concealed her disappointment, and by the end of the game, everybody was happy and laughing. The sky clouded over at the very end, and a few drops of rain started to fall.

"No afternoon tea on the lawn, I'm afraid," Arabella said apologetically. "We'll take it in the drawing room, instead. Your Grace, do you think we ought to knock on Henry's door and see if he wishes to join us? It's worth a try, don't you think?"

Lydia had to look away from the hopefulness in her friend's face.

Say yes, say yes, she silently urged the Duke.

He smiled and bowed. "I shall do my best, Lady Fernwood. All my meagre powers of persuasion shall be bent that way."

She smiled in relief, and the Duke turned and strode away across the lawn, heading towards the house. The rest of them left their mallets to be packed up by the servants and hurried after him.

Lydia found herself watching the Duke go. He was a strongly built man, broad-shouldered, with no need for the padding and elaborate corsetry that gentlemen favoured at the moment. Poor Mr Bolts, a pleasant-looking and good-humoured man, had quite clearly employed a corset to tuck in his waist, instead of embracing his soft belly. Lydia thought wryly of her mother and her dislike of stick-thin beauties and wished that Mr Bolts had a similar parent.

"I was thinking of hosting a party at our house, too," Lady Anne Everard spoke up hesitantly. "I'll be going into confinement soon enough, and William and I were hoping to host something beforehand."

"Oh, how thrilling," Arabella laughed. "You two are so serious, I can hardly imagine you hosting a ball."

Lord Everard chuckled, not offended. "It wouldn't be a ball. We were thinking of a literary evening. Lots of reading and poetry, and that sort of thing."

He glanced around, a trifle nervous, gauging what the others thought.

"I think it's a capital idea," Mr Bolts said stoutly, and his sisters agreed. "Something nice and intelligent, for us poor fools to learn a thing or two."

Lord Everard smiled in relief, glancing at his wife. "Well, we'll send out invitations soon, then. Naturally, you are all invited. Lady Fernwood, you *must* bring Henry along."

She smiled thinly. "If he can sit quietly and read a book in a corner, I'm sure he'll agree to attend."

Lydia winced while the others laughed. It wasn't a joke, unfortunately.

Chapter Eight

"Miss Waverly is Edmund's cousin."

Charles said it casually, almost as an afterthought, over breakfast. Anne was taking her breakfast in bed, and William and Charles were eating together. They were staying at William and Anne's new home, in the centre of Bath, a pleasant if not overlarge townhouse. It was entirely suited to their needs, and full of books.

William did not flinch. "I know," he responded shortly, helping himself to another piece of toast.

"She doesn't know who I am."

"I know. I wouldn't recommend you tell her."

Charles swallowed thickly. "If she finds out…"

"Why would she? You bore no blame in the man's death, Charles."

Charles looked away and said nothing. As always, William refused to understand. Charles had told him, of course – told him how he'd nearly grabbed Edmund's hand, nearly pulled him to safety. But William didn't seem to agree that Charles was at fault.

"You tried your best," he said firmly, whenever the question came up. "Nothing more can be said."

Charles gave up trying to explain. It *was* his fault, and there was nothing to be done about it, and his guilt didn't rely on his brother to be real. Charles *knew* that he should have died in the water rather than let his friend drown, and if William didn't agree, then there was nothing to it.

William glanced up at him, thoughtful.

"I hope you're not going to dredge up all of this at the literary evening," William said, sounding peeved. "Anne is so excited. It's not often we host things, and once the baby is here, we'll have even less time. I want tonight to go smoothly."

"I'll help, of course I will," Charles responded, a little insulted.

He'd been invited to stay there the night before and the night after, and he had accepted after a little thought. If William and he were going to bridge the awkwardness which had sprung up between them, they'd need to spend time together, it was as simple as that. Josephine had been a little peeved at her son leaving her alone, but she was coming to the literary evening too, and was quickly mollified at that.

Charles wasn't sure he was looking forward to it. He *should* be. Miss Waverly was coming, and he would be lying if he said he didn't enjoy her company.

The game of Pall-Mall earlier in the week had been fun, even though Charles had come last. They'd talked to each other, swapped jokes, talked about everything and nothing, and the hours had flown past unstoppably.

Of course, there'd been the incident with Henry in between it all. Henry had been conspicuous by his absence, although everyone was too well-bred to comment on it.

While the others gathered in the drawing room, Charles had made his way to the study, and rapped gently on the door.

"Henry?"

"Charles? What are you doing here?"

"Your wife invited me. We've finished playing Pall-Mall."

There was a moment of silence. The door did not open, and there was no invitation to come in, so politeness kept Charles standing in the hallway.

"I know," Henry said, after a pause. "I saw you from the window. You played terribly, by the way."

"Yes, we came last. We're going into the drawing room for tea. Why don't you join us?"

There was another pause, longer than the last. Charles made himself stay still and wait.

"I don't think so," Henry said at last. "I don't think my wife particularly wants my company."

"Oh, Henry, don't be such a fool. She asked me to come and request your company."

"I'm quite happy here, thank you. I have work to do."

"Henry..."

"I'm alright, thank you."

Charles sighed. He knew his friend well enough to recognize the tone. Henry had been pushed as far as he would allow, and now it was time to leave him alone.

"Very well," he said after a pause. "But if you do want to join us, you know where we'll be. I think we'd all like to see you."

The was no reply, and after a few moments, he'd taken his leave and returned to the drawing room. He saw how Lady Fernwood's face dropped when he returned without Henry, although she quickly composed herself.

They'd spent the next few hours discussing the upcoming literary evening, and which books and poems might be recited.

Henry did not join them.

Back in the present day, sitting at the breakfast table with his brother, Charles sighed to himself and raked a hand through his hair.

"Lord and Lady Fernwood are having difficulties," he said after a pause.

William barely glanced up. "I'm aware. They're poorly matched."

"Don't be so harsh. I think they could make a good thing of it. They do love each other, but..."

"But neither will compromise. I'm sorry for it, Charles – I know he's your friend, but marriage isn't all roses and romance. Hard work is required, and neither of them seem inclined to work hard."

Charles pressed his lips together. He wanted to argue, but he didn't know Lady Fernwood well enough to claim otherwise, and since Henry had gotten married, they hadn't been as close as before.

"Perhaps you're right," he said at last. "What are you planning to recite for the literary evening tonight?"

"I thought I'd do a reading. Something from *Ivanhoe,* or perhaps one of Shakespeare's. What about you?"

"*The Rime of the Ancient Mariner,* I think. It's the only poem I remember in its entirety from school, and I think it's a firm favourite with most people."

They fell to discussing literature, and the subjects of Miss Waverly, poor, dead Edmund, and the mismatched Lord and Lady Fernwood were no longer discussed.

Of course, that didn't mean that Charles stopped thinking about them.

***

Anne had done an excellent job of decorating the library for their purposes. The literary evening was not a ball, full of chatter and music and dancing. Charles was pleasantly relieved to see that the young Society belles who'd attended Lady Fernwood's party were just as excited and happy to be here, discussing books, as they were to dance the night away in a ballroom.

Miss Bolt and Miss Tabitha were good-naturedly arguing about who would recite the favourite speech from Shakespeare's *Much Ado About Nothing* – a speech of Beatrice's, he thought, about tearing out a man's heart – and Anne was quietly reciting *A Red, Red Rose* in the corner.

The light in the library was warm and inviting, not bright, but light enough to easily read. A few young ladies and gentlemen were over at the bookshelves, pursuing the titles on the spines, and William was eagerly showing Henry his collection of fine, leather-bound works.

Anne got to her feet, clapping her hands and moving towards the head of the room. The others immediately found their seats – gilt, red-velvet chairs, tastefully arranged in a semicircle around the corner of the room which held the piano and a low, square platform – and waited, expectantly.

"I'm so glad you are all here," Anne said, smiling nervously around. "Lady Fernwood was to start off our evening, although she informs me that she is sure she will forget her words and ruin the poem. I think she does herself a discredit, but she has offered to play the pianoforte for us instead, to set the tone. Isn't she kind, everyone?"

There was good-natured applause, and Lady Fernwood made her way to the pianoforte, smiling apologetically. She took her place at the piano and started off with a slow, gentle arpeggio, not loud enough to drown out any voices, just enough to provide a little background music.

Charles glanced over at Henry and saw him sit up a little straighter, clearly listening to his wife's playing.

"Instead, we'll start with Miss Waverly, who will be receiving William Blake's delightful poem, *The Tyger*."

There was applause, and Miss Waverly got to her feet and made her way to the platform. Now it was Charle's turn to sit up a little straighter, craning his neck to watch her.

She smiled around at them, clearing her throat, and began.

Tyger, Tyger, burning bright,
In the forests of the night;
What immortal hand or eye,
Could frame thy fearful symmetry?

In what distant deeps or skies,
Burnt the fire of thine eyes?
On what wings dare he aspire?
What the hand, dare seize the fire?

And what shoulder, and what art,

Could twist the sinews of thy heart?
And when thy heart began to beat,
What dread hand? and what dread feet?

What the hammer? what the chain,
In what furnace was thy brain?
What the anvil? what dread grasp,
Dare its deadly terrors clasp!

When the stars threw down their spears
And water'd heaven with their tears:
Did he smile his work to see?
Did he who made the Lamb make thee?

Tyger, Tyger, burning bright,
In the forests of the night:
What immortal hand or eye,
Dare frame thy fearful symmetry?

    It was a well-known poem to most of them, not too long, rich with imagery, painting a vivid, terrifying picture of *the tyger*. She recited it well and smoothly and received good applause at the end.

    Anne clapped hard, beaming. She looked relieved that her evening was going well, and Charles met her eye and gave her an encouraging smile.

    Miss Waverly returned to the audience, only to find that her seat had been taken by a young lady, urgently whispering to her friend about the recitation they were meant to do together. Miss Waverly hesitated and glanced around the seats.

    Her eye fell on the empty seat beside Charles. He saw reluctance flash in her face, but only briefly.

    She moved over and sat beside him, flashing a quick, nervous smile.

    She smelled richly of lavender and rose water, and Charles was hard-pressed not to breathe in deeply.

    "You did very well," he said, in a low voice, so as not to disrupt the next recitation.

    "Thank you, your Grace. I wasn't thrilled at having to go first, but I am glad that it's over with."

    "Is it your favourite poem?"

"One of my favourites. To be frank, I think I prefer prose over poetry. A good poem is hard to find, you know. Still, I don't feel that reciting a passage from a book is quite as moving as poetry, when it comes to literary evening. We rarely have these in London, you know."

He glanced down at her. "Really?"

"Yes, this sort of thing is saved for outside the Season. The Season is all fine soirees and balls. If there are any sort of recitations or musical evenings, they aren't done for the beauty of the thing. They're done so that ladies can display their accomplishments. There's no joy in it at all. It's almost like a competition."

The disdain in Miss Waverly's voice was palpable. Her lips were pressed together, her chin raised, and her eyes focused on the nervous, bespectacled young woman on the platform who was reciting a sonnet of Shakespeare's. She finished on a flourish and was greeted by applause.

Miss Waverly clapped too; her expression thoughtful.

"You seem to dislike London, and the Season." Charles said, earning himself a sharp look.

"Most people do, your Grace. They just pretend otherwise. Still, I suppose I'll have to go back and participate in the Season sooner or later, so I might as well enjoy Bath while I can."

A pang went through him. He'd known, of course, that Miss Waverly wasn't going to stay in Bath forever, but that didn't do anything to hide the disappointment.

"I hope you aren't going anytime soon," he said after a pause. "We all enjoy your presence very much."

She glanced up at him, and he could almost feel her gaze boring into the side of his face. He didn't look at her, preferring instead to watch Anne announce the next speaker, while Lady Fernwood played a gentle, lilting classical piece.

"I'm glad to hear it," Miss Waverly said at last. "I'm enjoying myself here very much. Very much indeed."

***

And I had done a hellish thing,
And it would work 'em woe:
For all averred, I had killed the bird
That made the breeze to blow.
Ah wretch! said they, the bird to slay,

That made the breeze to blow!

The rhyme went round and round Charles' head, almost as if it were being recited by somebody else.

He wished he'd chosen something else, anything else, but *The Rime of the Ancient Mariner*.

Edmund and he hadn't gone to school together, but like all schoolboys, they were obliged to memorize it, verse after verse. The story had given Charles nightmares at first, and he'd always wondered what had possessed the Mariner to shoot the albatross. Surely, the bird hadn't done anything wrong?

***

He tossed and turned in his bed, the story tangling in his mind along with the literary evening, the candles gleaming in Charles' memory. He hadn't recited the whole of the poem – it was long, to say the least – and now it felt like the story was unfinished, the words queuing up in his throat, desperate to be spoken.

He saw Edmund in his dreams, in the place of the Mariner, with a dead albatross hung around his neck and his lips all dry and cracked with thirst. Charles was trying to swim to him, but no matter how hard he struck out, he couldn't get an inch closer. Despite the heaving seats, the plank of wood that Edmund balanced on didn't move, and Edmund watched him with blank, unseeing eyes.

Day after day, day after day,
We stuck, nor breath nor motion;
As idle as a painted ship
Upon a painted ocean.

Water, water, every where,
And all the boards did shrink;
Water, water, every where,
Nor any drop to drink.

"Give me your hand! Charles, give me your hand!"

He twisted in the water, salt stinging his eyes, and saw none other than Lydia, leaning over the side of a small dinghy, her gloved hand extending towards him. He opened his mouth to try and explain that he needed to save Edmund – in the logic of dreams, Lydia could not of course bring her boat to her cousin – but whenever he tried to speak, ice-cold salt water poured down his throat, making him gag and retch.

He understood, in a vague sort of way, that if he kept going towards Edmund, or tried to speak, he would drown. His choices were to drown, or to accept Lydia's hand.

He stretched his hand out of the water, inches from her gloved fingers. So, so, close, and then...

Charles sat bolt upright in bed, gasping for breath, tangled in the bed sheets. It took him a moment or two to realize where he was, and what was going on. He passed a shaking hand over his head and glanced around his dark bedroom.

It was the middle of the night, and Charles was so thirsty that his throat felt like sandpaper, his mouth as dry as if he'd been diligently eating sun-baked soil.

Or perhaps swallowing gallons of salt water.

Shuddering, he reached for the candle beside his bed, sighing in relief at the warm, reassuring glow. There was a carafe of water and a glass beside his bed, and Charles gulped eagerly from it, feeling the cool water pool in his stomach.

When he was more or less satisfied and the carafe was two-thirds empty, he replaced the cup and sank back onto the pillows.

It wasn't the first he'd dreamt about Edmund and the sea, and it would probably not be the last. It was the first time that Lydia had appeared in a dream, and of course the first time that Charles had had the opportunity to save himself from the sea.

If only his dreams could arrange themselves so that Edmund could survive, too.

He swallowed hard, closing his eyes.

One thing was sure, however. As soon as it was morning, Charles was going to his library to remove every copy of *The Rime of the Ancient Mariner*. He would throw the wretched poem in the rubbish, or perhaps give them away to somebody who would appreciate a tale of bad luck and shipwreck.

He shuddered, deciding not to snuff out the candle. It wouldn't do him any harm to sleep with the candle burning, just for tonight. Just until the sun started to rise.

Chapter Nine

Lydia had never much liked embroidery.

Oh, she could admire the art of it well enough, and the beauty. Some women were skilled in embroidery, could create patterns and pictures with their needle and thread to rival any painter's. It was a real talent, and one to be ranked alongside singing, pianoforte or harp playing, or painting.

Unfortunately, Lydia was not one with such talents. She found embroidery, and indeed any sewing, to be tiresome and tedious. It would be wonderful to have the skill of making her own clothes from scratch, instead of leaving it to the maids and modistes. She knew the *necessity* of sewing, of course. It was contemptuously deemed *woman's work* by some gentlemen, all of whom no doubt assumed that their replaced buttons, hemmed shirts and trousers, and intricately embroidered handkerchiefs sprang from nowhere, like a sort of miracle.

But knowing the importance of sewing was not quite the same as *enjoying* it. Lydia pricked her finger on her needle yet again and stifled a yelp, bringing the pad of her finger to the lips and sucking at the wound.

Arabella, who was adding a veritable flower garden along the bottom of a neat little white dress, ideal for rambles in the garden, put her work aside and came hurrying over.

"My dear girl, that's the third time you've pricked yourself today. You must give over, or else your work will be all splattered with blood."

She paused, glancing down at Lydia's sampler, and the horrifying tangle of red and pink thread.

"How lovely," she managed, unconvincingly. "What... what is it?"

"It's a rose," Lydia said wearily. "Or at least, it's meant to be. It's gone all lopsided."

"Samplers are very outmoded now, anyway," Arabella said tactfully, whisking the unfortunate sampler away and settling down beside her friend on the sofa. "Really, only debutantes and girls getting ready for their coming-out need to worry about samplers. You have many other skills, like your recitation last night. Your *The Tyger* was very good indeed, everyone said so."

"Everyone's poems and recitations were good," Lydia said firmly. "Your pianoforte playing was beautiful, and frankly I think it *made* the evening."

"Yes, I was pleased with it," Arabella said with a grin, leaning back in her seat.

They were seated in the conservatory, with a view out onto the valleys and fields at the back of the house. It was early enough in the year that they could sit in here without being boiled alive. Summertime meant that the conservatory was more or less shut up, except perhaps very late in the evening on exceptionally cool days, with the doors and windows open. During midday, when the room got hot even if it were cold outside, a few flushed and sweaty maids were sent in, armed with dusters, brooms, and cloths, to polish and sweep and dust away cobwebs as quickly as they could before darting out again.

Lydia had often thought it strange that, while ordinary folk lived in houses with perhaps just one or two rooms, and maybe not even a dedicated bedroom, people like herself and her friends had entire rooms that were ignored for months on end. It didn't seem *fair*, somehow.

Not that she would dare mention it to Arabella, who had gleefully described every room in the house she was to have when she married Henry.

"Did you enjoy yourself?" Arabella prompted, breaking the silence. "I saw you sitting next to the Duke of Northwood. His recitation of *The Ancient Mariner* was very good, if a little gloomy."

She shot an arch, pointed look at Lydia, who was a little horrified to realize that she was blushing.

"I had a nice time," Lydia said, ignoring the comment about the Duke. "It made a lovely change to the usual hustle and bustle and dancing that I'm used to."

"Really? I would have preferred a little dancing, but I know Anne isn't much in the mood for it, especially in her condition. And don't pretend you don't notice that the Duke likes you."

Lydia shot her a quick, baffled look. "What?"

"You are so *demure*. I've seen him looking at you. I believe he has a little fancy for you."

She pressed her lips together, raking through her memory. So far, the Duke had been nothing but pleasant to her, but it would be unfair to make simple pleasantness and gallantry for something more.

"He's kind to me, and I believe we are friends," she said hesitantly, "but that's all. Don't make him uncomfortable by trying to push us together, Arabella. Don't you remember how gentlemen would make us talk to them, in our first Season, and we were obliged to be polite, and then they would use that to claim that we were *encouraging* them? Don't you remember how aggravating it was, to have common politeness taken as something more, when you were all but *forced* to be polite?"

Arabella sniffed. "I think that only really happened to you," she said tartly. "I stuck by my chaperones, who would usually save me, or else I'd simply act too demure to say a word."

"Ugh. I could never manage that."

"I know. Gentlemen used to call you *spirited*, until you said something to offend them, and then they'd call you *shocking*."

Lydia got to her feet, shaking out her skirts and moving over to the window. It was a fine day, deceptively sunny, but she knew from experience that it was ice-cold outside. She wanted a walk. Her legs were stiff and cramped from sitting so long.

"You could capture him, you know, if you exerted yourself," Arabella opined after a brief pause.

Lydia swallowed hard. "Arabella..."

"Don't snap at me. You *could* catch the Duke if you put your mind to it, you know."

"I don't like this talk of catching and *getting*. Marriage is a serious business, not a wild dash or a competition. If I do marry – and it is a large *if*, Bella! – it will be for a better reason than simply because I am getting older and other people think that I ought to. I truly think that if more ladies had the chance to slow down, catch their breath, look around themselves and get something of an education, they wouldn't be in such a great hurry to marry. A good marriage is lovely, I know that, and for ladies like us there's not much else to do, but a bad marriage is truly unpleasant."

Lydia paused after this speech, drawing in a deep breath. She glanced back over her shoulder and found that her friend had gone white, with her lips pinched together.

"So is that what you think of me, then?" Arabella said at last. "That I'm a silly girl who rushed to the altar before she could think about it properly? A brainless fool?"

"What? No, Arabella, no! I thought Henry and you were so well matched. I'm sorry if that was how it sounded, it was not my intention."

Lydia hurried back to the sofa, sinking down beside her friend.

"Arabella, talk to me. Please tell me you aren't angry."

Arabella blinked, giving her head a little shake. Her ringlets, impeccably if unnaturally curled, bounced and shook around her head, making her look even younger than her not-quite-twenty years of age.

"Of course I'm not angry, Lydia. I'm peevish and snappy because I have a headache, that's all. Let's not talk about Henry and me."

"I believe Henry loves you very much, and I think you love him. If you would only..."

"The Duke," Arabella interrupted, getting to her feet and pacing around the room, "is going to be at the Bolts' party this evening. There's to be no dancing, more's the pity, but still, there will be *opportunities*."

It was clear that she wanted to change the subject, and Lydia gave up. She leaned back in her seat, folding her arms.

"Arabella..."

"You don't have to be *artful*, my dear. You obviously enjoy his company, so why not seek it out a little more? Does his scar not bother you?"

"His scar? No. I think it looks rather dashing. I heard he got it on a sea-voyage."

Arabella threw herself down in an armchair with a sigh.

"Yes, it was a horrible thing, I've heard. Henry told me parts of it, but the Duke is very private about what happened. His friend and he had gone on a Grand Tour, and I believe their ship got into difficulties. I'm not sure whether he was knocked over or struck by something, but he was injured. He came home directly after and hasn't travelled again. He said once that he'd rather die than get back in a boat, and I'm not sure I blame him."

Lydia bit her lip. It was impossible not to think of Edmund.

"Travelling is so dangerous," she murmured. "I wonder how anyone can bring themselves to take a Grand Tour at all. It's a pity, because the Duke seems well-travelled. He told me all sorts of things about different countries. I quite envied him and his travels."

Arabella shuddered. "Ugh. Myself, I don't care to travel. Where's the enjoyment about being sick over the side of a boat, or being shaken to death in a carriage on truly awful roads, hoping that you'll find an inn which isn't *entirely* infested with fleas to sleep in."

"That sounds more like your experience of travelling than the general idea," Lydia pointed out tactfully, and her friend rolled her eyes.

"Henry did not enjoy it either. He confessed that he thought *I* would like it and would have been happy enough with that." She paused, picking at the arm of the chair. "I wonder when he stopped caring about my happiness in such a way?"

"He hasn't, Arabella, believe me. He..."

"Oh, no, no, enough of that! Ignore me and my maudlin ramblings. Let's talk about what we shall wear tonight. Now, as there's to be no dancing, we needn't bother with dancing slippers. I hate those things. They're so delicate I feel as if somebody is about to step on my foot and crush me at any given moment. There'll be cards, so if I were you, I should try and join the table the Duke chooses, so that you can play alongside him. Ooh, a pairs game would be ideal. You did very well, securing him as your partner for the game of Pall-Mall earlier. Poor Miss Bolt would have gotten him, if she could."

Lydia sank back in her seat, feeling a little dizzy at her friend's babble of conversation.

"I didn't *deliberately* secure him for my partner, Arabella. Truly, I didn't. He asked me."

"Did he really? Well, that's excellent. Well done, Lydia."

"Don't say *well done*, I haven't done anything," Lydia said, starting to feel tired already.

She enjoyed the social events, but Arabella's hunger for parties and gatherings never seemed to be satisfied. She stayed as late as she could, and they were usually one of the last or perhaps the last guests to leave. It was as if she were starving, and stuffing herself with food because she had no idea when she would eat again, or even if she *would* eat again.

It was a sad state of affairs, and Lydia felt entirely hopeless.

She rose to her feet, glancing at the clock. "I suppose I'd better go and get ready. I'm going to write a letter to Mama first, to see when Clara and she will be coming."

"Oh, good Lord, yes, we had better get a start on dressing." Arabella did a little twirl in the middle of the room. "I shall wear my midnight-blue silk, and Henry will simply *have* to admit that I look beautiful."

My Dearest Mama

I look forward to Clara and you arriving in Bath. I'm so sorry to hear that you've been bothered by a cold, which has prevented you from arriving earlier.

You asked in your last letter whether I am settled and enjoying myself, and I can answer yes to both. Arabella is such a gracious host, and we are quite friends again. Her husband, Lord Fernwood, is a good and kind man, and I like him very much. However, he does not much enjoy parties and dances, which is a pity, because Arabella loves to see people and spend time with them.

I am enclosing a letter to Clara, in which there is a more detailed description of what we have been doing and who I have been meeting. Arabella is looking forward to seeing Clara and invites her to come and stay with us in her house.

It will be almost like old times, she says.

We have a great many amusements planned – dances, soirees, trips, picnics, and more. Arabella is quite in her element, although poor Lord Fernwood seems greatly troubled at so much socializing. I hope he will feel comfortable soon enough.

This is not a long letter, as we are going out again in just a few hours, to a party at the Bolts'. You don't know them, but I shall make the introductions when you arrive.

Your Loving Daughter, Who Looks Forward To Your Arrival,
Lydia

PS. It's remarkably cold here, so be sure to wrap up well. Arabella's house is exceptionally pretty and well-arranged, but very draughty. It was designed and decorated, I believe, by the Dowager Lady Fernwood, Lord Fernwood's mother, and he is loath to make any changes.

Arabella is not pleased at this, but we have high hopes that she will soon be allowed to redecorate the drawing room and some of the bedrooms.

Chapter Ten

Charles eyed his reflection with resignation.

His valet had done a good job, well enough. Or rather, William's valet, a pinch-faced, nimble-fingered man who was clearly not thrilled at having to wait on someone beyond his master but was also willing to do as he was told and not make a fuss.

He was wearing a mustard-coloured evening suit – the Bolts were known to be free and easy over matters of fashion and what was 'proper' to wear – with a gold, pink, and blue waistcoat underneath, with mother-of-pearl buttons polished to a high shine.

It was a rather garish choice, but it made Charles feel – well, almost like his old self. His hair was neatly brushed and glossy with pomade, he was freshly shaven, and in the forgiving candlelight, his scar was not quite as bad as it was usually.

It was still *there*, of course, right there on his face for anyone to see, but somehow, Charles didn't much mind tonight.

After all, everyone who *mattered* didn't care about his scar. His brother and sister-in-law barely noticed it anymore, Henry didn't care, and Miss Waverly… well, if he didn't know better, he'd say that Miss Waverly found it *dashing*.

Careful, Charles, he warned himself. *Don't get carried away. Don't set yourself up for disappointment.*

William might think otherwise, but Charles was fairly sure that if she knew he was the one who'd let her beloved cousin die, all of his hopes would be at an end. She would never speak to him again, never look at him. The scar which she did not seem to mind would now remind her of his abject failure, how he'd let her cousin, brother to her in all but name, die.

He swallowed hard, closing his eyes.

No.

It wasn't that surprising that the family had not known that Edmund and Charles were travelling together. They hadn't planned to travel together. They'd met each other through their clubs, but their families moved in different circles. He had never met Edmund's family, and vice versa. It didn't much matter. Edmund was a monster when it came to writing home to his family, and Charles was fairly sure that he had never been mentioned much in his friend's letters, only as 'my companion'.

He had attended Edmund's memorial service back in England, of course, but he'd huddled in the back, and not gone to the luncheon after.

No, Miss Waverly did *not* know. Some might argue that not telling her the truth was deception, and Charles studiously avoided those thoughts.

A rap on the door made him jump.

"Are you ready, Charles?" William asked, voice muffled. "Anne's not coming tonight, but she insisted I go. Are you ready? We can travel together."

"I was going to ride."

"Jacobs tells me you're wearing the monstrosity of a multicoloured waistcoat. He seemed to like it, but I imagine I'll get a headache as soon as I look at you. Anyway, you can't possibly ride in that. You'll get covered in mud and horsehair. Take the wretched carriage."

Charles smiled wryly. "If you insist, my dear brother."

"I do, Charles. I *do*."

Moments later, the two brothers were sitting opposite each other in the carriage, rumbling through the dark landscape. Charles could see the Bolts' home high on a hill, windows ablaze, and he swallowed hard, wishing not for the first time that he'd stayed at home.

"Cheer up," William said awkwardly. "It's just you and me again. The two brothers, rattling our way through Society. Although of course I'm a married man now, so I don't need to feel jealous when the ladies all flutter around you."

Charles smiled mirthlessly. "No fear of that. The ladies aren't fond of me at all these days, and I think I can guess why."

William bit his lip. "Not true. Miss Bolt likes you."

"Miss Bolt is a likeable young woman and a decent friend, but she has solely mercenary aims in marriage. She wants a rich man, ideally a titled one, and *that* is why she likes me."

"Miss Waverly seemed to like you."

Charles flinched at that. It was cruel of William to say so, although of course his poor brother didn't know what he was doing.

"Miss Waverly is kind to everyone," he said airily, as if it didn't much matter either way. "I don't think she'd like to have her politeness interpreted as encouragement."

William snorted. "Well, it's not like I can understand the female heart. Still, I think you're in with a chance, there."

Not once she knows I let her cousin die.

The carriage slowed down, approaching the house, and Charles leaned forward in preparation for the evening.

He still wished he'd stayed at home.

***

The kindly candlelight of his own dressing-room was gone. The Bolts' huge drawing room, which had rooms opening off it to serve as cardrooms, was very well lit, and a fire burned in the grate. There would be no soft, friendly light to hide Charles' scar, and his clothes seemed ridiculously garish.

Mr Bolt enthusiastically complimented Charles' waistcoat, and begged to know where he'd got it, but really, Charles was sure he was just making fun of him. Miss Bolt and Miss Tabitha also complimented him, but again, they were just being kind. He was sure of it.

The amiable Lady Fernwood, kind as always, *also* told Charles his waistcoat was pleasant. Humiliated, he snatched up a glass of champagne and looked around for a card-table needing another player.

Henry, who had been dragged out of his study and spruced up nicely, came and stood next to him.

"You seem down today," he commented.

"I feel like a fool. What possessed me to wear these clothes, and this waistcoat? They must all be laughing at me."

Henry blinked at him. "I think you look nice. Arabella noticed it as soon as you came in, and started telling me I needed a waistcoat like that. Everybody is complimenting you."

"They don't mean it, they're all being kind."

Henry made a *disapproving sound*. "Ah, yes, everybody in this room, all members of Society where unnecessary kindnesses are frowned upon, they are all trying to spare your feelings. Of course."

Charles gave him a look. "I don't appreciate the sarcasm, my friend. And what brings you out of your home? You hate socialising."

Henry swallowed hard, seeming intent on his drink, swirling round and round in the glass.

"I suppose I ought to make an effort to accompany Arabella," he said at last. "I rather made a fool of myself over the game of Pall-Mall. I don't want to seem like a tyrant. I think she believes I'm deliberately trying to stop her enjoying herself. I'm not, I just... well, she doesn't believe that I don't enjoy this sort of thing."

"It can be hard, if one enjoys a pursuit, to understand that others may not. Why not talk to her about it?"

"I don't want her to think that I'm a weak fool."

"I'm sure she won't."

Henry shook his head, glancing around. "Shall we get a card-table? I fancy a game. Get us a table, and I'll round up some players."

"Agreed."

The men parted ways, with Charles eventually finding a green-baized rectangular table in the corner of the room, with a pack of cards left out on it.

He wondered, briefly, who Henry would bring. The man had few enough friends.

He didn't have to wait long to find out.

Barely had Charles gotten himself settled when he saw Henry trotting across the drawing room towards him, with Miss Waverly following him. Charles swallowed reflexively, half lifting his hand to cover his scar before he remembered that it was foolish and replacing his hand.

"Arabella didn't want to play," Henry said, a touch unhappily. "But Miss Waverley agreed. What shall we play?"

Charles swallowed hard. "Three is an odd number. What can we play with three?"

"Plenty of games, of course," Miss Waverly said, laughing. "What about Brag? Do you all know the rules."

"I can pick it up easily, I'm sure," Henry said, with unwarranted confidence.

"I know how to play," Charles responded, smiling nervously. He hadn't expected to have such an intimate card game with Miss Waverly, but...

"What's that?" came an unpleasantly familiar voice. "A game of Brag? How lovely."

Charles glanced up at Sir Gregory and wholeheartedly wished him to perdition. Sir Gregory beamed down at him.

"Don't mind if we join, do you? Mrs Habit and I, that is."

There was really no polite way to say *no*, so Charles smiled thinly, and the two uninvited guests sat down.

"Right. Well," Henry said, looking annoyed that people he did not know were joining them. "Miss Waverly, shall we get some champagne for the table?"

She nodded, and the two scurried off towards the refreshment table, leaving Charles alone with Sir Gregory and Mrs Habit.

The lady seemed bored and began to pick at her fingernails. Sir Gregory, on the other hand, looked positively gleeful. He leaned close to Charles, resting his elbow on the table.

"Do you know, your Grace, I've finally made a thrilling connection. Miss Waverly and you have a mutual friend. I beg your pardon, actually you *had* a mutual friend. It's that dear chap you went on your tour with, Edmund something-or-other. Everyone knows how much it hurt the poor dear to lose her cousin. The family was nigh inconsolable, I heard. How odd that he was killed in such a shocking manner, and yet you survived. Strange, is it not?"

Charles glanced immediately over at Mrs Habit, but she didn't seem to be listening.

He said nothing, and Sir Gregory leaned back in his seat with a secretive smile. As Miss Waverly and Henry returned to the table, he ostentatiously placed a finger to his lips.

The cards were shuffled and dealt, and the game began. It was a simple enough game, and since it was a genteel event, the stakes were kept low. The first phase of the game passed without incident or even much conversation. Mrs Habit yawned openly, and Miss Waverly glanced between the sullen faces, obviously wondering why the atmosphere at the card table was so tense.

The second phase arrived, and now the players were able to up the stakes of the game, in more ways than one.

"I brag," Sir Gregory announced, shuffling his cards, and placing a stake. "Come now, who wants to challenge me?"

The eldest at the table was, presumably, Mrs Habit, so she would have the chance to challenge him first. She winced, glancing at Sir Gregory's exultant expression.

"No, thank you. I daresay you have a marvellous hand. I shall pass."

He gave a laugh. "Perhaps I do, dear Mrs Habit, perhaps I do."

"Or perhaps he is bragging," Charles spoke up. "It is the game, after all."

Henry winced, eyeing his cards, and shook his head. Miss Waverly would be the last to have a chance to challenge him, and judging by the way she was looking at her cards, it would not be worth her while.

Charles leaned forward. "I'll challenge you."

He placed a stake, obliging Sir Gregory to up his own stake considerably. The man pursed his lips and did so.

The stakes were raised and raised, until a modest pile of coins and chips lay in the middle of the table.

"I'll see you, then," Sir Gregory said, smiling. "I can see by your face you don't have much of a hand."

Charles smiled tightly and turned over his hand, as did Sir Gregory.

The smile fell from Sir Gregory's face. His hand was good, but not quite good enough.

"Three threes!" Miss Waverly gasped. "That's the best hand one can get in this game, isn't it? You win, your Grace. Well done!"

"It's luck," Sir Gregory snarled, obviously put out. Charles held his breath, half-afraid that an accusation of cheating would be made.

Sir Gregory was a fool, but not *that* much of a fool. He pressed his lips together and shook his head.

"I'm tired of this game," he announced. "Mrs Habit, let's have a turn around the room."

The woman sighed, rolling her eyes, and set her cards face-up on the table. She got up and took his arm, but Charles noticed that all of her smiling adoration from their previous meeting was gone. She was bored of Sir Gregory, and he was too proud to notice that she was.

Oh, well.

"They left in the middle of the game," Henry said, shocked and a little angry. "We'll have to start again."

"It's impolite," Miss Waverly said. Her eyes were fixed on Charles, as if she *knew* something. He swallowed hard, avoiding her eyes.

"We should play something else," he said lightly, scooping up the cards and shuffling them again. "Not Brag, I've had quite enough of that."

"Aren't you going to collect your winnings?"

Charles glanced at the modest pile on the table and suppressed a smile. It *did* feel good to beat Sir Gregory at anything, even if only a card game.

He scooped up the money and began to shuffle the cards while Henry went for more refreshments.

"I meant to say to you earlier," Miss Waverly said, in a rush, "but your waistcoat is ever so nice. It's so unusual and colourful, and it suits you very much."

He swallowed hard, not daring to meet her eye.
"Thank you, Miss Waverly. Thank you."

Chapter Eleven

Arabella was in a bad mood. Lydia winced as her friend went stamping past the open door to the morning-room, whispering angrily under her breath.

She made herself sit still, waiting patiently. No doubt Arabella would tell her what was going on soon.

Lydia was right. Another five minutes and Arabella came stamping back, flouncing into the room and plopping down on the sofa beside her.

"I am outraged, Lydia, *outraged*. Just listen to this. Henry's mother – who has made nothing but trouble for me since we were married – has heard about the archery and tea party arranged for this afternoon, and wrote to Henry, inviting herself. Can you imagine it? He just told me now, and said that she'll have to be accommodated, as this was once her house, and he is her son. I'm furious, Lydia."

Lydia winced, closing her book – she hadn't turned a page for several minutes now – with a snap.

"Oh, dear. That is troublesome, Arabella. I don't suppose you can tell her not to come, since she *is* your mother-in-law."

Naturally, there were some people in town who either pressured their hosts into inviting them to events, or simply turned up anyway. It was, needless to say, shockingly bad manners, and Polite Society would name those people as vulgar, entirely too forward, and Not Proper Persons. It was a damning judgment, and generally not worth the icily polite reception and cold shoulders that one would receive at the event. It was generally a thing done by desperate people – ladies who were willing to risk their reputation to catch one specific gentleman, or gentlemen who needed access to high-stakes card tables, and other such uncomfortable situations. Besides, one ran the risk of being turned away at the door, or worse, asked to leave.

There wasn't a great deal one could do if it was one's *mother-in-law* shouldering her way into a party. Nobody would believe such a thing of a well-respected widow, in any case.

"What are you going to do?" Lydia continued.

"Why, nothing. I can't do a thing. I am heartily tired of that woman, Lydia, I can tell you. I suppose it will be the first time you meet her, and..."

"Arabella?" Henry appeared in the doorway, visibly nervous, shifting from foot to foot. He smiled wanly at Lydia. "May I have a word?"

Pressing her lips together, Arabella rose wordlessly to her feet and sailed out into the hallway. Lydia didn't *mean* to listen, but it *was* very quiet, and she couldn't quite help *hearing*.

"I'm sorry about Mother, Arabella. I should have been firmer with her, and I wasn't." Henry said, his voice low. "If you like, I'll send a message to her immediately and tell her not to come."

"Oh," Arabella responded, and Lydia could almost hear the surprise in her friend's voice. "Well, you don't need to do that."

"I don't? But you were so upset."

"I *am*, but I don't want you to look ungenerous towards your mother. I am *not* pleased, but then, we haven't had her over to dine for a while. Perhaps she just wants to see you. I was in a bad temper this morning, you see. Let her come. What's the worst that could happen?"

Henry gave a sigh of relief. "I'm glad you said that. Thank you, Arabella. I appreciate it. I suppose I had better go and dress, now."

"Yes, I think so. I shall see you soon."

Lydia heard Henry's footsteps retreat, and after a moment or two, Arabella returned to her seat, looking pensive.

"Is everything alright?" Lydia asked sweetly.

"Hm? Oh, yes, everything is fine. Henry was going to write to his mamma, but I think it would look shabby if we were to uninvite her. At least, that is what she'd tell other people, and I won't have her making Henry look unkind. He is *not* unkind. I don't much care what she says about me, but Henry is her only child, and I won't have her being cruel to him."

Lydia smiled and said nothing. Sniffing to herself, Arabella snatched up a book and angrily turned the pages for a minute or two, until she mumbled something about changing her dress and stormed out without another word.

Interesting, Lydia thought. *It's a good sign, isn't it? Henry is willing to compromise for his wife, and Arabella is giving her husband the credit he deserves. Yes, a very good sign indeed, I think.*

***

The sport of the day, Arabella announced, was archery. A section of the garden had been fenced off, angled well away from the lawn where the other guests were relaxing, and a handful of gentlemen were already flexing their bows experimentally, and choosing arrows.

It was all gentlemen, so far. The ladies and a few other guests reclined on seats set out for that purpose, sipping tea and eyeing the targets.

The Dowager Lady Fernwood, affectionately known as Dowager Fernwood to her friends, had taken the centre seat, a large wicker chair in the very middle of the circle of chairs, and appeared to be holding court.

Or trying to, at least. A great many of Arabella's friends had moved their chairs to sit by *her* instead, leaving a disgruntled-looking Dowager Fernwood with the matrons instead.

She was a portly woman, very tall, with little resemblance to her son. She had small, sharp, beady eyes which flickered everywhere, missing no detail. That gaze had raked over Lydia and dismissed her of no interest, not bothering to speak any further. She glanced continually at Arabella, and her lips pinched tighter and tighter with every glance.

"Arabella," she said, at one point, "why do you not have finger-cakes out here? Every picnic must have finger-cakes. Can your cook not make them?"

"This is not a picnic, madam," Arabella responded calmly. "I don't much like finger-cakes. There are plenty of other foods – I am not afraid of my guests going hungry."

"You *must* have finger-cakes, Arabella. Must she not, Mrs Typh? See, Mrs Typh agrees with me. Arabella, find a good recipe for finger-cakes. Perhaps your cook could make some for us to have before we go. It's simply shocking for a picnic not to have finger-cakes."

Lydia watched a muscle flutter in her friend's jaw.

"I do not like finger-cakes," she repeated placidly.

This was not what Dowager Fernwood wanted to hear. The woman's lips pinched tighter, almost disappearing.

"A good hostess does not think of what *she* wants, only the comfort of her guests. Really, Arabella."

Arabella, rather wisely, pretended not to hear this. Conversation had all but dwindled away, due to Dowager Fernwood's booming voice, and in a desperate bid to restart it again, Lydia leant forward towards Miss Bolts. Miss Bolts was sitting straight-backed, craning her neck at the archery fields, looking miserable.

"Miss Bolts, why don't you have a go? Arabella tells me you're a remarkable shot."

Miss Bolts flushed red and glanced warningly at Dowager Fernwood. She was too late. The dowager sucked in a breath and leaned towards Lydia.

"Archery is not a proper sport for ladies," she said severely. "There are *some modest* card games which a lady can properly play, but outdoor sports are quite inappropriate. There is nothing wrong with cheering on the men, but I can see nothing ladylike in a game of archery. In fact, I heard recently that you, Arabella, arranged some game of *Pall-Mall*. I must counsel you firmly against such nonsense. In fact, I would go so far as..."

Lydia bounced to her feet, attracting all attention her way.

"I think I'll play archery," she said sweetly, trying not to meet Dowager Fernwood's outraged glare. "Do excuse me, Arabella."

Arabella, who was trying unsuccessfully to hide a grin, inclined her head gracefully. "Of course, Lydia. Have fun!"

Lydia turned, and without a backwards glance, strode across the lawn towards the area fenced off for the archery. There were several targets at differing distances, and the only one unoccupied was the longest one. Lydia took her place there and picked up a bow.

She heard a man sigh theatrically and come plodding towards her. She recognized him as Mr Barnes, a cousin of Henry's, who had accompanied Dowager Fernwood. He was a skittish, self-important man, and nobody seemed to like him.

"I do believe that the Dowager disapproves of ladies playing archery," he said in a stage whisper, wincing as though she were making a faux pas.

Lydia smiled brilliantly. "And *I* do believe that this is *not* the Dowager's house."

He flushed. "Well, yes, but..."

"*Lady Fernwood* has arranged all this, and I know for a fact she intends for ladies and gentlemen to play at archery."

The man glowered at her for a moment, then made a bid to save his wounded dignity. "Well, now I suppose that somebody must teach you how to play. Perhaps..."

"I will."

The voice was familiar and sent shivers down Lydia's spine. She nocked an arrow, glancing briefly over her shoulder.

Mr Barnes eyed the Duke of Northwood with barely concealed dislike, then spun on his heel and stalked towards Dowager Fernwood and her entourage.

Lydia glanced up at the Duke, who was watching her with a strange, guarded expression.

"I'm not sure who decided that archery was only for men," he said, "but I apologise. Shall I show you how to pull back the string? It requires more strength than people think, but I'm sure you can do it."

"If you like," Lydia said. Out of the corner of her eye she saw Miss Bolt gathering her courage then striding up towards them, intent on playing a little archery herself. She smiled. Miss Tabitha would follow wherever her older sister led, and then probably Arabella would too, if only to escape from her mother-in-law's carping.

"You hold the bow here, with *this* hand," the Duke murmured, standing at her shoulder. It was perhaps a little too close, and Lydia found herself holding her breath. When she risked a glance at his face, however, he was intent on her hand and the bow. "And then with your hand gripping the string and the arrow like *so*, you pull back. Be sure to brace your first arm, however."

"Like this?"

"Yes, exactly so. You are a natural, Miss Waverly. Now, sight down the length of the shaft towards the target. You've chosen a long distance, but I shouldn't worry about that. Don't worry about hitting the target at all – archery takes practice."

"Am I ready to shoot?"

"You are, Miss Waverly." He stepped back, and Lydia found herself missing the warmth of him. "Whenever you are ready."

She sighted down the shaft, adjusting her hold minutely, and let the arrow go.

It sailed noiselessly through the air, embedding itself into the very centre of the target with a *thud*.

There was a brief silence. Lydia noticed that the other gentlemen had gone quiet too, along with the gleeful Miss Bolts.

"Well, I..." the Duke managed, and Lydia grinned.

"Beginner's luck, perhaps. Shall I try again?"

Without waiting for an answer, she nocked another arrow and let it fly, the arrow thudding into the target within an inch of the first. She lifted an eyebrow.

"Again, perhaps?"

The Duke let out a huff of laughter.

"Am I correct in assuming you are already very good at archery, Miss Waverly?"

She gave a modest curtsey. "I have played archery before, yes."

"Hmph. Serves me right for assuming. Well done, Miss Waverly. I can assume that you are the best shot here, much to these gentlemen's horror."

Lydia glanced around at the other gentlemen. Miss Bolts was thrilled, of course, and a few of the men looked admiring, at least. Most of them, however, were regarding her with disgust and dislike. She winced.

"I forgot that gentlemen hate women who outshine them in anything," she muttered, half to herself.

The Duke heard and took a step closer.

"Then you know which gentlemen to avoid," he murmured. "They have saved you the time and trouble of getting to know them. For my part, I admire people who excel at anything, and I know from experience that archery is not easy."

"Would you like a turn?"

He smiled down at her, and Lydia felt her treacherous heart flutter. She handed over the bow, and just for a moment, their fingers brushed against each other. The contact sent shivers along her skin, and she withdrew her hand as if it had been burnt.

If the Duke noticed, he showed no signs of it. He nocked an arrow and expertly took aim. His shot was good – not as good as Lydia's, of course, but still good – and he let off two arrows before handing the bow back to her.

They continued in this manner, measuring their progress against each other, for a few moments. The world around Lydia began to crumble away, and all she knew was the smooth wood of the bow beneath her hand, and the ripple and shimmy of the arrow as it launched towards her target.

That, and the Duke of Northwood, standing at a respectful distance behind her, and yet always *there*, always leaving her aware of him. She shivered, and her latest shot went a little awry.

She winced, watching the arrow quiver in one of the outer circles of the target.

Before she could comment, however, Arabella came bouncing up to them.

"May I have a turn?" she asked sweetly, and the Duke immediately gave up his turn to her. "By the way, I had better warn you both that my dearest mother-in-law is planning a musical evening later this week, and we will be obliged to attend. All of us. Oh, curses, I have missed."

Chapter Twelve

The Dowager Lady Fernwood's musical evening was not shaping up to be an enjoyable occasion. Charles had very much wanted to avoid it, but William insisted. Anne was going; she was one of the nervy wives and soon-to-be mothers who were all too aware of the hold women like Dowager Fernwood had on Society.

"She's tried and rejected at least four dresses," William had muttered earlier that evening, as they sat and waited in the carriage. "Don't expect tonight to be fun."

Charles adjusted his expectations accordingly.

Dowager Fernwood lived in the widow's house at the edge of the estate, although she had tried her best to stay living in the main house when her daughter-in-law had first moved in. Charles didn't listen too closely to gossip, of course, but he had it on good authority that there was bad blood between the current Lady Fernwood and the Dowager, and poor Henry was caught in between, and that Dowager Fernwood had left the main house in a tremendous temper.

The widow's house, he saw as they approached, was a large building, well-constructed, with large, airy windows and extensive grounds. It was smaller than the main house, naturally, but still large and pretty.

The three of them were ushered through the high-ceiling hallways by a blank-faced footman, and were shown into a large, well-decorated, and overheated drawing room. There was a large pianoforte in a corner, with a harp beside it, and chairs arranged in a semicircle.

The Dowager herself held court in the middle, wearing a costly gown of rustling black silk, dripping with diamonds, pearls, and impossibly expensive lace.

She rose gracefully to greet Charles and the others, encouraging them to take a seat and enjoy some of her famous finger-cakes.

Beside her sat Lady Fernwood, looking miserable and dull in a dark-blue satin gown, trimmed with lace. Her husband sat on the other side of his mother, looking for all the world like a little boy again, not daring to speak up lest he contradict his mother.

Charles felt heartily sorry for him.

"Our musical program is all arranged, your Grace, and I think you shall be thrilled. Lady Thomasin is going first, playing a delightful aria of her own composition on the harp. She is such a wonderful player, with the neatest arms and elbows you ever did see. Be sure to pay attention, your Grace. I should exhort Lord Everard to pay attention, too, although I know that *he* is a married man." Dowager Fernwood tittered, to show them that it was a joke, and they all laughed politely.

Charles sat beside his brother and he was uncomfortably aware that he was the most eligible man there, and one of the few single ones. He could see a few familiar faces – the Bolts, all crammed in together behind the door, and Mrs Habit, in the middle of smothering a yawn. There was no sign of Sir Gregory, for which Charles was relieved.

There was one particular face he longed to see, and it took him a few long moments to find her.

Miss Waverly had been, rather cruelly, separated from her friends. She was not seated near Henry or Lady Fernwood, or even the Bolts siblings. Dowager Fernwood had curated the seating arrangements, and Miss Waverly had been put in a cluster of matrons and widows, all gossiping freely among themselves and shooting disapproving stares at Miss Waverly's Parisian-style yellow gown.

She looked thoroughly bored. Perhaps sensing eyes on her, she glanced up and met his gaze. He gave her a nod and a half smile, which was returned.

Then Dowager Fernwood laid her hand on his arm, and Charles was obliged to lean in to listen to her.

"Now, you are such a dear friend of my Henry's, I am quite determined, you Grace. You shall be married by the end of the Season. I have half a dozen pretty, suitable young ladies for you to view."

Charles' heart sank. "I thank you for your kindness, madam, but..."

"No need to thank me. We widows must do our best."

Lady Fernwood leaned forward. "Madam, I don't believe that his Grace wants a match made for him. He wants to pick his own bride. In fact, Henry said..."

The Dowager rudely cut her off, not even glancing her way.

"Hush, now. Lady Thomasin is about to start. Look at those wrists. So finely turned."

A prim-faced lady with an air of irrepressible smugness glided up the harp and began a mournful-sounding aria. When he could, Charles leaned over to William.

"I thought we were meant to be listening to the music, not looking at her arms."

William smothered a laugh. "Incorrect, dear brother. For a single gentleman or a single lady, this sort of occasion is *never* about the music. All you must do is play well enough and look good doing it."

Charles winced.

Lady Thomasin's performance seemed to go on forever, and when she finally finished, she lingered at her harp as if she hoped to be asked for an encore. She was not.

Dowager Fernwood glanced over at Charles, and caught him smothering a yawn. She clapped her hands, rising to her feet, and Lady Thomasin flushed and scurried back to her seat.

"Now, Arabella, you may go next."

There was a hint of triumph in her voice. Charles glanced at Arabella in time to see the colour drain from her face.

"I...you said I would not have to perform," Arabella said anxiously. "I have not practiced."

"Not practiced? Nonsense. You must have done. Play us a little something on the harp, won't you, Arabella?" Dowager Fernwood sank down onto her seat, not even looking at Arabella.

"I really cannot," Arabella said urgently, trying to attract her mother-in-law's attention.

Dowager Fernwood shot her a tight-lipped smile. "Come, come, girl, don't be so impolite. It does not behove Lady Fernwood to disoblige her hostess. Come, play us a song."

Charles swallowed hard. He knew from Henry's tales that Arabella did not excel at music. Once, she'd played something on the harp for them, as a comic turn for a few private friends, to display how bad she was. It was amusing then, to hear her twanging and warbling, but here, in front of her mother-in-law and her friends... the humiliation would be intense.

Which, of course, was the intention.

Charles opened his mouth to speak, and saw Miss Waverly half rising to her feet, out of the corner of his eye.

Henry beat them all to it.

"If Arabella does not want to play, Mother, I'm sure there's no need to insist," he said, his voice quiet but carrying well in the uncomfortably silent room.

Dowager Fernwood shot him an annoyed look. "It has been arranged, Henry," she snapped, as if that decided it all. Henry tilted up his chin, just a little.

"She doesn't want to play, Mother. I know you won't be so unkind as to insist."

There was a taut silence in the room. Early in Lady Thomasin's performance, Dowager Fernwood had quelled a few whispers of conversation with a staunch glare, and the result had been absolute silence. The silence continued, and the whispered conversation was clearly heard.

"There will be a gap in the performance if she does not play," Dowager Fernwood said, irritation starting to creep into her voice. "Who else is going to play, if Arabella chooses not to..."

"I'll play. Sing, rather."

There was a general rustling sound as everyone turned to see who had spoken. Charles, of course, knew exactly who.

Miss Waverly was on her feet, ignoring the angry hisses of the matrons around her, and a few clumsy attempts to pull her back onto her seat. She met Dowager Fernwood's eye and smiled sweetly.

"I can sing, if someone can accompany me on the pianoforte."

"You weren't asked to play," Dowager Fernwood responded, a little ungraciously.

"I know. But I don't mind."

Charles found himself getting to his feet. "I can play the pianoforte well enough to accompany you. I'm not exactly accomplished, but I'm sure that between the two of us we can make a decent performance."

She met his eye and smiled. "I think so."

Dowager Fernwood, pouting like a child, made a sharp gesture.

"Very well, very well!" she snapped, and leaned back in her chair, arms folded.

The heat of the room was more intense up on the platform. Charles' legs carried him up there, and he found himself wondering what on earth he'd done. No doubt Miss Waverly could sing well enough to reassure herself that she *could* manage, but he hadn't touched a piano in weeks. What if he made a fool of himself? It was all to save Lady Fernwood, who so far as he could tell, didn't even *like* him very much.

Miss Waverly took a step closer, and he focused on her, rather than the audience, all peering eagerly at them. No doubt this debacle would be the most exciting thing to happen all night, and everyone was keen not to miss a thing.

"Do you know the tune to *The Ash Grove*?" she asked urgently.

He blinked. "I... I think so, but it's not perfect. It's a sad song, is it not?"

"More to the point, it's a short song. I don't consider myself beholden to provide good entertainment for the dowager and her friends, but neither do I want to embarrass myself. It's my friend's favourite, and Clara can't sing, so we used to perform it together. Do you think you can do it?"

Charles, under his breath, hummed a few bars of the tune, and she let out a breath.

"Yes, yes. That's it. Excellent. Let's get this over with, shall we?"

Charles smiled wryly at her, and something flashed between them, something unusual and simmering, almost a flash of heat.

Then the moment was gone, and Charles had to settle himself at the pianoforte while Miss Waverly turned to face the audience. From his seat at the piano, he could see their faces, glistening in the candlelight, all upturned to watch her. She stood straight, head held high, shoulders back, preparing to start.

He played the introduction. She sang, and her voice was clear and confident, if not brilliant.

"The ash grove, how graceful, how plainly 'tis speaking;
The harp (or wind) through it playing has language for me,
Whenever the light through its branches is breaking,
A host of kind faces is gazing on me.
The friends of my childhood again are before me;
Each step wakes a memory as freely I roam.
With soft whispers laden the leaves rustle o'er me;
The ash grove, the ash grove alone is my home.

Down yonder green valley where streamlets meander,
When twilight is fading I pensively rove,
Or at the bright noontide in solitude wander
Amid the dark shades of the lonely ash grove.
'Twas there while the blackbird was cheerfully singing
I first met that dear one, the joy of my heart.
Around us for gladness the bluebells were ringing,
But then little thought I how soon we should part.

My lips smile no more, my heart loses its lightness;

No dream of the future my spirit can cheer.
I only can brood on the past and its brightness;
The dear ones I long for again gather here.
From ev'ry dark nook they press forward to meet me;
I lift up my eyes to the broad leafy dome,
And others are there, looking downward to greet me;
The ash grove, the ash grove again is my home."

She ended the song, and Charles finished the music without a flourish. It wasn't a song of triumph, or of a great love or a great passion, but something smaller and yet infinitely more meaningful. Of course, the singer *had* been in love, and of course then lost that love, but the song was too reserved, too resigned for any real spirit. It was a woman who'd suffered great loss, and for whom death no longer held any real fear.

Like so many of the popular songs at the time, the singer – always a woman – died at the end.

There was a pause at the end. There was no denying that Lady Thomasin's harp playing was more skilled than Charles' playing, and Miss Waverly's singing, but somehow that didn't *mean* anything.

Lady Fernwood led the applause, bouncing to her feet and clapping happily. Henry joined in, obliging his mother to slap her hands together a few times.

Miss Waverly seemed to sag where she stood, and glanced over her shoulder at Charles, face alight with relief and triumph.

A few of Dowager Fernwood's friends were feigning boredom, or clapping half-heartedly, but most of the audience were not. They smiled at them, applauding hard.

Dowager Fernwood got to her feet, clapping loudly and glowering around herself for silence. She got it.

"Yes, yes, very nice, Miss Waverly. A little short and simple for our taste, I think, and I'm not sure that *Welsh folk-songs* are proper for a dignified English drawing-room. But, no matter, well done. Now, where is Miss Timmins? Ah, Miss Timmins, you have the finest taste I ever encountered! So many young ladies do *not* have a refined taste these days, but never mind, never mind!"

The message was clear. Charles got up from the pianoforte and made his way back to his seat. Miss Waverly had already gone back to hers, and was sitting straight-backed among the matrons and widows, who were firmly ignoring her.

Before he sat down, Charles met her eye across the room. Something passed between them, a sort of understanding, and she flashed a quick, lopsided smile.

The smile sent heat coursing down into Charles' chest. He cleared his throat, composing himself just in time for Dowager Fernwood to lean in close to him again.

"Listen to Miss Timmins, your Grace. Now *she* has impeccable taste, let me tell you. Are you listening? You must listen *closely*."

"I am, my lady."

Chapter Thirteen

The song wound itself into her dreams.

Down yonder green valley where streamlets meander,
When twilight is fading I pensively rove,
Or at the bright noontide in solitude wander
Amid the dark shades of the lonely ash grove.
'Twas there while the blackbird was cheerfully singing
I first met that dear one, the joy of my heart.
Around us for gladness the bluebells were ringing,
But then little thought I how soon we should part.

She heard the song, sung in her own voice somehow, echoing around the beach. She dreamt that she was crunching her way across the sharp sands, barefoot, towards where the grey sea crashed and raked across the shore.

"The Ash Grove," Clara had said once, eagerly, "is *not* necessarily about romantic love, you know."

"They're all about romantic love, Clara."

"No, but listen. *'Twas there while the blackbird was cheerfully singing, I first met that dear one, the joy of my heart'*. That *could* be about a lover..."

"It *is* about a lover."

"...but it could be a friend that she met, couldn't it?"

Lydia sighed, turning over. It was one of those strange dreams where she knew she was sleeping, knew she was in bed, and yet she found herself darting between her bed and the tangled sheets and the beach, where the grey tide crept further and further up towards her.

"I suppose."

"The song," Clara continued, "is about *loss*, many losses, and the poor girl cannot handle it. That's why she dies."

"Of heartbreak? Ugh."

"Don't be so *callous*, you wretch."

Then Lydia was back on the beach, watching the foamy edge of the tide lap at her feet – which were bare for some reason – and felt the cold climb up her legs, higher and higher until the hem of her skirts were soaking wet, dragging her down.

My lips smile no more, my heart loses its lightness;
No dream of the future my spirit can cheer.

I only can brood on the past and its brightness;
The dear ones I long for again gather here.

    She glanced up, craning her neck, fancying that she could see a ship on the horizon. Was that a dark head, bobbing in the water? A man, drowning?

From ev'ry dark nook they press forward to meet me;
I lift up my eyes to the broad leafy dome,
And others are there, looking downward to greet me;
The ash grove, the ash grove again is my home.

    The waves surged forward, knocking Lydia to the ground, drowning her, dragging her back out with the unstoppable, irrepressible tide, and she was lost, nobody to save her, nothing but the cold sea and...

    "Lydia? Lydia, are you awake?"
    She sat bolt upright, gasping for breath. Her throat was hoarse, her breaths coming in ragged as if she'd been holding them for too long. She blinked stupidly around herself, taking in her surroundings.
    She was in her bedroom at Arabella's home, of course, a familiar place. Light streamed in through the window, showing that the morning was well along, and the sheets were twisted around her legs, for all the world like an anchor ready to drag her down. She shivered, kicking herself free.
    "I'm awake, Arabella," Lydia responded, "But not up yet."
    The door creaked open and Arabella slipped in, dressed in her nightgown and a robe. She darted over to the bed, curling up on the bottom.
    "I never had a chance to properly thank you for saving me last night," she said quietly. "That woman was keen to humiliate me. If Henry hadn't stood up for me, if the Duke and you hadn't taken my place..." she bit off the sentence, shaking her head. "I haven't thanked Henry, either. I should."
    "You should," Lydia agreed, pulling her hair out of its loose plait, which had more or less come undone during the night anyway. "It was awful, wasn't it?"
    Arabella shuddered. "All that harp-twanging gave me a headache. The Duke and you performed so well, everyone said so. Not in the dowager's hearing, of course."
    "Ours was just a simple song."

"And that is why it sounded better, I think. Everyone else's pieces were so... so *showy*. Yours was short, sweet, and heartfelt. That was Clara's favourite song, wasn't it?"

"Yes, that's how I knew it."

"Ooh, I almost forgot. Your Mamma and Clara arrived in town only this morning. They're coming over for breakfast."

Lydia perked up. "They're here? That's wonderful! I'd better get ready."

Arabella chatted on while Lydia darted around her room, pulling on her clothes and twisting back her hair into a respectable knot and tying it with a ribbon. After a few moments, Arabella fell silent.

"You could ring for your maid, you know."

Lydia chuckled. "I don't mind dressing myself."

"Well, if you end up being a *duchess*, you'll never have to dress yourself."

Lydia paused, caught in admiring herself in the mirror. She met Arabella's eyes above the shoulder of her reflection. "A duchess? Me? What are you talking about?"

"Oh, don't be so demure, it's so boring. I'm sure that the Duke of Northwood likes you. Why else would he offer to play the pianoforte for you?"

"Well, because he disapproved of the Dowager's treatment to you, of course. And because he knew I'd need help to perform. He's a kind man, Arabella."

Arabella pursed her lips, inspecting her fingernails. "I'm sure that he *is* a kind man, make no mistake. But he likes you, Lydia. I'd wager that he does."

"Well, please don't, because you would waste your money. He's a Duke, and he'll marry accordingly. We move in very different circles outside of Bath, I warrant you."

Arabella pursed her lips, not looking as if she agreed at all.

"Well, a little modesty will only make you look better to him," she said at last. "I wish you would apply yourself a little more, Lydia. You did this all through our Season, you know. So many gentlemen liked you, and all it would have taken was a little *encouragement*. Gentlemen don't need much, you know. Just enough to assure them that you *are* interested, and that they aren't going to make a fool of themselves and damage their delicate sense of pride. It's the easiest thing in the world."

Lydia sighed. "I don't believe that finding the love of one's life *should* be easy, Arabella. I want to be happy. You loved Henry when you married him, did you not? And you still do, I believe that."

Arabella looked away. "I do," she admitted quietly. "But love gets in the way, you know. It's troublesome. You care entirely too much, and you don't think logically. Sometimes I wish I'd applied cold, cool reason to my Season, instead of seeing Henry and immediately losing my head. Although," she added reflectively, "not a man in London was a patch on him. He *was* one of the most handsome men of the Season."

Lydia suppressed a smile. Love was indeed blind, then. While Henry was pleasant looking enough, nobody but Arabella and possibly his own mother had considered him the most handsome man in London, by any stretch of the imagination.

Before they could talk further, Lydia heard the crunch of carriage wheels on the drive. With a squawk, Arabella bounced to her feet.

"Oh, Lord, they're here, and I'm not even dressed! Lydia, you go down and greet them first, as soon as you can. I shan't take longer than a moment."

Robe billowing in a most ungraceful manner, she skittered out of the room and down the hall, leaving the door swinging.

Lydia shook her head and smiled and shot a quick glance at her own reflection. She wore a plain white dress decorated with blue ribbon, matching the one in her notably disheveled hair. It wasn't exactly *fashionable*, but then, it was only Clara and her mother.

In truth, Lydia thought to herself, *I have missed them more than I thought.*

***

Clara and Lady Pemshire waited in the hall, unpinning hats and handing shawls and coats to the footmen.

Lydia came rushing down the stairs, crushing Clara to her first, then turning to her mother.

"I am so glad to see you," she gasped, beaming until her cheeks hurt. "Arabella has set out a spread in the dining room. You must be hungry. How was your journey? Are things getting started in London? Ooh, how is Papa? And Clara, guess what song I sang only last night?"

"One at a time, one at a time," Lady Pemshire said, laughing. "With all your inquiries, I find myself in a situation akin to being interrogated by a panel of stern judges."

"Lady Pemshire!" Arabella announced from the top of the stairs, apparently having gotten dressed in record time. She was wearing a grand dress, all silk and sequins, in shades of pink and red and embroidered with silk roses around the hem and bodice.

In short, it was entirely too much for an informal breakfast with friends, even though she did look very pretty.

"And Clara too," Arabella reached the bottom of the stairs and beamed around at them. "I'm so glad you're here. I wish you would have stayed with us."

"The house in Bath needs looking to," Lady Pemshire admitted. "Clara, of course, may stay wherever she likes."

"Of course. Well, are you starving hungry, or would you like the tour? It's a fine house." Arabella glanced around hopefully.

"I will see it," Clara said, smiling.

Lady Pemshire pursed her lips. "Your house is beautiful, Arabella, and I look forward to seeing it, but I'm an old woman and I have seen many fine houses in my life. For now, might I have a word with my daughter?"

"Of course, of course. Lydia, take Lady Pemshire to the morning room. It's very pleasant at this time of day, and you won't be disturbed."

Then Arabella and Clara sailed off, arm in arm, leaving Lydia alone with her mother.

Lady Pemshire playfully pinched her cheeks. "You're looking well."

"I'm enjoying myself, Mama. Really, I am."

"I'm delighted to hear it. Now, let's see this fine, private morning room, shall we?"

Lady Pemshire settled herself into a comfortable armchair and looked around.

"Arabella has done well for herself," she remarked. "I hear good things about Lord Fernwood, and this is a fine house. She seems well settled."

"She is, although I believe his mother – the Dowager Fernwood – is making trouble for her."

Lydia recounted the events of the musical evening the night before, including the dowager's attempt to pressure Arabella into performing. She downplayed herself and the Duke's heroic rescue, but of course, her mother latched onto it immediately.

"The Duke of Northwood, you say?" she said thoughtfully. "Well, How interesting. I'm glad you've made his acquaintance. For a man of his age – a *duke,* no less – to be unmarried is certainly a cause for talk. People say he's looking for a wife this Season."

"Oh, not you too, Mama."

"Not me too? What does that mean?"

She fidgeted, avoiding her mother's eyes. "Arabella keeps pushing me towards him, too. I wish she wouldn't. I couldn't bear it if he thought I was one of the grasping young women, trying to *catch* him."

Lady Pemshire sniffed. "Well, in a world like ours, where a woman can do nothing beyond secure herself a good husband, I hardly think it's fair to make fun of them when they *do* try to find good husbands."

That was a fair point. Lydia shifted in her seat. The truth was, unmarried women – cruelly called *spinsters* or *old maids* – were generally seen as a nuisance, something to mock. Ladies who were blessed with an independent fortune were considered rather eccentric for being unmarried but could go on to lead ordinary lives.

But woe betide women whose fortune rested on fathers, brothers, or some other male relative. Lydia knew women whose fathers had died, leaving them at the mercy of a brother, who hastily threw them out of the house to eke out a living as best they could while they brought in a wealthy wife.

Or perhaps they would let her stay, with the unspoken knowledge that she was a burden, and had better not start to get above herself and show ungratefulness for their generosity.

She shuddered. The law favoured men, just like the rest of the world. Lydia would have some money on her father's death, and some on her mother's death, but not enough to keep up the lifestyle she was used to.

If she didn't marry, she'd come to financial straits soon enough.

It wasn't *fair.*

"Darling," Lady Pemshire said quietly, leaning forward. "You've gone white. Are you well?"

She nodded, not meeting her mother's eye. "I do not approve of this haste to wed, Mama."

"Yes, it's unpleasant. But let's put the foibles of Society to one side for now. This gentleman – the Duke of Northwood – is being exceptionally kind to you. One would argue that he is singling you out."

"He's just polite, Mama. He's a kind man."

Lady Pemshire nodded. "That is good. But what do *you* think of him, darling? Do you like him? Answer me honestly, now."

Lydia did not hurry to respond. Her mother waited patiently while she gathered her thoughts.

"Truly?" she spoke up at last, voice wavering. "Truly, I think that perhaps I do. But I daren't admit it, in case it all goes wrong and I find myself with a broken heart. Sometimes I think that he *does* care for me, but then other times I think otherwise. I don't know what to do."

Lady Pemshire nodded again, reaching out to take her daughter's hand.

"Be yourself," she said firmly. "That's what you must do. I'm here now, and I shall be watching. Watching *carefully*."

Lydia smiled at her mother. "I'm glad you're here, Mama. Really, I am."

Chapter Fourteen

There were a few blessed days free from social events.

And Charles could not even enjoy them.

He kept replaying that night at Dowager Fernwood's musical evening over and over in his head. He could feel the smooth, cold ivory of the keys beneath his fingers, and he could hear Miss Waverly's voice lilting up and down around the words. He could hear the sadness in her voice, the story unfolding in just a few verses.

He wanted to see her again.

There had been little time to speak at the musical evening. Dowager Fernwood had planned everything out vigorously. To invite her son, of course she *had* to invite Lady Fernwood, and to invite *her*, she was forced to invite Miss Waverly. Charles was fairly sure that was the only reason Miss Waverly was there at all, although she had pointedly not been asked to perform.

The evening, of course, had not gotten better. Performer after performer climbed the low platform, all in Lady Thomasin's style. Harp players twanged their way through dreamy arias which seemed to have no discernible beginning, middle, or end, pianoforte players thumped diligently through well-memorized tunes, sometimes singing. The songs were all genteel ballads, all fashionable, all well-known.

Afterwards, they retired to the dining room for refreshments, where the seats were picked out, and Charles was seated well away from Miss Waverly, who had once again been separated from her friends.

He'd received several cards and invitations from the mammas of some of the ladies introduced to him, and he had steadfastly ignored all of them.

None of the invitations were from Miss Waverly, or from the Fernwoods. He hadn't seen her now for over three days.

Well, that was the way things were here. In London, one might run into the same person every day in a week, at balls, soirees, picnics, and so on. Bath was a little more subdued.

What now, then?

It bothered Charles that he was so keen to see her again. What good would it do him? Miss Waverly – he'd started calling her *Lydia* in his head, even though that was probably a bad idea – would hate him as soon as she found out who he was. Even if everybody else told Charles that he wasn't to blame for Edmund's death, Lydia would believe that he was.

He groaned, leaning forward to rest his elbows on his desk.

It was barely eight o' clock in the morning, and Charles had not slept well. Eventually, he'd given up. He got dressed and gone down to his study, where there was work aplenty to keep him busy.

He hadn't *done* any of the work, of course. He couldn't focus. Whenever he perused an important letter, opened a ledger, or even put his pen to paper, he found himself thinking of Miss Waverly. He thought of the way she'd looked, what she'd said, the inflection in her voice, the way his music and her voice had mingled so perfectly together...

He swallowed hard, closing his eyes.

I'm falling in love with her, he thought desperately. *That is, if I'm not already in love with her. Oh, this is too much!*

A tap on the door woke him out of his reverie, and he glanced up.

"Who is it?"

The butler opened the door and peered around it, looking Displeased with a capital D.

"Do forgive my intrusion, your Grace. Your valet assured me that you were up and awake, otherwise I would have sent the gentleman away at once."

The hairs on the back of Charles' neck prickled.

"Gentleman?" he repeated warily. "What gentleman?"

The butler frowned. "The man in question claimed that you and he had an appointment set up for this morning. I assumed... I beg your pardon, your Grace. I'll turn him away at once."

"That you will not."

A familiar and distinctly unpleasant voice drifted in from the corridor, and somebody shouldered past the outraged butler and stepped into Charles' study.

He felt mildly sick.

"Sir Gregory," Charles said grimly. "I should have known."

"Your Grace, please accept my apologies!" the butler babbled. "I made it clear this man was to wait in the hall. Come this way, sir, at once!"

The butler – a portly man past middle-age, of middling height – made to lay hands on Sir Gregory and drag him out. Sir Gregory pulled back his fist, making as if to strike the man, and the poor butler pulled back with a squeak.

"Don't lay a hand on my butler, or I'll make you regret it," Charles said sharply. "Evans, thank you. This gentleman has barged his way in, unfortunately I do know him, and we'll see what he has to say. You may go, thank you."

The butler – Evans – regained his composure, straightening his waistcoat and glowering at Sir Gregory.

"Very good, your Grace. I shall *not* bring tea."

The insult was poignant, although no doubt Sir Gregory did not understand it.

Evans left, closing the door behind him, but Charles knew that the faithful butler would be within shouting distance.

Even so, that didn't make him feel much better about being restricted in his study with Sir Gregory.

It was a bit like being shut in a room with a crocodile. You *hoped* it wasn't hungry, but you weren't sure what you would do if it *was*.

"The next time your man lays a hand on me," Sir Gregory said conversationally, "I'll break his head."

Charles clenched his jaw. "And if you do, I'll see you in gaol. Understood?"

Sir Gregory snarled. There was something unfocused about his eyes that made Charles worry that he was drunk. The man stalked across to the fireplace, beside which was a whiskey decanter and a pair of glasses. Charles' heart sank when Sir Gregory poured himself a generous glassful, but besides striding over there and knocking it out of his hand, there wasn't a great deal he could do.

Sir Gregory drank back the entire glassful in a series of large gulps. He sighed in satisfaction, poured himself another, and ambled back towards Charles' desk. As expected, he threw himself down into a chair without waiting to be asked.

"Good whiskey, this," he said pleasantly, lifting the glass. "I should have poured you some."

"It's eight o' clock in the morning," Charles responded testily. "What do you want, Sir Gregory?"

Sir Gregory sighed, and took a deep sip of his whiskey.

Well, *Charles'* whiskey, really.

"Do you recall that game of Brag we played together?" he said, after a pause.

Charles frowned. "Of course."

"Hmph. You had a run of luck, there. Three threes, eh? One might even suspect cheating."

There. He'd said it. Charles stiffened, then forced himself to relax. Sir Gregory was in *his* study, with no other witnesses to his words, and he was clearly saying it to provoke.

The man was famously good at dueling pistols, even if Charles were stupid enough to try him.

"That's a bad accusation to make," he said evenly. "I'm glad you didn't say such a thing at the party."

"No, no, of course not. I'm gentle as a lamb, your Grace, gentle as a lamb. I should never want to cause trouble." He took a deep drink of the whiskey, and thoughtfully swirled the liquid around the glass. "No, I do not want to cause trouble. I'm a fair man, and if trouble *must* come about, I always like to give the persons involved a good, fair chance to get out of it. If they don't take the opportunity, well, that's hardly my fault. A great many people don't understand what's good for them, though, and then how can I be blamed?"

The hairs on the back of Charles' neck were prickling, warning him. Wherever this conversation was going, it was not good.

"I see," he responded neutrally. "And what has this to do with me, Sir Gregory?"

It was a not-so-subtle hint for him to get to the point of his visit.

Sir Gregory ignored him. "You see, when you won that game of Brag, I'm afraid I stormed away in rather a huff. I'm an excellent player, you see. I have a talent for cards. Mrs Habit will tell you, although I think she's tired of my company of late. Not that it matters either way. Still, even the most *talented* players must come in with a run of bad luck sooner or later, eh, your Grace?"

"Please do get the point, Sir Gregory. I'll be taking breakfast with my brother and his wife soon, and I'm not sure William is a friend of yours."

Sir Gregory winced. "Ah, yes, Lord Everard. He's always rather brusque with me. Well, what can you do? I shall get the point at once. As I say, I have a talent at cards, but I *have* had a run of bad luck lately. Entirely unexpected, nothing to be done. I find myself with a horrid pile of Notes Acknowledging Debts and very little ready cash."

There was a pause. Sir Gregory had his eyebrows lifted expectantly. Charles, on the other hand, felt as though he were in a particularly ridiculous dream.

"Let me be clear," Charles managed at last. "You want to borrow money from me? Even though we are not friends, and that you have always been markedly unpleasant to me?"

Sir Gregory winced. "Old friend, really..."

"We are not old friends, Sir Gregory. We are not friends of any kind. We are barely acquaintances, and even that is a reluctant business. I can tell you at once that I will not lend you any money. I'm sorry for your troubles, but you got yourself into them, and I think you must get yourself out of them."

There was a long pause. Sir Gregory, his expression inscrutable, swirling the last mouthful of whiskey around his glass.

Did he truly think I was going to lend him money? Charles thought, baffled. It made no sense. What was the point of all this?

"I thought you might say that," Sir Gregory said, with a hearty sigh. "I thought I'd give you a chance to be a gentleman."

"And what is that supposed to mean?"

Sir Gregory took his time in responding. He drank the rest of his whiskey in a long, messy gulp, and set the glass down with a *clack* directly onto Charles' desk. A few drops of spilled whiskey rolled down the side of the glass, soaking into the green-tinted leather surface.

"My friend, Mrs Habit, was at a musical evening a few days ago," he continued, conversationally. "There was some business about a girl who didn't wish to perform, and our mutual acquaintance, Miss Lydia Waverly, volunteered to sing in order to spare the lady. Very gracious, don't you think? And now I'm sure you know who kindly volunteered to play the pianoforte to her warbling. None other than you, your Grace."

Charles swallowed hard. He knew where this was going now.

"And what is your point?" he managed.

Sir Gregory pursed his lips. "Well, there are theories that perhaps you are fond of the said lady. Care to comment?"

"If I was, I would not confirm it to you. I think you have said quite enough, Sir Gregory."

Charles rose to his feet, but Sir Gregory did not move. The man stayed where he was, picking at his fingernails. Charles felt oddly out of place, as if *he* were the uninvited guest.

"The lady has a tragic past," Sir Gregory said, almost absent-mindedly. "A dear cousin of hers went travelling and never returned. I do so hate a tragedy, so I did some digging. I learned that the cousin was indeed *your* companion. Since one of you returned from the trip and one did not, it raises questions, does it not? I have it on good authority that in fact the lady does not even know that it was *you* who accompanied her cousin. I do hope you didn't push him, your Grace. Two friends travelling together can start to argue after a while, you know."

Charles felt vaguely sick. "You're accusing me of killing my friend?"

The other man smiled sweetly up at him. "No. Actually, I am accusing you of hiding your part in the man's demise, no matter how innocent it may be. If you had nothing to hide, then Miss Waverly would know that *you* were her beloved cousin's companion on that fatal, final voyage, don't you think?"

There was a long, protracted period of silence. Sir Gregory, entirely unperturbed, sniffed.

"Of course," he continued, almost to himself, "if I knew you were a *gentlemanly* sort of man, I'd know that you were not hiding anything, and so would not be necessary for Miss Waverly to know the truth. I do hope you can prove to me that you *are* a gentleman, your Grace."

Charles found his voice. "Get out," he managed.

Sir Gregory gave a twisted, malicious smile. He pulled a pile of Notes Acknowledging Debts out of his pocket, dropping them unceremoniously on Charles' desk.

"Handle these for me, old chap, won't you?" he said lightly, rising to his feet. He was unsteady, his eyes unfocused, and it was clearer than ever that he was drunk and had been before he arrived.

The two men stared at each other for a long, tense moment.

"Evans!" Charles suddenly rose his voice, and had the brief satisfaction of seeing Sir Gregory flinch.

There were running footsteps, and the door flew open. Evans, subtly armed with a candlestick, stood poised in the door.

"Your Grace?" he gasped, sharp eyes running across the room to make sure that nothing was amiss.

Charles met Sir Gregory's eye and did not look away.

"This man is leaving. Show him out."

"This way, sir," Evans said sharply. "Look lively, if you please."

Sir Gregory sneered. "Such a gentleman, your Grace. *Such* a gentleman."

Chapter Fifteen

From the window of his study, Charles watched Sir Gregory stumble down the driveway, with Evans watching him go sternly. It was embarrassing to watch. The man stumbled on his own feet, landing face-first in the gravel. Charles' suspicions that he was drunk were clearly well-founded.

The butler sighed, gesturing to a pair of footmen. The men strode pointedly down the drive, bending down to grab an arm each, and hauled Sir Gregory to his feet.

The man had chosen to ride in, and the glossy black mare watched her master approach with a sort of resignation.

In the end, Charles had to turn away from the spectacle of Sir Gregory trying to mount his horse, with the footmen taking turns to push and pull him up into the saddle.

He hurried into the hallway, where Evans was still observing, and gestured him over.

"That man is not to be admitted again," Charles whispered.

"Understood, sir."

"Where might I find my brother? It's early in the day. Is he up yet?"

"I believe Lady Everard and he are taking breakfast together in the dining room."

Charles winced. He'd have to disturb their breakfast. Still, there was nothing for it. He needed advice, and he needed it now. He thanked the butler, who went back to make sure that Sir Gregory really did get off their property and took off at a run towards the dining room.

As promised, William and Anne were in the dining room. They glanced up and smiled as he entered, and Charles felt a twinge of regret at breaking up such a domestic scene.

The dining table was a long one, of course, fit to seat many people, but William and Anne sat together at the end, side by side. They were reading something in a newspaper, Anne pointing and William chuckling, their forks poised above their breakfast plates, food forgotten.

"Sit down, Charles," Anne said, smiling. "Cook has made the most delicious scrambled eggs. She says it's a new recipe, and I'd love your opinion on it."

Charles swallowed hard. "I'd love to, but I really must talk to William."

William's smile wavered, taking in the tension in his brother's face.

"Can't it wait?"

Charles shook his head. "I'm sorry, but it can't."

Anne seemed to sense the atmosphere, the smile fading off her face. Charles felt like a monster, crashing in on their happy breakfast scene.

William got up and followed Charles out of the room, back along the corridor into the study.

He frowned at the whiskey glass, picking it up and wiping at the ring of spilled whiskey underneath.

"It's a little early," he said, tactfully. "Charles, I..." he trailed off once he spotted the pile of crumpled Debt Notes. "Charles, I *know* those are not yours."

"They aren't. And the whiskey wasn't mine, either. We had a guest. Well, perhaps *guest* is too kind a word. I'm sure that Evans will tell you all about it later."

William pressed his lips together in a thin line. "Why do I think that this is not good news?"

"Because it isn't. Sit down, and I'll tell you what happened."

Charles told the whole unpleasant story as succinctly as he could, while William leafed through the Notes.

He let out a sigh at the end of the story. "Blackmail, then. Plain and simple."

"Yes, I suppose so. Even if I was to pay him off, there would be more gambling debts soon enough, and perhaps a request for a regular payment. He's a greedy man, and I can't see where he would draw the line."

William leaned over and rang the bell, folding up the Notes. He slipped them into an envelope, sealing them well. When Evans appeared, eyebrow raised questioningly, William handed over the envelope.

"Can you find the address of Sir Gregory Simms, please? That is, the gentlemen who just left?"

"I'm sure I can, sir."

"Excellent. Return these to him, won't you?"

Evans bowed and took the envelope, holding it between thumb and forefinger as if he didn't much want to touch it. Despite everything, Charles fought to suppress a smile. Once Evans had gone, William absently wiped his palms on his trousers.

"I counted close to a thousand pounds in debt there," he murmured. "A colossal amount. A run of bad luck, indeed. The man's a gambler, through and through. There will be more soon enough, of course. You did the right thing, sending him away. As to his threats, I shouldn't worry about it. What has he to tell Miss Waverly, anyway?"

Charles felt sick. "That I travelled with her cousin, and that I wasn't able to save him. It's my fault he died, William."

"Well, I'm sure that Miss Waverly will see straight through that."

"Do you think so?" Charles responded bitterly. "She adored her cousin, and it's my fault he is dead. She'll never forgive me."

William pursed his lips. "I can see that I'll never convince you otherwise. But think of this, at least. If Sir Gregory tells Miss Waverly what he clearly thinks is a shocking truth, what then? He will have nothing to hold against you. You're not obliged to pay him a single half penny. He wouldn't be so foolish."

"He's a malicious and spiteful man. If he believes I won't help him, then why would he not tell her?"

"Then, let him tell her!" William leaned forward, suddenly animated. "Do you recall the lady I was engaged to, Ruth Harvey? How it was broken off between us and there was so much bad feeling?"

"I remember."

"Well, for a while, I tried to hide it from Anne. I thought she'd be upset that I was engaged before, or even feel engaged. I worked hard to keep it from her. At last, she found out, and she was angry – but not for the reasons I'd thought. she didn't care that I was engaged before. She was upset that I'd lied to her, tried to keep it from her. We talked it through, and it all ended well, of course, but that's not the point. The point is that honesty is crucial, Charles."

"Miss Waverly and I do not have an understanding, the way Anne and you did."

"But you might have one. She likes you, Charles, I know it. Everyone is saying so, and I know that *you* like her. You can't convince me otherwise."

Charles swallowed hard, trying to compose himself. "William, I know you're just trying to help me, but really, this isn't going to work out. It's not. I know Miss Waverly enough to know that she has a firm sense of right and wrong. She... she won't forgive me. I'm sure of it."

William sighed. "At least *talk* to her, brother. We can put off this Sir Gregory for a while, dodge him at parties and so on. You have plenty of time to talk it over."

Charles flashed a brittle smile. "What happened with Edmund keeps me awake at night, William. I could have saved him. I should have saved him."

"You almost did. You couldn't possibly have managed it."

"You don't know how close I was. I've already decided what I'm going to do."

There was a pause. William eyed him warily.

"And why do I think that what you have decided won't please me at all?"

Charles snorted. "Because you know me too well. I'm going to leave Bath."

There was a taut pause.

"I beg your pardon?" William managed.

"I'm leaving Bath, Will. I'm going to pack up and go before the end of the week, before Sir Gregory knows what I've done. I doubt he'll find me in London. In Bath, he might be accepted into higher circles than he's used to, but I'm fairly sure I won't have to see him much in London. If at all, really. I might write to Miss Waverly and explain the whole thing, but honestly, that's the only thing that's coming to mind."

There was a longer pause, and William opened his mouth to speak.

He was interrupted by the door flinging open with a *bang*.

The two men whipped around. Anne stood there, hands on her hips.

"What are you doing?" William said, bewildered. "Were you *listening* at the door?"

"I was, yes," Anne said, entirely unabashed. "Don't look at me like that, Will. You two snuck off so secretly, you can't blame me for being curious. I just listened to some of it to start with, and decided that it was important enough for me to keep listening."

"Of course you did," William muttered. He didn't look *very* shocked, though.

Charles sighed, raking a hand through his hair. "Well, I don't have any objections to you knowing too, Anne. It doesn't exactly put me in a good light, but..."

"That it does not." She strode into the room, one hand resting over the swell of her belly. Soon, she wouldn't be able to go into

Society at all, and Charles fully believed that she was relieved about that. "You cannot possibly go running off to London because one drunken fool of a gambler threatens you."

"He hasn't threatened me, exactly. He just promised to tell the truth to... to a lady who I esteem highly."

"Esteem highly? Tosh! You're in love with the lady, Charles. Be frank with us."

Charles swallowed reflexively, bouncing to his feet. He moved over to the window and stood looking out, arms crossed. It was a frosty morning, with ice spread over the lawn, glistening like dew. Soon enough, the sun would shine over the icy lawn, and melt the frost away. For all there was no real power in the sun at this time of year, it was bright enough. One could feel the heat of it on one's skin, if it wasn't too breezy.

"I do love her," Charles murmured, half to himself, half to Anne. "And because I love her, I want her to have peace. Knowing that I could have saved her cousin, but didn't quite manage it, would be worse than thinking that there was never any hope. To come so close to being saved and have it whisked away..." he trailed off, swallowing again and shaking his head. "I have to leave, Anne. You must see that."

She crossed the room, her steps slow and uneven with the growing weight at her front and rested a hand on Charles' shoulder.

"I can't imagine how you felt, watching your friend drown in front of you, despite your best efforts," she said quietly. "Just like I can't imagine what poor Miss Waverly felt like, waving goodbye to her cousin and then never seeing him again. But one thing I do know is that it's worse never to know at all. If you leave now, and Miss Waverly never knows why..."

"I'll write to her," Charles insisted, but she shook her head.

"No, you won't. I know you, Charles. With the best will in the world, you won't tell her. You'll convince yourself it's for the best, and simply slip away, assuming that she'll forget you in a moment. She won't. She *won't*, Charles, I can promise you that. I won't go so far as to say you owe her the truth – the truth is a tricky thing to say the least – but I will say that running away is not the solution. It's cowardly, and it solves nothing."

Charles bit his lip. He wanted to turn away from Anne's firm, unblinking gaze, but *that* seemed like cowardice, and after braving so many insults from Sir Gregory, he was desperate to prove himself *somehow* at least.

"What would you suggest, then?" he asked.

She sighed. "Stay."

"I just said that I cannot."

"Stay for a while, then. Give yourself six months..."

"That is too long."

"Four months, then."

"A week."

"That is *not* enough time."

He lifted an eyebrow. "Do you really think it will take Sir Gregory a full six months to act?"

She winced. "Perhaps not. But you must give it a little while. Running away at once is not the solution."

"How about this," he said at last. "I'll stay until you go into confinement. You have another two weeks at least, I believe. At the end of that time, the Season will be getting into swing in London, and people will be leaving. Perhaps Sir Gregory will be among them, in which case he'll want to unload the rest of his debts onto me first. What do you say to that?"

Anne pursed her lips. "Two weeks. That does *not* give us enough time to work with, but I can see by your face that you won't budge. Two weeks, but you can't hide yourself away. You must go to all the parties and social events, and you must *not* keep yourself from Miss Waverly. William and I will work on the Sir Gregory problem, and you will concern yourself with seeing how you really feel about Miss Waverly."

I know how I feel, he thought numbly. *That's half of the problem.*

Aloud, he said, "Done," and extended a hand for her to shake.

Grinning, Anne shook his hand, as firmly as any man would.

Over by the fireplace, quite forgotten, William pointedly cleared his throat.

"Is anyone going to tell me what's going on," he demanded peevishly, "or should I just guess?"

Chapter Sixteen

It was fairly clear that poor Lady Fernwood – who had begged Charles to call her *Arabella*, since he was the closest friend of her husband's – was throwing party after party to make the most of things. Already, people were starting to leave Bath for London, as the Season gradually got into swing.

Charles wondered if Arabella and Henry would go back to London. He would be surprised if they did – Henry hated London, and the Season. But then, Arabella loved it, so a compromise would have to be made.

They'd discussed it earlier, in Henry's study. Charles had arrived early, at his friend's request. The house was a hive of activity, with last-minute preparations being done, and servants flying here and there, making things perfect. Charles had weaved his way in and out of the chaos, somewhat apologetic, and had gone straight to Henry's study.

And here they were now, taking their ease, an hour at least before the earliest guests would begin to arrive.

"Do you think I compliment my wife enough?" Henry asked suddenly.

Charles, who had not been expecting that question, blinked. "I beg your pardon?"

Henry sighed, shifting in his seat. "Well, I think Arabella is the most beautiful creature to ever walk the earth. I thought it the moment I saw her, and I think it still. I assumed she knew. But perhaps... perhaps I've been a little neglectful. I've seen her come alive over the past few weeks, with all these parties and nonsense. I've always known that she loved that kind of thing, I just thought that once we were married, I would be enough for her."

Charles leaned forward, resting his elbows on his knees.

"I don't think it's as simple as you *not being enough*, as you put it. Arabella is a social woman. She loves the company of others, loves conversation and excitement and going out. There's nothing wrong with that, and there's also nothing wrong with you wanting to stay at home and lead a quiet life. She loves you, I know it, but that doesn't mean that she can't have a life outside of her marriage."

Henry closed his eyes. "I didn't mean that."

"I know what you meant, Henry. I'm not going to tell you what to do, or how to manage your marriage, but you should know that Arabella's character will not change. Just like yours will not. She loves people, you prefer to avoid them. You love each other, and that is the most important thing."

Henry nodded, rubbing the frown line between his brows. "I suppose you're right. We were talking about it yesterday evening, and I thought... I thought that we could spend a few months in London, for the Season. We could do that every year. I don't need to go to *every* party, but Arabella would be able to spend time with her friends and enjoy socialising. What do you think?"

Charles smiled wryly. "I think that's a very good idea."

But that was half an hour ago, and Henry had since gone to dress. Arabella was dressing, of course, and he assumed that Lydia was too.

Miss Waverly, he reminded himself firmly.

The preparations were almost done. Charles wandered around the house, all dressed for the party, and wondered how to entertain himself. He found himself in the ballroom, where the musicians were already seated, tuning up their instruments, ready for later in the evening. A cluster of footmen were discussing something in the corner, and a maid was putting the finishing touches on a spectacular garland of flowers and greenery draped over the mantelpiece.

Aside from those people, the ballroom was empty. It was strange, being in a place which was designed to host hundreds of people. Alone.

Charles wandered to the centre, where the parquet floor was patterned in a circle spreading outwards and tilted back his head to inspect the marvelous carved ceiling, far above his head.

"Beautiful, isn't it? And yet people so rarely look up."

He flinched, glancing behind him.

Lydia stood there, head tilted back, looking up thoughtfully.

She was wearing a pale blue, gauzy gown, cut rather shockingly low over her shoulders, but just on the cusp of propriety. She wore a bluish sort of diamond on a pendant around her neck, and matching earrings. Pale blue glass flowers glittered in her hair like starlight.

In short, she looked beautiful, and Charles found himself short of breath.

"Miss Waverly," he managed. "You startled me."

"I do beg your pardon. I didn't know you were here."

"I came to see Henry. I assumed that Lady Fernwood and you would be dressing."

"We are. Well, Arabella still is, but I'm ready. The guests will be arriving soon, I think. She wanted me to make a few last-minute checks, but I'm not sure that it's necessary. The housekeeper and the servants always do such a marvellous job."

"Indeed they have," Charles agreed. His heart was pounding. What on earth had she done to him?

"I remember," Lydia said, slowly and uncertainly, head still tilted back to look up at the ceiling, "how my cousin and me would creep down before a party to dance in the ballroom."

A shiver rolled down Charles' spine. "Your... your cousin?" he stammered.

She nodded, not looking at him. "His name was Edmund. He was my cousin, but really, he felt like my brother. He sometimes attended those parties, but I was too young to do so. So, he'd sneak me downstairs to show me the refreshments, the decorations, the flowers, and see the ballroom all ready for dancing. Sometimes the musicians could be persuaded to play us a little music, and we would dance together. He loved parties, and he was tremendously popular."

I know, Charles thought, feeling sick. *I know how well-liked he was. He was my friend.*

Before he could say anything, before the whole awful story could tumble out of his lips, Lydia carried on, seemingly lost to the world.

"When I was little, I thought that he really was my brother. It was a blow to find out that he was *only* a cousin – because that was how I thought back then, you see. I remember asking my mother if it really made a difference, and she laughed and told me of course it didn't. Edmund grew up with me, and we were going to do my first Season together. He would introduce me to people, and we'd dance together, and gossip together, and he'd help me find a good match – because of course that was what I thought about at that age – and it was all so thrilling. I used to imagine making a very good friend in Society, and he would make a very good friend, and then we'd marry each other's friends and have a double wedding, and it would be perfect." She paused, giving a short huff of laughter. "Silly, isn't it?"

"It's not silly," Charles said firmly. "It's sweet."

She glanced fondly at him, and heat flared in Charles' chest. He had to look away, before he found himself telling her everything.

I could have saved your Edmund, if I'd swam a little faster, a little harder, I could have saved him. If I hadn't let them tug me back to the ship. I should have untied the rope. I should have stopped him going up on deck. I should have...

"I know it's not at all the thing for ladies to ask gentlemen to dance," Lydia said impulsively, "but if you're not busy, your Grace, perhaps we might dance together."

He swallowed hard, glancing over at the musicians. They were huddled together, deep in conversation, tuning their instruments. "I don't think they'll play for us."

She smiled wryly. "We could always imagine the music."

"Agreed," he offered a hand, and she took it. Her fingers were warm through the sheer, dark blue gauze evening gloves she wore. "We'll have to imagine the same music, though."

She gave a snort of laughter. "In case one of us tries to dance a waltz and the other a jig? That would be disastrous."

Charles had to grin at that, imagining them trying to hang onto each other, their feet working at rhythms, one trying to twirl and skip and the other to promenade.

"Might I suggest," he said, coming close and taking both of her hands in his, "We think about that new piece that is being played everywhere? I can't for the life of me remember the name, but it was played by a Miss Whirl at that dreadful musical evening."

"Ah, I recall. It goes like this..." she hummed a few bars, and he grinned.

"That's the one. Shall we?"

"On the count of three. One – two – three. Go."

Her hands rested on his shoulders and his around her waist, unlike any dance they'd ever done before. It probably resembled a waltz most of all, but Charles quickly gave up trying to perform any proper dance and contented himself with stepping neatly around each other in slow, lazy circles, while Lydia hummed the tune under her breath.

Everything melted away. The quiet ballroom, the gentle hum of conversation, the smart clicks of the musicians' heels on the parquet floor, and the soft thumps of the velvet-soled servants' boots.

There was nothing except Lydia, who was looking over his shoulder with a faraway expression in her eyes. A sort of melancholy settled in Charles' chest, tightening around his ribs.

I love her, he thought dizzily. *I am in love with her.*

It seemed obvious, when he thought about it.

"He drowned," Lydia said suddenly, and then the dizzy, adoring feeling melted away, replaced by cold fear. "He was coming home from his Grand Tour, and the ship ran into a storm. The captain said that he was washed overboard, and they couldn't save him. Mama was heartbroken and raged terribly. She said that they probably hadn't tried, hadn't even tried to bring the ship around. She said that since they had his money for the return trip, they didn't care about his safety, or else they'd have made him go below decks."

"They did," Charles said, and flushed when she glanced sharply up at him. "That is, I'm sure they would have done. Even if they hadn't, I'm sure your Edmund would have gone below decks of his own accord. He was a clever man."

She tilted her head to one side. "You knew him?"

He swallowed. "Yes, I knew him."

"For the longest time," Lydia continued, the faraway expression returning to her face, "I thought that it couldn't be real. He couldn't be dead. Not *Edmund*, who was so full of life and energy. I was quite sure that he'd arrive on our doorstep one day, grinning like a fool, with all sorts of stories to tell us about his adventures, and how he swam to shore. I used to stare at the map of the world for hours. I'd put a pin in the sea where the captain said he'd gone over. It was a terrible distance from land. Terrible. No islands nearby, but I used to imagine an undiscovered one, where he was living quite happily, waiting to be picked up by a passing merchant ship. Silly, isn't it?"

"It's not silly to have hope," Charles said, firmly.

They danced on for a few minutes, with Charles now wrapped up in his own thoughts. It had occurred to him, more than once since his return, that men and women who had not travelled did not understand how vicious the sea could be. They imagined a flat, blue ocean, or at worst the lapping grey waves of a beach.

It wasn't like that at all. It wasn't even close. When he closed his eyes, he saw the iron-gray troughs of water, deep as a house, rearing up out of the sea. He saw the sailors silhouetted against the rigging, a bone-white sky without a hint of sun, and the captain at the helm, holding the ship with its prow pointed towards a towering wave.

"*It must hit us head on,*" he was shouting to his men. "*If it hits us broadside, we're finished.*"

Charles shuddered. Lydia must have felt it, as she glanced up at him curiously.

"Are you alright, your Grace? Are you cold? It is a little cool in here."

"It'll warm up once the guests start arriving," he said, with forced cheerfulness. "I shouldn't worry."

"I won't, don't worry. I daresay we won't see each other at all once people start arriving. Arabella's invited the whole of Bath by the sounds of it."

He chuckled, but the joy of their dance was gone. He longed to hug Lydia close to him, to press his cheek into the top of her head and tell her that he loved her.

He did not, of course. It would be shocking, and already the musicians and retreating servants were shooting them curious glances.

They had warning before Arabella burst in, her clacking heels echoing on the well-polished floor. They had pulled apart when she came gliding in, glistening satin skirts trailing around her.

"There you are," she said brightly. "Now, I think the first guests are going to be here soon. Lydia, my love, will you come and help me redo one of the garlands? I think it needs a little sprucing up."

"Of course, Arabella." Lydia moved to follow her friend, but on impulse, Charles clutched at her hand. She glanced back at him, eyebrows raised inquisitively.

"Thank you for dancing with me," Charles managed, and again it seemed like he couldn't catch his breath.

He lifted her gloved hand to his lips and kissed the knuckles. He thought he heard her draw in a sharp breath, but when he glanced up, her face was smooth and smiling again.

"And thank *you,* your Grace," she said, dropping down into an elaborate curtsey.

"Lydia!" Arabella called from the dining room, and Lydia was obliged to hurry after her, leaving Charles standing alone in the empty ballroom.

Chapter Seventeen

The party was going well, Lydia thought. It wasn't Arabella's best – there were too many people there for comfort – but it was enjoyable. As always, Lydia found herself more or less on the outskirts. She didn't feel like dancing – her feet were sore, and the ballroom was crowded beyond comfort anyway. It was a modern song, a bright jig that was enjoyable to listen to but tiring to dance along to.

She met Arabella's eye, surrounded by friends and with Henry at her side for once, and flashed her friend a smile. Arabella smiled back, and before she could elbow her way out of her adoring crowd, Lydia melted away.

She'd hoped to find Charles, although that was silly. She had to remind herself to stop looking around for him, to stop standing on her tiptoes to look for a familiar head of glossy black curls and a peacock-blue coat.

The dance from earlier left Lydia feeling... well, confused. It was too bold to ask him to dance like that, in an empty ballroom, and she was glad nobody had seen them. Perhaps he was put off by her forwardness. But then, she could almost still feel the press of his lips on her knuckles. There had been moments when she thought...

Stop it, Lydia told herself firmly. *Getting your hopes up too soon is a recipe for disaster. Besides, the Duke blows hot and cold, you know that. One moment he looks at you as if you were the loveliest thing in the world, and the next, he has the oddest faraway look on his face, and looks perfectly pensive.*

She sighed to herself, draining her glass of champagne. There was no sign of the Duke. It was silly to imagine that he was avoiding her – the crush was so bad that she couldn't see *anyone* – but Lydia was conscious of a slight disappointment. She had hoped that he would find her.

She stumbled out of the crowd, finding a rare corner of space. The reason for the space was clear – a portly gentleman was sprawled in the only chair in the corner, head tilted back and snoring loudly. How the man had managed to fall asleep, Lydia had no idea, but there he was. She suppressed a smile and shook her head, looking about for a place to put down her champagne glass.

She wanted to sit down, but short of turning the poor gentleman out of his sleeping place, her options were to sit on the floor, plough through the crowd to find the seats where the matrons sat and hoped that one would be available, or simply keep standing. She sighed, shifting from foot to foot. The Duke might even have gone home. She would find Henry, she decided, and casually ask. If he'd gone home, she might as well go to bed. There would be plenty of outings and parties later. She would see him another time.

Before Lydia could brave the crowd again, a man staggered out of the crush and flashed a tilted smile at her. He was clutching an empty champagne glass in both hands, and she had the strangest idea that he had been drinking both at once.

The man was unpleasantly familiar. She recognized him at once, and flashed a quick, polite smile.

"Well, well, Miss Waverly. What a pleasant surprise."

"Sir Gregory," she responded curtly. "Are you well?"

"Well enough, and I'll be better yet once I get some more champagne. Good stuff, isn't it?"

"I thought it was rather strong," she said, eyeing him. He was clearly in his cups, although not to the extent that would shame him publicly. He was unlikely to vomit over somebody's skirts or collapse. Not yet, at least.

He gave a harsh, barking laugh. "Strong? I'm afraid not. It's weak stuff, but I suppose if you only care about quality, it's nice enough. May I get you a glass of champagne?"

"No, thank you."

"What, then?" he shot back, sounding faintly irritated. "Punch, then? Wine? Don't say that you want lemonade."

"I'm not thirsty, Sir Gregory."

He snorted. "Oh yes, I forgot. You're a lady, and ladies can't be seen to eat or drink."

She lifted an eyebrow. It wasn't a good idea to encourage conversation with him, she knew that, but that was really just too much.

"Ladies don't eat or drink, do they? Goodness, how shocking."

He grinned wolfishly, and Lydia knew that she'd made a mistake. It would have been better just to have pretended she hadn't heard him, or else flung herself back into the crowd.

"My friend, Mrs Habit, makes a point to eat so slowly that it looks like she isn't even chewing. Takes her a full hour to eat a moderately full plate, if not more than that. No wonder you ladies all have such tiny waists."

Lydia didn't consider herself to be easily shocked, but really, talking about ladies' waists in the middle of a crowded ballroom was simply not done. She pursed up her lips, and moved away.

Or rather, she tried to move away. In a blink, Sir Gregory was at her side, leaning too heavily on her shoulder and drawing her arm through his. Short of pulling it rudely away, there wasn't a great deal Lydia could do. He held her hand tight in his elbow, making it clear that she couldn't pull away even if she tried.

Lydia swallowed down a twinge of panic.

"I believe my friend is waiting for me, Sir Gregory."

"What, Lady Fernwood? Oh, I don't think so. Last I saw, she was surrounded by her adoring friends, chatting away with great volubility. She'll scarcely notice you're gone. How about a dance, Miss Waverly?"

"I..."

"Already engaged? Surely not. Let me see."

Without waiting for permission or even a response, Sir Gregory grabbed at the dance card tied around Lydia's wrist with ribbon. It had precious few names on it, and naturally there was no name down for the upcoming dance. He grinned at her, wolf-like, and Lydia's heart sank.

"I'm not sure I feel up to dancing," she said hesitantly. She'd hoped that the Duke and she could have a dance, but he wasn't here, and he'd probably understand her keen need to avoid dancing with Sir Gregory.

It didn't work, of course. He leaned close to her, his breath smelling strongly of champagne and something that was worryingly like brandy or whiskey, and his smile widened.

"Now, now, Miss Waverly, it's bad form to refuse a dance, unless you're otherwise engaged."

"I... I don't feel well. I was about to take my leave."

He snorted. "Of course you were. Don't be such a prim and uptight individual, Miss Waverly. Come let us partake in a dance."

Without waiting for a reply, he dragged her through the crowd towards the dance floor, which was filling up with couples for the next dance.

Lydia's face was crimson with anger. He would never have gotten away with such rudeness ordinarily. Half a dozen ladies and gentlemen would have come to her rescue, and while she would *not* have been able to dance with anyone else for the rest of the evening, she would have been safe from Sir Gregory. But the hall was full of people, all of them talking loudly and intent on themselves and their friends, and none of them had even glanced her way. There was to be no rescue, then.

It's just one dance, she told herself firmly. *One dance, then you can take your leave.*

Or so she hoped. With the mood Sir Gregory was in, she wouldn't put it past him to try following her out into the hallways.

Much to her displeasure, the dance was another jig. Most of the couples dancing the previous reel were leaving the dance floor, gasping and pouring with sweat, shaking out stiff and aching feet, making a beeline for the refreshments table. New couples were taking their places, all but vibrating with excitement and ready to dance.

"Ready to fly, Miss Waverly?" Sir Gregory whispered, over-loud, in her ear, making her cringe away from him.

Thank heavens it is not a waltz, was all that Lydia had time to think, before the music started up with a flourish, and she was forced to dance.

There were some benefits to dancing a jig. For one thing, nobody had breath to talk. She was scarcely in her partner's arms, and only had to hold his hand occasionally. She caught glimpses of Sir Gregory's face through the dance, and saw that he looked sour and displeased.

Why was he dancing with her? With a wrench of memory, Lydia recalled that Mrs Habit had left for London only a few days ago, and so would not be attending. Perhaps he'd had high hopes of the woman, but if she were there and he were here, that was a sign that they hadn't reached the understanding he'd hoped.

Surely he doesn't have his sights set on me, Lydia thought, with a flare of panic. *The man is an infamous fortune hunter, but I am not that rich.*

The dance hurt her already sore feet, but it could not last forever. Soon enough, the music ended with a flourish, and the exhausted dancers stumbled to a halt and clapped at each other, eyes glazed and panting for breath.

Sir Gregory didn't smile.

Lydia turned away, intending to dive into the crowd and disappear, but he was on her at an instant, her arm trapped in his again.

"You can't possibly say that you're not thirsty after that," he rasped. "An uncomfortably quick dance. I think a quieter one is next. One can only hope for a waltz, eh? I saw that you don't have a partner for the next set. What say you and I stand up together again, then?"

A flash of panic rolled through Lydia. "I really must take my leave now, Sir Gregory. I... I am not feeling well. I think I'll go to bed."

"Nonsense," he said brusquely.

"I am tired, Sir Gregory."

"You can sleep when you're dead. One glass of punch each, then back on the dance floor, shall we?"

She tugged ineffectually at her trapped hand, but it didn't even move an inch. When it was clear that he really was dragging her towards the refreshment table, Lydia began to worry.

"Sir Gregory, you know that we can't dance together again."

"Why not?"

"Well, it's rather *singular.*"

He flashed a quick, unpleasant smile. "You ladies. Concerned about your reputation, are you? A dance won't kill you."

Lydia swallowed hard. Of course it wouldn't *kill* her. A lady *could* dance twice with a man in one night, but everyone would assume that she was trying to catch him, or that he was hoping to be caught. She would share equal blame. And two *consecutive* dances? That was akin to announcing one's engagement then and there. It was a *remarkably* bad idea. It would be all over town tomorrow, and on the front page in the gossip columns, that Miss Waverly and Sir Gregory were on the cusp of announcing their engagement, despite his recent *entanglement* with Mrs Habit.

She shuddered to imagine what they would say.

"I really can't dance with you a second time, Sir Gregory," she said, as firmly as she could. "Please let go of me."

Lydia glanced around, hoping for help, but she saw only strangers around her. Nobody looked at her, and if they did, their eyes quickly glanced away. Nobody was interested.

"Sir Gregory..." she tried again, and he rounded on here.

"Look here, you stupid little girl," he hissed. "I have had quite enough of your nonsense and excuses. You should be grateful that anyone is paying any attention to you. You're not getting any younger, you know, and I can't imagine that you were ever a beauty. That's the trouble with you ladies – you don't recognise a decent gentleman when you meet one. Now be quiet, drink your punch, and let's dance, shall we?"

Her cheeks flared red, she opened her mouth to say something – or scream, perhaps, Lydia wasn't entirely sure – when a figure stepped neatly out of the crowd, hand landing heavily enough on Sir Gregory's shoulder to make him jump.

"I think you're squeezing Miss Waverly's hand a little, Sir Gregory," the Duke said pleasantly. Lydia's heart did a traitorous little skip, and she found herself swallowing hard.

Sir Gregory's expression hardened. "Miss Waverly and I are about to dance."

"You've already danced together. I saw you."

He bared his teeth. "We're dancing again."

"I don't wish to dance again," Lydia said, her voice a little squeakier than she would have liked, but at least it didn't wobble. "I have told Sir Gregory that I intend to retire for the evening, but he seems to have some trouble understanding me."

Sir Gregory shot her a quick, sharp look of loathing.

The Duke smiled serenely at him. "You heard the lady, Sir Gregory. Perhaps you ought to find another partner of the dance."

"This is none of your concern."

"When I fetch Lord Fernwood and tell him that you're in your cups before ladies and polite Society, do you think it will be my concern then? I should leave now, if I were you, Sir Gregory. If you leave in the next ten minutes, I see no need to tell our host and hostess of your behaviour. If not, I shall tell them, and you can endure the humiliation of being tossed unceremoniously out. Would you like that?"

Sir Gregory's face flared red. He muttered something that sounded none too polite and let Lydia's hand drop. Without bothering with goodbyes, he shouldered his way past the Duke, and vanished into the crowd. After a moment, Lydia saw him heading towards the foyer, where hopefully he would leave altogether. She let herself heave a sigh of relief and turned back to the Duke.

"Thank you," she said frankly. "He was being... being troublesome."

The Duke nodded. "I saw as much. I am surprised that Lady Fernwood isn't by your side."

"Arabella has so many friends, so many people to speak to. I can't expect her to mind me all the time. Besides, I think Sir Gregory was just bored and... well, and in his cups. I don't believe that he had any real interest in me."

Although perhaps if he'd dragged her onto the dance floor for a second time and the scandal sheets announced them engaged, he might decide that a smaller portion was better than none and try and trap her into marriage. Fortune hunters of Sir Gregory's age and temperament tended to get desperate very quickly. There was a rumor that the man needed money.

"That's not the point," the Duke said firmly. "I am sorry that he treated you that way. I was looking for you, Miss Waverly, but the crowd is so dense..."

"I know," she answered regretfully. "There's nothing to be done."

He nodded, hesitating. For a moment, Lydia thought he might ask her to dance. Technically, she should *not*, but Sir Gregory was likely gone, nobody would know.

Then he smiled faintly, and said, "Well, I bid you goodnight, Miss Waverly. Shall I escort you to the stairs?"

Lydia remembered that she had said she was going to bed. Disappointment flashed through her, but she did her best to swallow it back.

"No, thank you," she responded. "I shall be fine by myself. Goodnight, your Grace."

"Goodnight, Miss Waverly. Sleep well."

I won't, Lydia thought, but of course she didn't say it.

Chapter Eighteen

Charles left the party early. He didn't usually leave early, as it tended to look rather singular and almost rude, but tonight he'd had quite enough.

The anger he'd felt at the sight of Sir Gregory dragging Lydia around the dance floor hadn't quite simmered down. How dared he treat her like that?

Sir Gregory is plumbing new lows, Charles thought grimly. *Even he wouldn't have dared to treat a lady so badly in full view of the world before. And now, here he is, trying to strong-arm a woman into dancing with him twice in a row. Something must be done.*

"Shall I summon your carriage, your Grace?" the butler asked demurely, and Charles shook his head.

"No, thank you. I'll walk around the side of the house."

"It is a cold night, your Grace."

Charles smiled wryly, shrugging on his coat and pulling on his gloves. "It'll be brisk. Do convey my goodbyes to Lord and Lady Fernwood, won't you?"

"Of course."

With no further ado, Charles stepped out into the ice-cold night.

It was somewhere after midnight, he estimated. The night was cold and crisp, with a glittering layer of frost covering the gardens. The gravel under his feet crunched as he walked, and once he rounded the corner of the house, it was much darker.

There was of course not enough room for all the guests' carriages and horses to rest in the stables, so the carriages were lined up on the gravel drive in front of and around the house. The coachmen were clustered together in groups, eating and drinking food provided for them, chatting in low voices. On a night like tonight, they would likely have much preferred to sit in the kitchens, but there was likely not enough room, not with the house in an uproar, keeping the party supplied with food and drink.

Charles spotted his carriage at the back of the queue, although his coachman was nowhere to be seen. He spotted the man chatting with a group of acquaintances, and gestured to indicate that he should finish his conversation and his meal before coming to drive Charles home.

He had one hand on the door of the carriage when a figure swept around the side of the vehicle. Charles stopped short.

He recognized the figure at once, despite the poor light.

"Sir Gregory," he said bluntly. "One might almost think that you were lying in wait for me."

Sir Gregory grinned mirthlessly. "I thought I'd have a long, cold wait for you out here. I thought you'd be pressing your advantage with Miss Waverly, now that you've strong-armed me into leaving. Hardly gentlemanly behaviour."

"Gentlemanly behaviour? How can you say such a thing, when you were all but dragging the poor woman onto the dance floor? And if you must know, Miss Waverly retired to her bed, as she had mentioned repeatedly to you that she wished to do. She is tired."

He snorted. "She's tired when it suits her. I suppose neither of us are of real interest to her, then."

Charles tilted up his chin. He was *not* going to show Sir Gregory of all men that his words had hurt him.

"That is no concern of mine, or of yours. Get out of my way, please."

By way of answer, Sir Gregory leaned more pointedly against the carriage door. Charles glanced over his shoulder and was dismayed to see that his coach driver was still chatting, his back turned to them. If anyone was to glance their way, they'd see two gentlemen engaged in conversation, with nothing to ring any alarm bells.

Curse the man, Charles thought. *He's clever, at least.*

"I've been meaning to talk to you," Sir Gregory said, as if they had all the time in the world. "I'd have dropped by your home, but I have a strange feeling that I would not be welcome."

Charles smiled grimly but said nothing. Sir Gregory would certainly not have been admitted through the front door and would likely have been kicked down the steps by the dutiful butler.

"So," Sir Gregory continued, "I thought now would do. It's much quieter out here, don't you think? You and I can talk properly. Like gentlemen."

Ah. So this was where the conversation was going. Charles clenched his teeth.

Delay, he thought. Once his coachman was back, Sir Gregory would be obliged to step aside, and Charles could leave. There was no need to entertain him any longer.

"I have no idea what you are talking about," Charles responded sharply.

Sir Gregory narrowed his eyes. In a flash, he was standing toe to toe with Charles, almost crowding him back against the side of the carriage in front.

"Don't play games with me, *your Grace*. You had your man return those Notes Acknowledging Debts."

"Yes, they were yours. I can't think what possessed you to leave them at my home."

"Don't be such a raging fool. You were meant to pay them."

"Oh? Was I?" Charles said, with studied surprise. "Well, they are not *my* debts."

"If you want to play the fool, then fine. It suits you, to be frank. If you wish me to keep my mouth shut about what I know of you, and keep Miss Waverly's opinion of you clear and pure, you will oblige me, as a gentleman should. There's no need to make such a business of it all. I ask a simple favour, and I'm sure you can afford it. Pay my debts, and all of this will go away. It's the simplest thing in the world. I'm a reasonable man. There's no need to blast your hopes of Miss Waverly, although what you see in such a prissy little thing as that, I have no idea."

Charles clenched his jaw. "If I were you, sir, I would get out of my way. I don't appreciate this sort of talk."

Sir Gregory narrowed his eyes. "All I need is your word, as a gentleman, on your honour that you will arrange this small business which I've spoken to you about. Not too much to ask, I fancy."

Charles gave a bark of laughter. "I might as well tell you now, Sir Gregory, that I would rather Miss Waverly never speak to me again than I should deceive her and pay you a blackmailer's fee into the bargain. You are wasting your time, I'm afraid."

Surprise flashed across Sir Gregory's face, followed rapidly by anger. He darted forward, faster than Charles would have imagined. In an instant, his fists were twisted in the lapels of Charles' coat, shoving him back against the carriage with a dull *thump*. The back of Charles' head hit the carriage, and there was a flash of pain. He had no time to cry out, because Sir Gregory thrust his face up to his, forcing him to press back as much as he could.

"Now, you see here," Sir Gregory hissed. "I was to come into money soon, but that damned woman has up and gone back to London, and there go my hopes. If you think I'm going to sit plaintively around and wait for whatever crumbs you throw my way, you're mistaken. Now, you could have settled those Notes like a gentleman and a friend..."

"We are *not* friends." Charles managed to spit out. Sir Gregory continued as if he hadn't spoken.

"... but no, you decided to make it all a ridiculous business. Do you think I'm funning, *your Grace*? Do you think I won't tell Miss Waverly all I know?"

"I think," Charles managed, his voice tight, "that Miss Waverly would not believe you."

Surprise flashed over Sir Gregory's face, quickly gone.

"Perhaps she would. Perhaps she wouldn't. But I can tell you for sure that she certainly would think about it after I'd gone. I shouldn't give much of your chances. But if you've lost interest in her – men of your rank do tire quickly of people, I have heard – then perhaps we can come to a new arrangement. Perhaps if you don't mind Miss Waverly thinking the worst of you, you'd care about the unscarred side of your face. I think a new scar would suit you, don't you think?"

A flash of fear rolled down Charles' spine. Surely Sir Gregory wasn't about to whip out a penknife and carve a line into his face. Not here, outside a perfectly respectable party at a perfectly respectable home, with coachmen and various servants within shouting distance.

Then he saw the glazed, unfocused look in Sir Gregory's eyes, and realized that once again, the man was in his cups. Dangerously so. And like far too many men in their cups, he was capable of just about everything. It was just as likely that he would crumple to the ground and go straight to sleep as it he would whip out a knife, but those were even possibilities, and Charles did not fancy his chances.

He wrapped his fingers around Sir Gregory's thick wrists, preparing to shove him away and defend himself on the count of three, two, o...

"What is going on here?"

Both men flinched. Sir Gregory released Charles and backed away, and Charles let out a breath he hadn't even realized that he was holding.

Henry stood there, his breath misting out before him in cold, silvery-white puffs. His expression was just as frosty as his breath.

"Arabella saw you leaving, Charles," Henry said, his eyes fixed on Sir Gregory. "I came out to see what was wrong, and here I find an uninvited guest making trouble."

Sir Gregory's cheeks burned. Of course, it stood to reason that he hadn't been invited. What fool *would* invite Sir Gregory to a party?

"I must be mistaken," Sir Gregory responded, flashing a smile which he clearly hoped was charming. "I believed I *had* been invited."

"Mm-hm," Henry said, obviously not convinced. "What is going on here?"

"Nothing," Sir Gregory said, keeping the smile on his face. It was a little mechanical now, rather frozen in place. "Just a friendly chat between gentlemen. Isn't that so, your Grace? Nothing to concern you, Lord Fernwood. Feel free to go back inside – you must be missing your party."

Charles immediately knew the mistake Sir Gregory had made. Strangers often mistook Henry's reticence and reserve for... well, for stupidity. They assumed that a man who didn't enjoy making witty and brilliant conversation with persons he did not know simply *had* no witty and brilliant things to say.

They would, of course, be wrong. Attempting to pull the wool over Henry's eyes never ended well. Sir Gregory clearly believed that Henry would shrug and go skipping back inside, or else would not have the backbone to stand up to a man like Sir Gregory.

He would be wrong on all counts.

Henry narrowed his eyes and took a large step closer. The smile on Sir Gregory's face wavered a little.

"You invite yourself to my wife's party," Henry said slowly, "You drink my wine, eat my food – plenty of both, if the footmen are to be believed – and cause trouble for Miss Waverly, who is my own house-guest and a close friend of Lady Fernwood's. And now, you follow my own friend outside and threaten him. Is that the gist of it?"

"Lord Fernwood, I..."

"I am speaking to his Grace."

Charles swallowed. It wasn't good to get in Henry's way at times like this. He had a temper – everyone did, really, to some extent – and he had clearly reached the end of his patience.

"That is right, Henry. Sir Gregory requires money from me."

Henry pursed his lips tightly. The smile was entirely gone from Sir Gregory's face by now.

"Is that so?"

"Not exactly," Sir Gregory said, with a short, tentative laugh. "The truth is..."

"The truth is, Sir Gregory, you've made a great deal of enemies in Bath in a very short period of time. Now, I couldn't possibly guess what information you have that keeps Charles listening to you instead of laughing and turning you over to the constables but let me tell you what information *I* have."

There was a steely edge in Henry's voice, and Sir Gregory visibly wilted. Footsteps crunched on the gravel, but Charles didn't dare glance over to see who was approaching.

"I know of your debts," Henry continued, as if he were remarking on the weather, "I know about the ones you have no intention to pay, and no means to pay. I know how much money you get in a year, and how it is considerably less than you tell people. I fancy that the moneylenders who have been searching for you would be distressed to know that you have exaggerated your income. I think they would also be pleased to know your true address, not the incorrect one you gave them. I do believe you also gave your creditors the impression that you were about to make a great match, did you not? A widow, you said, by the name of Mrs Habit. Well, I think they would be shocked to learn that Mrs Habit cut off all contact with you and left for London. Your prospects, which were never illustrious, have dwindled to nothing, I fancy."

Sir Gregory had gone entirely white. The gossiping coachmen had gone quiet and were staring over at them. Henry did not glance at them. He stared at Sir Gregory, unblinking.

"I think," Henry said, his voice as level and cool as it had always been, "that Bath is not the town for you, Sir Gregory. Now, so long as you leave my friend alone, and I do not see you again, you shall be quite safe. I have no intention of causing trouble for you – I think you have managed quite enough trouble of your own. But if I were you, I should leave town as quickly as possible, before your creditors and moneylenders lose patience. They are not quite as *gentlemanly* as Charles and myself."

Sir Gregory swallowed reflexively. He opened his mouth to speak and managed a squeaky sort of noise. Henry sighed.

"You may leave, Sir Gregory. At once."

The spell was broken. Suddenly cowed, Sir Gregory scuttled between them, head down, heading towards the front of his house. It didn't surprise Charles to see that he had not come by carriage or horseback.

He gave a start at the figure standing behind them, watching Sir Gregory dive past with large eyes.

"Arabella," Henry said, seeming a little taken aback. "I didn't know that you'd followed me."

"Lydia told me that Sir Gregory bothered her tonight," Arabella said, eyes on her husband. "I came to give him a piece of my mind, but I see you've done that already."

Henry flushed. "I am sorry you had to hear that."

Arabella gave a tiny, shy smile. She seemed almost awed, and certainly impressed. Well, *Charles* was impressed by his friend, too.

"I thought you did very well, Henry. I was proud of you."

Henry blinked, then broke into a small, hesitant smile. He glanced at Charles.

"Are you well, Charles?"

"Quite well," Charles said, recovering himself. "I'm leaving, but you two should go back inside, and enjoy the rest of your party."

Henry smiled and turned to offer his arm to Arabella. Arm in arm, they made their way back around the front of the house. Charles watched them go thoughtfully.

The coachman appeared at his elbow, and Charles recovered.

"Ready to leave, your Grace?" the man asked.

"More than ready," Charles murmured.

Chapter Nineteen

Another party, yet another one. Bouncing around in the carriage on the way to the home of Lady Josephine Everard, the Dowager Duchess of Northwood. Charles' mother.

Lydia was exhausted. She would have given anything for an evening in, to sit and read and take her ease. Even Arabella looked a little tired. Henry was not with them tonight, but Arabella hadn't complained about it once. Lydia thought the pair were getting on a little better than before, which was of course excellent news.

If only it lasted.

"I doubt there will be dancing tonight," Arabella observed, smothering a yawn. "The Dowager is a little old-fashioned when it comes to things like waltzing. I'm afraid it won't be a remarkable evening tonight. She's pleasant enough, and we couldn't *not* attend, but it'll be a dull evening."

Lydia sighed. "I wish I'd stayed at home. I am exhausted, Arabella."

Her friend pursed her lips. "Well, Lady Everard is the Duke's mother."

Lydia shot her a sharp look. "And what is that meant to imply?"

"Oh, I don't know," Arabella responded, shrugging lightly. "But it can't hurt to impress her, can it?"

Lydia bit her lip. She had met the Duke's mother before, if briefly, and it wouldn't be the worst thing in the world if the woman liked her, would it?

She didn't say so, of course. The evening was going to be a dinner, some music afterwards, and doubtless light, polite conversation in the drawing room before and after.

Thrilling.

They arrived on the dot of seven, which was the arrival time carefully outlined in the invitation. Lydia had learned that Bath was a little stricter about punctuality than London. In London, at the height of the Season, a popular lady or gentleman might hop from party to party, spending an hour or two at each, starting at dusk and ending shortly before dawn.

Lydia had done it herself once or twice. It was exhausting. It meant that arrival times meant nothing, and one's host or hostess wouldn't mind if you left only two hours after arriving, or less.

In Bath, that simply was not permitted. Not that it mattered, of course.

Lydia smoothed out her skirts, and Arabella and she entered. Arm in arm, they were ushered by a pale-faced butler into a large and well-arranged parlour, full of muted conversation and the tinkling of some bored-looking young lady on a pianoforte in the corner.

Lady Everard sat in state in the centre of the room, resplendent in dark blue satin, so dark as to almost be black, pearls clinking around her neck. Dowager Fernwood sat beside her, and the Duke himself on the other side.

Lydia's heart skipped a beat at the sight of him, and she swallowed hard. She still remembered the quick press of his lips against her knuckles, and the way he'd so gallantly rescued her from odious Sir Gregory – who, by all accounts, had left town, and Lydia was relieved to hear it. She found herself searching out his gaze. When their eyes met – he was already looking at her – a shiver rolled down her spine.

"Miss Waverly, Lady Fernwood, how lovely!" Lady Everard cooed, rising to her feet and holding out her arms. "How nice. Lady Fernwood, come and sit beside your dear mother-in-law. Miss Waverly, will you favour us with a recital on the pianoforte? We were all charmed with your performance at that musical evening."

Was it Lydia's imagination, or was there a flash of malice in that comment? No, surely not. For all Lady Everard was Dowager Fernwood's friend, she was said to be a kind and well-liked lady.

She forced a smile. "I am not much of a pianoforte player, Lady Everard. I would rather not perform, not when I am sure there are so many other accomplished players here tonight."

Lady Everard smiled tightly. "What a modest young lady. That's a rare thing to find, you know. A *truly* modest woman, in our age. You must tell us your secret, Miss Waverly."

Lydia was beginning to feel rather beset. She glanced around, uncertain. The rules for this sort of gathering were clear – the hostess assigned seats, and therefore conversation groups. Arabella was sitting beside her mother-in-law on a footstool, which seemed something of a breach of etiquette to Lydia, seeing as how Arabella was Lady Fernwood, not the Dowager. No seat had been pointed out to Lydia, so she was obliged to stay standing, feeling like something of a spectacle.

The polite conversation around them had dimmed, and most people were eyeing her curiously, and then glancing over to Lady Everard, who was also standing.

"I... I don't understand, your Grace," Lydia stammered, feeling stupid.

Lady Everard smiled tightly, glancing over at Dowager Fernwood, whose eyebrow flickered. Lydia's heart sank. It was going to be a long evening, she thought.

The Duke had said nothing, and looked rather helpless, gaze flitting between his mother and Lydia.

"Are you familiar with *Polonaise? Beethoven*, you know. It's a favourite of mine, but I really can't play it alone. You must join me at the pianoforte."

Lydia swallowed again. It was a far from simple piece, but she *did* know it. It was a music instructor's favourite to teach a student.

"Yes, but I am really out of practice, your Grace."

"Then you must brush up on your pianoforte skills, Miss Waverly. The height of the Season is nearly upon us. Are you intending to go back to London?"

"Now, what a silly question, Josephine," the Dowager interrupted, before Lydia could say a word. "No sensible young lady would stay away from London during the Season. Bath will be empty in a month, perhaps less, and if Miss Waverly is to find herself a husband..." she trailed off meaningfully, and Lydia felt her cheeks heat.

Lady Everard smiled thinly and moved over to the pianoforte. Lydia had no choice but to follow her. The lady at the piano got up with an air of relief, and the two women settled side by side on the piano seat, which was really a little too small for two.

Thankfully, Lady Everard had the sheet music for the piece, and Lydia's stiff fingers gradually remembered their rhythms. There were harder pieces to play, and Lady Everard's confident playing overshadowed Lydia's occasional wrong notes.

"My son and I used to play this," Lady Everard said, after a full page of music had been performed, and light conversation had sprung up in the room. "Charles is such a wonderful pianoforte player. Of course, you know that – you and he performed that interesting piece at that musical evening. I was surprised – it's not at all like Charles to volunteer to perform."

A response was clearly expected, judging by the quick, thoughtful glance shot her way. Sitting side by side as they were, with her eyes on the piano keys, Lydia couldn't look at the other woman to gauge her expression. It was starting to feel as if she were being watched, strangely enough. She suspected that if she looked over her shoulder, she would see Dowager Fernwood with her eyes firmly fixed on her. It's not as if she would have been talking to *Arabella*, of all people.

"I believe he had the same motivation as I," Lydia responded. She was not going to let herself be cowed by this room of powerful widows.

"Which was?"

"To prevent Lady Fernwood from being embarrassed."

"Oh?" The surprise in Lady Everard's voice was all affectation. "I can't think what you mean."

"I think you can, your Grace," Lydia responded coolly, pausing her playing to turn the pages. "The Dowager Lady Fernwood was pressuring Arabella to play. An innocent mistake, I'm sure, but Arabella had not prepared anything."

"Ladies ought always to be ready to display their accomplishments," Lady Everard said gently. "Especially a Lady Fernwood. The Dowager is simply concerned that her son's wife is presenting a proper face to the world. I do worry that young Arabella is managing things badly, you know."

Lydia clenched her jaw. "Times are changing," she responded smoothly. "Presenting a proper face to the world is no longer a matter of doing what one is told and playing flawless pianoforte pieces."

"Lady Fernwood – whom I love dearly, of course – does not quite understand how things are meant to be done, and sometimes…"

"If the younger generations decide to dispense with traditions that no longer serve them, there is not much to be done about it, I think. After all, traditions are here to serve us, are they not?"

There was a taut pause. "I strongly disagree," Lady Everard said, some of her composure gone, "But you young people must have your foibles, I'm sure. You will see the way the world works soon enough, I suppose. Or suffer the consequences."

She was probably meant to ask what those consequences were. It was a small rebellion on Lydia's part to keep her mouth shut, but she was gratified when Lady Everard shot her a quick, annoyed glance.

The piece seemed interminably long.

"Have you met Lady Deane?" Lady Everard said suddenly.

Lydia blinked. "No, I have not."

"Oh, I *must* introduce you. This will likely be your last chance. She is going back to London for the Season, and I daresay you will move in vastly different circles."

That was an insult, and it stung, the way it was intended to, but Lydia kept a smile on her face.

"That would be lovely. I have not heard of Lady Deane. Was she in London last year?"

"No, this is her first Season. And her last, I daresay. She is a remarkable beauty, and has a great fortune besides, to say nothing of her charms and accomplishments. She'll be snapped up at once, you know. The best women never last more than a Season."

Another calculated insult. Lydia kept a serene smile on her face. Only one page left.

She heard a peal of laughter, the kind of carefully crafted, tinkling laughter that ladies learned at finishing schools.

That must be the darling Lady Deane, she thought sourly. The piece finished, and there was mild, scattered applause. Lydia got up, intending to go to Arabella and find herself a seat there, but Lady Everard firmly drew her arm through hers, steering her towards the Duke.

And towards a beautiful, fair-haired young woman sitting beside him.

She was no more than eighteen, with ferociously curled hair and a shockingly expensive-looking gown. She was sitting beside the Duke on the sofa, turned towards him, one hand resting on his forearm. He looked very stiff and wide-eyed, and deeply uncomfortable. He met her eye briefly, and a flash of understanding went between them.

Lydia felt anxiety drain from her. She had no right to expect anything of the Duke, of course not, but in that moment, she knew that Lady Deane's efforts – and Lady Everard's, for that matter – were in vain. The Duke was not for catching.

"Lady Deane, let me introduce Miss Waverly," Lady Everard said, a tinge of triumph in her voice. "Miss Waverly, I played that same piece with Lady Deane just before you arrived. You did very well – I am sure you did your best – but Lady Deane's taste is unmatched, I'm afraid. Is it not, Charles?"

The Duke blinked. "I'm sorry, Mother, but I'm afraid I was not listening to Lady Deane and you."

A flash of irritation crossed Lady Everard's face, and Lydia suppressed a smile. Lady Deane gave that high-pitched laugh again.

Without the sound of music to blur it out, it sounded a little nasal and somewhat irritating, not to mention entirely false.

"Oh, your Grace, you are *too much!*" she cried, slapping his shoulder with her closed fan. He flinched and smiled tightly. "Is it not terrible, Miss Waverly? Gentlemen have no notion of music, I do declare."

Lydia fidgeted from foot to foot. "I'm not sure that is entirely fair. I can't speak of all gentlemen, but I know that his Grace is an excellent pianoforte player."

"Oh, gentlemen are too rough and clumsy. Myself, I play the pianoforte and the harp, and I have been told that I sing remarkably well. Perhaps I could sing for you all later, if that's agreeable, your Grace?"

This was directed at Lady Everard, who smiled weakly. "Of course, my dear. Charles, why don't you play something with Lady Deane? Not the Polonaise, of course – we've already had that."

"Yes, twice, I believe," Lydia added smoothly, earning herself a hastily smothered glare from both ladies.

"I'd rather not, Mother," the Duke said slowly. "I'm quite tired. Lady Fernwood was suggesting a game of cribbage, though."

Dowager Fernwood, who was not technically part of the conversation, but who was leaning forward to listen anyway, gave a tut of annoyance.

"Cribbage! Before dinner! Hark at them, Josephine."

"I think not," Lady Everard said severely.

"Your Grace," Lydia said, rapidly reaching the end of her patience. "I wonder if I might sit? I am rather tired."

There was a brief silence. Of course, Lady Everard had not asked her to sit at all, and while *that* was a breach of etiquette in a gathering like this, it would be ruder still to sit unasked. Calling Lady Everard out in front of her guests was possibly a little more spiteful than was needed, but Lydia truly felt that her knees were about to give away.

The woman cleared her throat. "What? Of course, of course. I believe I invited you to sit when you arrived, my dear girl."

"You did not, Mother," Charles said, quietly but firmly.

Since no seat was pointed out for her, Lydia pulled up a stool to sit beside Arabella. That effectively cut her out of the conversation between Lady Everard, the Duke, and the ever-tittering Lady Deane, but that was just as well. Arabella looked miserable, and it was fairly certain that her mother-in-law had not spoken two words to her since she'd sat down.

Lydia leaned forward, dropping her voice so that nobody could hear them.

"In about ten minutes," she said quietly, "I am going to have a terrible megrim, and will need to leave immediately. You, of course, will need to accompany me."

Arabella bit her lip. "Have a care, Lydia. You don't want to offend them. The matrons quite run the town here."

"Arabella, if I have to spend another hour here, I am going to throw a cup of wine on somebody. I have done it once, and truly, I shall do it again."

Chapter Twenty

The evening had dragged on. Cribbage was duly played after dinner, and Charles found himself entirely unable to escape the determined Lady Deane.

He wasn't sure whether she was making a play for him in earnest or was simply sharpening her skills before the Season began proper, but either way, he was not interested.

Miss Waverly had left early in the evening with a megrim, and her anxious friend followed her. Dowager Fernwood seemed disappointed not to have further opportunities to humiliate her daughter-in-law, but his mother was relieved, visibly so. Charles wasn't entirely sure why.

When the last guest – Lady Deane and her chaperone – had gone, Charles let himself sink down onto the sofa, and breathed a sigh of relief. His mother shuffled over and stood expectantly in front of him.

"Well?" she asked, impatiently.

He lifted his eyebrows. "What do you mean, *well*?"

"What do you think of her?"

"Her?" he echoed. Only one woman came to mind, and of course that was Miss Waverly. He remembered every note of her playing, the way she'd looked, even though she hadn't had a chance to speak a word to him.

"Yes, yes, Lady Deane! Beautiful, is she not?"

"Oh, yes, very pretty," Charles said, recovering. "Her laugh is rather grating, though. Not that it's her fault."

"She's extremely fashionable, my dear," Josephine pointed out, as if he were a silly child.

I'm sure she is, Charles thought, *but she's not exactly enjoyable company.*

He knew that his mother's parties were not exactly *exciting*, but there were plenty of opportunities to enjoy a little conversation, and he had been looking forward to speaking with Miss Waverly.

Of course, that hadn't happened. Even if she hadn't left so early, Lady Deane occupied all of his attention and conversation, and did not seem inclined to share. It had been full-time work to ignore her significant looks and fan-flutterings.

"If you were to marry," Josephine said, more bluntly than before, "you could do much worse than Lady Deane. She's an heiress, and so charming...."

"I will not marry Lady Deane," Charles said firmly. "I'm sure she's a very fine woman, but I have no interest in her."

Josephine frowned. "Well, why not? You've only just met her, you silly man. You need to allow *time* for this sort of thing. If only William and Anne were here, they would talk some sense into you. I'm sure that William would encourage a match between Lady Deane and you. You'll see her in London, and..."

"I am thinking of marriage, Mother," he said slowly, "But not with Lady Deane."

There was a taut silence.

"Miss Waverly," Josephine said, her voice flat.

Charles glanced up, a little surprised. He hadn't expected his mother to put two and two together so quickly. Was it that she was his mother, or was he simply *that* obvious?

"Yes," he managed at last. "I... I've known Miss Waverly for some time now, and I feel... I feel drawn to her in a way I've never experienced before. I think I am in love with her, Mother."

That was the first time he'd said it aloud, he thought. It was something of a shock to realize that it was true.

He was in love with her. He was in love with Lydia Waverly. It was a dizzying feeling, and he felt the urge to giggle like a schoolboy.

She doesn't know the truth, whispered a voice in the back of his head, but Charles was too exhilarated and giddy to care.

"No," Josephine said flatly.

That single word was like a bucket of cold water upended over his head. He blinked, glancing up at her. She was looming over where he sat on the sofa, arms folded tightly, lips pinched, face white.

"I... I beg your pardon? What are you saying, Mother?"

"You heard me, I think. Miss Waverly is not a suitable match for you, Charles."

Charles blinked again; the happy feeling gradually faded away. The doubts came thronging back, and Edmund's grinning face flashed up in his memory, replaced by the brine-soaked expression of fear on the man's face before the sea swallowed him up forever.

"Mother, I can't think what objections you would have to her. She's from a good family, well-bred, and even if she doesn't have much money – or even any – I can't imagine why that would matter. I have plenty of money of my own."

Josephine gave a tart huff. "Oh, Charles, you are too good-natured. Miss Waverly is entirely unsuitable. Did you hear how rude she was to me this evening? Everyone was shocked. Everyone was talking about it. Dowager Fernwood was about to give her one of her dressing-downs, and Miss Waverly may thank her lucky stars that *someone* at least has a sense of propriety."

Charles chewed the inside of his cheek. "She wasn't rude, Mother. She wasn't."

Josephine sat down beside him, clutching at his sleeve. He had the strangest impulse to pull away.

"She is not *proper*, Charles. She speaks without thinking, shows no respect to the older ladies, and is entirely too rude and unladylike. I am quite shocked at her, but then what else could be expected from a friend of that Arabella's?"

"Lady Fernwood," he said tightly. "She is Lady Fernwood, and the wife of my friend, Mother."

Josephine waved her hand dismissively. "As you like, as you like. But Charles, while I cannot stop you marrying who you like, I must make it clear that I will not give my blessing to you marrying this Miss Waverly."

"This is only because Dowager Fernwood doesn't like her, Mother!"

Josephine ignored this point, rising to her feet and shaking out her skirts.

"She's leaving soon, at least," she muttered.

Charles tensed. "What?"

His mother flashed him a wry smile. "Oh? Did she not tell you? She is leaving Bath. Her mother and friend came to collect her, and they only ever intended to spend a week here. They are leaving the day after tomorrow. I see that you did not know. You don't have to marry Lady Deane, of course, but I can't countenance you marrying Miss Waverly. I suggest you forget about her."

She swept out of the room, leaving Charles feeling hollow.

Sir Gregory had left town, he knew, but his time was running out anyway, it seemed. Before he knew what was going on, he had Edmund's pocket watch in his hand. He opened the cover, staring at the inscription.

Thank you for adventuring with me.

Chapter Twenty-One

"I can't believe you are leaving already," Arabella said, sounding genuinely miserable. "Today is your last full day in Bath, can you believe it? I'm so glad you came, Lydia. Henry says we can spend a few months in London for the Season, but we aren't leaving right away."

Lydia smiled weakly at her reflection.

"I can't believe it's my last day, either. I wish I hadn't saved that lovely green silk. I can't wear it today, and now I won't have a chance."

"Nonsense," Arabella said briskly. "You can wear it in London. I bought you that dress as a present, and you can wear it whenever you like. What are you going to wear today?"

"Something sensible, I suppose."

It was a fine day, cold but sunny, and a picnic by the lake had been arranged. There was talk of boating, and Arabella and Henry were determined to make everyone go out on the lake.

How long had it been since she spoke to the Duke? Tomorrow, Lydia was leaving for London, and there had been no word from him. No note, no letter, no visit. There had been no opportunity to talk to him at his mother's awful party the previous night, and Lydia felt as though she'd wasted her time.

He would be at the picnic, though. Or so she hoped.

And then what? A snide voice at the back of Lydia's mind inquired snippily. *Do you think he's going to propose in the middle of a boat?*

No, of course she didn't think that. If the Duke was interested in her – and sometimes she had felt so very sure that he was – he would have spoken to her by now. He wasn't a shy or diffident sort of man, so what was holding him back?

Perhaps she'd misinterpreted friendliness for something more. Perhaps she was just seeing what she wanted to see. Bath was not London, where every move was second-guessed and a smile of greeting between a man and a woman could set off a spiral of gossip.

She'd chosen a plain blue gown, sparsely ornamented, with no jewelry or lace. There wasn't much point, not for a picnic. Dressing finely wasn't going to make the Duke more likely to tell her that he had feelings for her.

Perhaps it was a mistake, she thought. *Perhaps it was a flirtation, and he had no idea I would take it so seriously. Perhaps I'm just a fool.*

No answer provided itself, and Lydia had no intention of telling Arabella about all this. If she was going to stay in Bath, it wasn't fair for Arabella to treat the Duke as if he'd broken her friend's heart.

I shouldn't have been silly enough to give it away so easily, then, Lydia thought bleakly. She pasted on a smile and turned to face her friend.

"I think I'm ready. When are we leaving?"

***

Arabella had selected a good place for the picnic. It was a hollow, surrounded by a glade of trees, with the lake lapping at the shore not too far away. There were ices to be bought only a short walk along the lake, and boats for hire. Already some of the young people were eagerly making plans to go rowing on the lake.

The footmen were setting out the blankets and food, although it would be some time before it would be ready. Arabella clapped her hands for attention.

"Well, since everybody is here, why don't we go boating now, and eat our picnic afterwards?"

There was a general murmur of agreement. Out of the corner of her eye, Lydia saw the Duke approach. His mother was clinging onto his arm, face pursed up in disapproval. Dowager Fernwood had been invited, but had not accepted, and Arabella had not bothered to hide her relief.

Arabella flashed a beaming smile all round. "So, boating now, yes? Right, well, it looks as if the boats for hire can only take two at a time. To make things a little more interesting, I thought Henry and I would assign us all into pairs. Many of us are leaving for London in the next few days and weeks, so this may be our last chance to get to know somebody new. What do we all say?"

This idea seemed to interest everyone, almost as if it were a game. Lydia, who had intended to go boating with Clara, pursed her lips a little.

Arabella clapped her hands again, her infectious grin spreading around the group. Lydia saw Henry smiling fondly up at her, and had to suppress a smile of her own.

"Now, I thought we could do chiefly male-female pairings, what do we all say?"

"Count me out," Lady Pemshire huffed, shaking her head. "I'm too old for boating."

A few others also demurred, leaving a crowd of young people all waiting to be paired up.

"Very well," Arabella said cheerily. "Clara, you can go with Mr Green, I think you two have a shared love of literature. Miss Bolts, you can go with..."

She listed names, carefully pairing those who had shared interests or were likely to enjoy each other's company. It was a clever idea, and Lydia saw that most people were smiling and pleased with their assigned pair. She flinched when her name was called.

"Lydia, you may go with... let me see, the Duke of Northwood. You two are already good friends, I think, and you'll have plenty to talk about."

Lady Everard sucked in a sharp, annoyed breath.

"Lady Fernwood, I think I should prefer to sail with my son."

Arabella cast a disinterested look her way. "You said you did not want to go boating, your Grace."

"I think perhaps my son and Lady Deane intended to go sailing together," Lady Everard persevered.

Arabella's eyebrows shot up. "Your Grace, are you quite well? Lady Deane is not here. I would have invited her, but I'm afraid I had no opportunity to make her acquaintance. If his Grace wishes to remain on shore, of course he may. I am not *forcing* everyone to go boating."

Lady Everard, who had gone quite red, closed her mouth with a snap. She glanced up at her son, tugging his arm, but the Duke was not looking at her.

"I am quite alright, Mother," he said, in an undertone which everyone craned to hear. "I'll go boating with Miss Waverly."

"But Charles..."

"Mother," he said, in a warning tone. "Please, do not."

She fell silent, and Arabella hastily began pairing people up again, to brush past the awkwardness of the moment.

Once all the pairs had been assigned, the young people hurried towards the boats, talking and laughing. Arabella and Henry were together, it seemed, arm in arm. Lydia had been briefly worried about Clara, but her worries faded away. She had been paired with a young man of her own age, with a head of vibrant red hair, a pair of round wire-rimmed spectacles, and an earnest expression. They were already talking eagerly and seemed entirely happy.

Lydia and Charles, on the other hand, were very quiet.

"I'm sorry about that business earlier," he said at last. "My mother has it in her head that Lady Deane and me would make a fine match."

Lydia cleared her throat. "And you think not?"

He smiled wryly. "Lady Deane is a fine woman, I'm sure, but she will not be the Duchess of Northwood anytime soon. I very much enjoyed your duet with my mother last night, by the way. I know you didn't want to play, but you performed admirably."

She flashed a quick smile up at him. "I think I preferred our duet."

Was it her imagination, or was there a dusting of red around his cheeks and nose? Was he blushing?

Perhaps. But then they were all filing along the wooden pier, two by two, gingerly climbing down into boats. Everybody was talking and laughing happily, but when Lydia glanced up at the Duke, he was white-faced.

She pulled him aside, taking his arm. He glanced down at her, his expression unreadable.

"Are you well, your Grace?" she asked quietly. "You seem… you seem distracted."

He smiled weakly. "I don't much care for being on open water. Not after…" he trailed off meaningfully, his hand creeping up to trace the scar on his cheek.

She bit her lip. "Let's go back, then. I don't want you to be uncomfortable."

"Of course not, Miss Waverly. *You* want to go boating."

"Not at your expense," she said firmly, but he shook his head.

"It does me good to do things that unsettle me, Miss Waverly. I can swim, so there's nothing to worry about."

She still felt uncertain, but now all the others had boarded their boats and were rowing away. The man whose boats stood at the end of the pier, was looking their way expectantly, the rope mooring the final boat hanging from his fist.

They moved towards him, and the Duke handed over the coins required for the hire of the boat. Lydia stepped in first, the boat rocking under her weight. She'd gone boating before, of course, but not in such a small boat, not with only one person beyond herself. The water of the lake was iron-grey and a little unsettled, the wind whipping the water into ripples and shallow troughs. She sat down heavily in the stiff wooden seat and glanced up at the Duke.

He climbed down nimbly, face still white, and settled himself with more grace than she had done.

"You've rowed before, sir?" the boat-man asked, and Charles nodded. Reassured, the man pushed the boat out, away from the shore and the pier, and Charles gripped the oars firmly, knuckles turning white.

"We needn't stay out here long," Lydia said, feeling a little guilty. "I'm sure Arabella didn't know how uncomfortable you were around the water."

"One can't spend one's life in fear," Charles said, his voice absent and pensive. "We live around water, besides. It's simply not practical to have a fear of water. I shall be fine, Miss Waverly, thank you. You are very kind."

She bit her lip at the compliment, feeling colour rush to her cheeks. He began to row, pulling the boat skillfully and powerfully across the water. They quickly caught up with the others, passing most of them.

It was cold out in the middle of the lake. A stiff wind blew, whipping up the water into stiff peaks, and disarranging Lydia's hair. Clouds covered the sun, and the warmth of the day, such as it had been, disappeared altogether. She wished she'd worn a thicker shawl, but of course it was too late for that. Trailing her fingers in the water, she found it was ice-cold. They bobbed up and down cheerfully, and after a while, Charles leaned on the oars and let the water take them where it willed.

They sat in silence, enjoying the lap of the water and the bob of the boat. At least Lydia was enjoying it. Charles no longer looked white-faced and afraid, but there was a pensive sort of preoccupation in his face now.

They'd floated out past the others by now, and Lydia couldn't decide whether it was peaceful or unsettling. Most had given up rowing and were leaning forward to chat with each other. Peals of laughter rolled over the surface of the water, the sound carrying easily. They passed Mr Green and Clara, who were deep in conversation. Mr Green was not rowing well, and the boat was moving rather too fast and erratically. He didn't seem to be watching where he was going, and of course Clara would not be paying attention. It was a relief to pass them by.

"I hear you are leaving for London tomorrow," the Duke said at last.

Lydia swallowed, drawing her thin shawl tighter around herself.

"Yes," she admitted. "Arabella would have me stay longer, but my mother wants me to take in the Season. Clara intends to take in the Season, too. We can't stay in Bath much longer. People are leaving, anyway. This was our agreement."

He nodded. Lydia found herself holding her breath. Was he upset that she was leaving? Indifferent? What? If only the wretched man would just *tell* her.

"What about you?" she asked, after a pause. "Are you leaving Bath?"

"No, I think not. I... I intended to, not so long ago, but now there's no reason to leave, so I think I am obliged to stay. I have a great deal of work to do."

Disappointment crashed over her, but Lydia did her best to hide it.

"That's a pity," she said, as lightly as she could. "I'd hoped to see you in London."

He smiled vaguely, and Lydia had the strangest idea that he was bracing himself to say something.

"I have not been entirely honest with you, Miss Waverly," he said at last.

Her stomach clenched. "Oh?" she managed, pleased to sound at least moderately unconcerned.

"I... that is, I knew that Lady Fernwood – Arabella – intended to pair us up for boating. Perhaps she might have paired us together anyway, but I wasn't willing to take the chance. I asked her to put us together as a pair."

A jolt ran through Lydia, and she leaned forward. "Why did you do that?"

He glanced nervously at her. "Are you displeased?"

"Am I...? No, of course not, but I have to ask why."

"I wanted to speak to you about something. It's important. I couldn't see any way of speaking to you about it before you left for London, and I know that if I don't tell you now, I never will. And you deserve to know."

He drew in a deep breath, eyes squeezing closed.

Lydia felt dizzy. She reached out to grab the sides of the boat, squeezing hard to steady herself. The rough grain of the wood scraped her fingers, splinters pricking her skin.

He wanted to speak to her privately. *Privately*, and he'd made arrangements to speak to her. That could only mean...

Steady, she told herself firmly, removing her hands from the side of the boat to fist them in her dress. *Stay calm and composed. How silly will you look if it's something entirely dull and ordinary?*

Although that would be unfair of him, she was sure. Surely, he must know what she would think of what he had said. Surely, he would know what she was expecting... she swallowed hard, tossing back her hair.

Why does he look so upset and serious? She thought. Surely a man about to make a... to make an *offer* would not look so upset. What is going on?

She leaned forward, frowning, and trying to look him in the face.

"Your Grace? Please, tell me. You seem upset. What can I do to help?"

He opened his eyes and smiled dully at her.

"I wish you would call me Charles. Although perhaps after this you won't want to call me anything."

Chapter Twenty-Two

Charles' heart was hammering hard against the inside of his ribs.

It had been easy enough to convince Arabella to pair him with Lydia for the boating trip. He suspected she'd already intended to do so, but he simply wasn't willing to take the chance.

He knew, beyond a shadow of a doubt, that if she left for London, he would never tell the truth. About anything – about the way he felt about her, or about what had truly happened to her cousin.

She deserved to know both. Although once she knew one thing, she might not want to hear the other.

He was barely aware of his own words as he spoke. He'd thought them all up beforehand – it was easier to speak if you'd already decided what to say. He avoided looking at Lydia while he talked. He couldn't bear to see the emotions flit across her face. Would she be hopeful and happy, thinking that he meant to declare himself, or uncomfortable? Best not to see.

"You remember that there was an accident on my Grand Tour, the one that left me with this scar?" he heard himself say. "Around the same time your cousin, Edmund, was sadly drowned."

He sensed Lydia tensing, sitting a little straighter and stiffer. He glanced up and saw that she was frowning at him, confused.

Now would be the time to stop talking. Now, I just stop all of this, and pretend that I had something else in mind. I could tell her that I loved her, that I wished to marry her, and she would never have to know any of this.

I would know.

He closed his eyes. The water on the lake was getting choppier, churned up by the sharp wind. Soon, the other rowers would start heading back to shore. Charles, for one, was hungry, and the others would soon start thinking about the picnic waiting for them and get tired of the chill wind prowling over the lake.

His opportunity would be gone.

Now or never, he thought bleakly.

Reaching into his pocket, he curled his fingers around the cool surface of Edmund's silver pocket watch.

Strange how I think of it as his, when it was bought as a gift for me, and engraved with my name. It's probably because he never had the chance to give it to me. After all these years, with my name engraved on the lid, I still feel as though I stole it, almost.

What would have happened if Edmund was still alive? Would they still be friends? Would they even now be in Society, laughing and joking about their adventures abroad, and pretending to be sad at their return to real life and real responsibilities. Would he have been introduced to Edmund's cousin, Miss Waverly, in her first Season? Would they have been friends? Would he feel the same way about her?

He thought perhaps he might, but that was getting lost in a world of *what ifs* and *maybes*. A waste of time. He drew in a deep breath and pulled out the watch.

Lydia's gaze automatically dropped to the watch, its chain dangling freely, the weak sunlight glinting off the silver cover. She frowned, squinting at it.

"Checking the time already, your Grace?" she said, trying for a joke. Charles didn't smile and didn't bother to ask her to call him *Charles* again.

"I have something to tell you, and you'll wonder at once why I didn't tell you right away," he said, and his voice sounded weak. "It's about your cousin. It's about Edmund."

Lydia's eyes widened in confusion. She opened her mouth to speak. Then, in the ensuing silence, Charles heard frantic shouts and commotion.

The boat had floated around so that his back was to the shore, with Lydia's end of the boat pointed out towards the middle of the lake. They'd floated a good way out, and the others were already heading back to the shore. Henry's voice came thundering over the splash of the waves.

"For heaven's sake, Mr Green, slow down!"

Lydia's gaze slid over Charles' shoulder, and her jaw dropped, panic widening her eyes further.

He turned and saw a boat coming towards them at full speed.

Out on the lake, a strong rower or a person not used to maneuvering a rowing boat could get up quite a speed. Out on the open water, it was easy to lose track of how quickly one's boat was actually travelling.

That is, until one started to return to shore and realized that one could not stop.

Mr Green was flailing around with the oars, sweat beading on his forehead and sunshine glinting off the wire rims of his spectacles. He was trying to turn the boat and slow down at the same time, and neither was happening. Clara was clutching the side of the boat, eyes wide, and it was gut wrenchingly clear that the boats were going to collide.

Charles reached for the oars, and just had time to curl his fingers around the time-smoothed wood before Mr Green and Clara's boat barreled into theirs.

The prow of their boat struck the side of Charles and Lydia's boat, the impact shoving both of them sideways. The boat rocked violently, turning onto its side. Only a few seconds could have passed between seeing the oncoming boat until the impact – perhaps less – but the time seemed to stretch out interminably.

Charles reached forward to grab Lydia, in the wild hope of steadying them both, but she was already falling sideways, arms windmilling, her shawl flying off her shoulders. The hem of her gown slipped through her fingers, then he fell too.

With a sickening *crack*, Charles' head bounced off the side of the boat, filling his world with blurred pain and flashing lights. He just had time to admire the irony of the situation – he survived a storm and the full power of the raging sea once, only to drown out here in a lake, on a calm day – before unconsciousness nibbled at the edges of his vision, and everything went dark. He just had time to hear his own name being screamed before the water swallowed him up, and then he knew no more.

***

The impact was sickening, and Lydia found herself hurled sideways. She hadn't really expected to fall into the water, somehow that seemed too ridiculous. And yet she fell in with a splash, icy water taking her breath away and soaking through her ridiculous layers of clothing. She remembered a flashing series of scenes – Clara's terrified face, Mr Green's white knuckles on the oars, Charles trying to brace himself on the side of the boat and reach for her at the same time, and the iron-grey sky above their heads.

Then she was in the water.

Lydia took in a reflexive gasp of air, and immediately choked on water. She clawed around herself, kicking her legs, tangled in her skirts. Her shoes came loose, although she barely noticed at the time, and her sodden clothes dragged her down.

She kicked again, determinedly, and came rushing up to the surface. It took a moment for her to recognize the dark cavern she found herself in. The boat had capsized, it seemed, and she was underneath it, the top of her head brushing the seat that she had been sitting on only moments ago. Treading water, Lydia drew in a few steadying breaths, trying to get used to the weight of her clothes around her. They were dragging her down, of course, but thankfully she'd chosen a light muslin dress and only a few under-layers today. It was not enough for a cold morning, but if she'd worn the green silk... Lydia shuddered.

She expected Charles to bob up beside her, but he did not. A sense of unease bloomed inside her.

I can't stay here, Lydia thought sensibly. She couldn't feel the lake-bed underneath her feet, of course, and her clothes seemed to get heavier by the minute. Taking a deep breath, she ducked underneath the edge of the boat, and came up in the open air outside.

It was all noise and chaos. Several boats were rowing towards them, and Mr Green had come to a halt a little way away. He was bone-white, and looked as though he were going to be sick. He gave a cry of relief when he saw her.

"There is Miss Waverly!" he called. "Miss Waverly, we are coming to you, just stay there!"

"You can't!" called another voice. It was Arabella, perched in the prow of the boat while Henry rowed rapidly towards them. "The boats only take two."

"I'll swim to shore," Lydia called, striking out.

"You mustn't! Lydia, it's not safe." Clara shouted, sounding shaken.

"What would you recommend? Should I tread water here, while somebody sails back to shore and drops off a passenger? Seems rather pointless. Or perhaps you'd like to swim back, Clara," Pausing, Lydia glanced around. "Where is Charles?"

She noticed that she called him *Charles,* rather than *the Duke* or even *his Grace*. Such formalities seemed silly at a time like this. Nobody else seemed to notice.

"He hasn't come up," Henry responded, his face grim, and Mr Green gave a moan of fear.

Panic tightened up Lydia's body, and she floundered for a moment, accidentally taking in a mouthful of lake water. She remembered a *bang*, of Charles being thrown sideways just as she tipped over the side.

"I... I think he knocked his head," she shouted, doing her best to swallow down the fear. It was not working.

Henry sucked in a breath. "He could be unconscious. Arabella, take the oars, I'll go in for him."

Lydia knew she should be conserving her energy, striking out immediately for shore, instead of wasting her strength treading water here and getting colder and colder, but she stayed where she was, frozen. Henry stripped off his jacket and waistcoat, tossing off his cravat, and dived neatly into the water near the upended boat.

"Oh, God, oh God," Mr Green moaned. "I've killed him."

"It was an accident," Clara was trying to soothe him. "He may yet be well."

"Lydia, come here and get into this boat," Arabella said, knuckles standing out white where she gripped the oars.

Lydia imagined herself floundering, half in, half out of the water, her sodden dress dragging her down. Arabella wouldn't have the strength to pull her up. And Arabella couldn't swim. If the boat capsized, there would be two people at risk of drowning, not just one.

"No, Arabella. It's too dangerous. I'm going to shore."

Arabella gave a squawk. "Lydia, *no!*"

"I have to, Arabella!"

Not waiting for a response, Lydia turned and struck out for shore.

It was quite possibly the hardest thing she'd ever done, turning her back on her terrified friend and Charles, possibly drowning in the freezing lake. It was the most sensible thing to do, but it didn't make it any easier.

People were gathered at the shore, craning their necks and muttering nervously. Lydia could see her mother there, practically in the water herself. She imagined that she would look quite a sight, trawling her way through the water, bedraggled as a half-drowned rat.

When she felt the lake-bed beneath her feet, Lydia twisted to see what was going on behind her. Mr Green and Clara were rowing back to the pier, with most of the other boats following.

Henry was swimming strongly towards the shore, towing Charles through the water. Charles was limp, his head lolling on his friend's shoulder. Arabella followed them, rowing determinedly. A pang of fear went through Lydia's heart, then a rush of current knocked her off her feet and made her worry about herself again.

Swallowing hard, she swam the last few feet to the shore, staggering upright towards safety.

"Oh, my poor girl!" Lady Pemshire gasped, rushing forward into the water, flinging her arms around Lydia. "We saw it all from here, and we couldn't do a thing. You can't imagine how terrified we were for you."

She shivered. "I'm cold, Mama."

"Of course you are, darling, of course. Here, take my shawl."

Lady Pemshire wrapped her shawl around Lydia, pulling her properly out of the water onto dry land. The others clustered around her, firing questions.

Lady Everard was up to her ankles in water, hands pressed over her mouth, watching Henry swim ashore with Charles. Lydia felt sorry for the woman.

"That wretched man," Lady Pemshire hissed. "That Mr Green. Just wait till I get my hands on him!"

"It was an accident, Mama," Lydia said, her teeth chattering. "Mr Green didn't mean to do it. If we'd been paying attention, we could have gotten out of his way." She felt oddly numb, not cold anymore, and suddenly there was a flurry of shawls and gentlemen's jackets swung over her shoulder. She pushed herself to her feet as Henry came stumbling ashore.

A group of the men hurried down to help, carrying the unconscious man ashore. A pang of fear choked Lydia when she saw the gash on the side of his head, watery blood streaking down his face.

They laid him carefully down on the beach, and Henry knelt over him, Arabella came splashing through the water, leaving the boat bobbing near the shore, and hurried over to her husband.

"He's breathing," Henry announced to nobody in particular.

"His head, his head!" Lady Everard moaned, but Arabella laid a hand on her arm.

"Head wounds often look worse than they are," she said firmly, and Lydia caught herself wondering how on earth her friend had come to learn that. "They tend to bleed a great deal, but that wound doesn't look deep or particularly nasty. Compose yourself, your Grace."

At any other time, Lady Everard would doubtless have taken great exception to being told to compose herself, but today she only drew in a few deep breaths and nodded vigorously.

"We should take him to a doctor," Henry spoke up. "Whose carriage is closest?"

A white-faced Mr Green, tailed by Clara, pushed through the crowd. "Mine," he gasped, "But I can bring it closer. It's a gig, and we can travel quickly. I know where the nearest doctor lives. Miss Waverly and you ought to dry off before you catch your deaths."

"Agreed," Henry responded bluntly.

On cue, Charles stirred, blinking water out of his eyes, squinting at the people around him with confusion. Lydia imagined that he would have a terrible headache. She wanted to edge closer, to lean into his field of vision to flash him a smile, but Lady Everard was there first, squealing pitifully and making as if to throw herself across him.

Once again, Arabella prevented herself.

"Don't smother him, your Grace," she said sharply. "Let him breathe. We will follow Mr Green to the doctor."

"I would like to come too," Lydia heard herself say, and her mother glanced sharply at her.

"Not until you're dried off and warmed up," she said brusquely. "Let the others handle the Duke."

Swallowing, Lydia turned to obey. Out of the corner of her eye, she saw something glint, half-buried in the sand of the shore. Frowning, she bent to get a better look.

Now, what is that?

Chapter Twenty-Three

"Lydia? Lydia, darling, come away from the water. Quickly, now. I don't want you falling in again."

Lady Pemshire's voice was high-pitched with worry, and she tugged ineffectually at her daughter's sleeve. Lydia didn't bother to point out that the water was barely ankle-deep at the shore, and she'd just managed to swim halfway across the lake without drowning.

Around them was all chaos. The boatman, having reassured himself that neither Lydia nor Charles was at risk of imminent death, had set about retrieving his boats, some of which had been left floating haphazardly everywhere. Lydia and Charles' boat was still upside-down in the middle of the lake.

The picnic was being packed up, and people were talking between themselves, in varying stages of shock and curiosity.

This event would feature strongly in the scandal sheets tomorrow, Lydia was sure of it. It wasn't exactly a *scandal*, but no doubt the papers would turn the accident into some sort of unorthodox duel, and promptly conjure up a rivalry between the Duke of Northwood and Mr Green. Perhaps they would put Lydia in the middle of it all, or perhaps Clara.

Really, the whole thing was ridiculous. Whenever Lydia closed her eyes, she saw Charles lolling against his friend's shoulder, face bone-white and his eyes closed. Arabella had said that his head wound looked worse than it was, but hadn't people died from hitting their heads before?

He could have drowned, Lydia thought, with a shudder. *We both could have drowned.*

The flash of silver which had caught her eye was half-buried in the sand, the water lapping around it. Clearly, the current was bringing things up to this part of the shore. She noticed a lady's bonnet, bobbing comically in the swell, and her own sodden shawl, partially submerged, a few feet away from the line of the shore.

She crouched gingerly down, inspecting the silver thing. It was a pocket watch, she saw at once, with a broken chain trailing back out into the water. She dug it out, the sand scraping at her cold-numbed fingers. It was heavy, and there was a pretty pattern engraved on the lid. She cleared away the sand, wondering why the thing looked so familiar.

"Lydia!" Lady Pemshire appeared at her side, snatching her arm. "You are going to catch your death out here, and I for one am not going to stand here while you get pneumonia. You need to come home immediately and change, there's no time to waste."

"I want to go to the doctor's," Lydia managed. She *was* cold, actually. Her brisk swim had warmed her, but not the chill was creeping back in, and she was hard-pressed not to let her teeth chatter. "I want to see Charles."

She hadn't called him *the Duke* or even *his Grace*, but if her mother noticed, she did not let on.

"And so you shall, my dear, but not right away. The doctor will want time and space to do his work, and *you* are going nowhere until you're warmed and thoroughly dried off. Now come on, let's go."

Lydia let herself be towed away. It was a short walk from their picnic spot to where the carriages were, as the walk was pleasant, and it had seemed like a good idea at the time. Now, the walk seemed interminable, the wind an icy blade which cut through Lydia's sodden clothes. They dragged down on her, heavy as stone, and sand seemed to have gotten into every crevice of her clothing, itching and scraping.

It was a relief to see their carriage up ahead, the door open, and the coachman waiting anxiously.

Lydia got inside, wincing as she spread her soaking skirts over the fine upholstery. Her mother barely seemed to notice, clambering in after her and spreading more shawls and blankets over her.

"I have sent the footman ahead," she explained brusquely, "So there will be a hot bath waiting for you, and of course dry clothes."

"But Charles..."

"Charles is not going anywhere," Lady Pemshire said firmly. "My darling, *you* are not going anywhere until you are warmed and dried off. This is really rather serious. I dare say folks will be talking about this for the rest of the Season. What a shocking thing! Poor Mr Green. It was an accident, of course, but I doubt he'll rest until he knows that the Duke and you have made a full recovery. Really, it is too early in the year to go boating. Why, only last week, the ice..."

Lady Pemshire rattled on, talking and talking as she always did when something serious had happened, or when she herself felt uncomfortable. Lydia allowed herself to sit back in her seat, careless of the soaked upholstery. She lifted the pocket watch, inspecting it closer.

It was a fine item, solid silver, and she could hear it ticking strongly. She opened the lid and was pleased to see that the glass cover over the clock face itself was not cracked.

And then she saw the inscription.

To Charles. Thank you for adventuring with me. Your Friend, Edmund.

Lydia felt dizzy and sick. So that was why the pocket watch looked so familiar – Edmund had bought it only a week before he left for his Grand Tour.

"But you already have a pocket watch," she'd pointed out, confused. Laughing, he'd ruffled her hair.

"But this is not *for* me, my dear cousin."

She'd assumed immediately that it was a gift – Edmund loved to give gifts – and now it seemed that she was right.

"Mama," Lydia heard herself say, the word slurred. Her lips were numb, whether from shock, cold, or a combination of both, she wasn't entirely sure. "Mama, did Edmund travel with a friend?"

Lady Pemshire frowned. "What's brought this on?"

"I'm just asking. I want to know, please."

She sighed. "He wrote home so rarely, and you know how terrible he was for writing letters. He mentioned a travelling companion, a young man he'd met along the way, but never named him. You know what Edmund was like for details."

Lydia swallowed reflexively. "I think it was the Duke of Northwood. Of course, he wouldn't have been a duke then."

Lady Pemshire blinked. "Oh. Well, I suppose a lot of young men went on their Grand Tours at the same time. Why do you bring it up?"

Wordlessly, Lydia handed over the pocket watch, indicating the inscription. Lady Pemshire frowned as she read it.

"Oh, I see. Well, they must have been travelling together, then. What a shame. Now I think on it, the Duke's father died soon after Edmund was... was lost, and it was mentioned that he had come home early from his own Tour. I wonder if they travelled together?"

Lydia swallowed hard. "They must have done. Don't you see, Mama?"

Her mother lifted an eyebrow. "See what? I really don't know what you mean, darling."

"The Duke must have been scarred in the same storm that drowned Edmund."

"Well, that *is* something of a leap, my dear."

"It is not! But why wouldn't he tell me? Why hide it from me, if he knew my cousin? I would have loved to meet a friend of Edmund's, especially if they've travelled together. Why didn't he tell me? I don't understand."

Lady Pemshire pursed her lips. She tenderly wiped the remaining sand from the pocket watch and closed the lid with a *snap*.

"Perhaps it slipped his mind," she responded lightly, handing it back to Lydia.

She shook her head. "No, that can't be right. I must talk to him about it."

She wasn't sure what she'd expected – agreement, perhaps, or even a shrug of disinterest. She hadn't expected to see the flash of pain in her mother's face.

"I know you won't let Edmund rest," Lady Pemshire said quietly, startling her daughter. "I know that you are looking for something, *anything* to give you the closure you long for, even if you don't know it. Lydia, life is rarely so neat. You must learn to let things go and move on. I know, I know – easier said than done. But if you want any peace, you must accept that Edmund is gone, and is not coming back."

"What does this have to do with…"

"Edmund would not want to see you suffering like this," Lady Pemshire interrupted firmly. "Bath was meant to refresh you, to invigorate you, to remind you that although our beloved Edmund is gone, life still remains. Enjoyable life, at that. I hope you haven't wasted your time here, my dear."

Lydia sank back, deflated. "I had a good time here," she admitted. "There were times when I thought…"

She trailed off, and Lady Pemshire tilted her head to one side. "You thought what, dear?"

Lydia shook her head. "Nothing. Just some hopes I had for… for something. It hardly matters now. Are we nearly home? I'm fair freezing to death."

Lady Pemshire's pursed lips indicated that her not-too-subtle change of subject had been noticed, but she asked no questions.

"Nearly," she responded, smiling kindly. "We're nearly there."

Chapter Twenty-Four

Charles jerked awake, head pounding. He felt sick and hollow, as if his insides had been unceremoniously whisked out.

Narrowing his eyes, he squinted up at the ceiling, trying to work out where he was, because *that* was not his ceiling at home.

Then a familiar face edged into his field of vision. It was a man in his sixties, with a bristling moustache, and old-fashioned pince-nez resting on the bridge of his nose. Charles smiled weakly.

"Doctor Figg, hello."

"Your Grace, I'm glad you're awake. How do you feel?"

"Ill. I feel sick, and as weak as a kitten."

"Hardly surprising, hardly surprising. I shall have some food brought to you. Nothing spectacular, mind, only bread and butter, until you feel better. You've had a nasty knock to the head, to say nothing of almost drowning. You had a lucky escape, your Grace. What do you remember?"

Charles winced, closing his eyes.

"All of it, unfortunately."

He remembered the boat ploughing towards them, the screams of people around them, and the panicked look on poor Mr Green's face when he realized he could not control the boat. He remembered the way the world had overturned, the *thump* of his head hitting the side of the boat, Lydia's frantic face...

He sucked in a breath, making to sit up. Doctor Figg tutted loudly, firmly pushing him back down.

"Have a care, your Grace, have a care! You need to sit quietly and rest. That head wound is not dangerous, but you can't go flailing about like that."

Charles sank back onto the pillows. He wanted to struggle, to insist on sitting up, but he really did not have the energy.

"Where is Miss Lydia Waverly?" he managed, a little shocked at how weak his voice sounded. "She fell into the water. Is she hurt?"

"Miss Waverly is quite alright. She fared better than you, I must say," Doctor Figg said severely. "I believe that she swam ashore. Unless she catches a chill – and frankly, she does not strike me as a young lady who tends to catch chills – she will be entirely unharmed by this misadventure. She has gone home, I believe."

Charles smiled weakly. "Yes, I can imagine her swimming ashore."

"A very enterprising young lady."

Doctor Figg bustled around the room, and Charles was left to his own devices for some time. His eyes got used to the clear, mid-afternoon light streaming into the room, and he was able to take stock of himself. He had been changed into clean, dry clothes, and was tucked tightly into the unfamiliar bed. He recognized the room now – it was one of Doctor Figg's rooms, kept for patients and the occasional guest. It was neat, clean, practical, and mostly unadorned.

"Where are my clothes?" Charles managed.

"Taken to be washed and dried, your Grace. Not to worry. Your valet has been here and intends to come home with a fresh change of clothes. Once I am satisfied that you are healthy enough to move, I believe you'll be taken home. You'll recover more quickly in your own bed, I'd warrant."

"Has my brother been notified? And my mother?"

"Yes to both. Her Grace the Dowager was given a sedative – she was quite upset, as you can imagine – and your brother is on his way, I am told. Now, your Grace, will you please stop worrying?"

I wish I could, Charles thought gloomily. "What of Mr Green?"

"The gentleman who rowed his boat into you? He's well, but understandably concerned. Frankly, I think that taking boats out on the lake in this deceptively cold weather was a mistake. It's too early in the year for swimming, and one might always find oneself swimming if one goes boating."

Charles grimaced. "I'm inclined to agree. Doctor, where are the rest of my things? Was there... was there a pocket watch among them?"

Doctor Figg paused, narrowing his eyes in an attempt to remember. "There was a watch in your pocket, I recall. The glass is cracked, I'm afraid, and it has stopped. It's a pretty, gold thing, I believe. I'm sure it can be fixed."

Charles swallowed. That was his own watch, the one he used every day, the one he had stuffed in his pocket before he left for the day.

That was naturally not the watch he was thinking of.

"Was a silver one found?" he managed. "Plain, with an engraved pattern on the lid and an inscription inside? I had it in my hand when the boat overturned."

Doctor Figg winced. "Ah. No, no such item has been found. I am sorry to say, your Grace, but it's probably at the bottom of the lake at the moment. Was it very valuable?"

"Sentimental value, mostly," Charles managed. He didn't speak again, the doctor continued bustling around the room.

He could remember the instant that the watch – Edmund's last gift – had gone shooting out of his hand into the dark water of the lake. He remembered how Lydia's eyes had widened with recognition when she saw it. He hadn't had the chance to show her the inscription and tell her the truth.

And now he never would, Charles knew that. He felt so weak it seemed likely he would spend days or even a full week in bed, recovering, by which time Lydia Waverly would be long gone, and his opportunity would be missed forever.

Perhaps it's for the best, he thought bleakly. *She can go on with her life, find a man more deserving. Enjoy London, and I can stay here and stew in my guilt.*

Hurrying footsteps along the hallway made him jump. Doctor Figg straightened up and glared at the door, ready to glower at whoever dared to enter. For one brilliant, breathless moment, Charles thought that it might be Lydia.

Of course it was not. The door opened and a breathless William staggered in.

"Charles!" he cried, dashing over to the bed. "Anne has the carriage, so I ran all the way here. What on earth happened? I'm his brother," he said briskly to Doctor Figg. "What did you do?"

"It was just a boating accident," Charles managed weakly. "Doctor Figg says that I will be fine."

William gave a sigh of relief, pulling up a stool. "What happened to your head?"

For the first time, Charles realized that a thick, white bandage was wound around his head. No doubt it looked rather comical, and something of an overkill for such a small cut.

At least, he hoped it was a small cut. Heaven knew that he didn't need any more scars.

"I banged my head on the boat, knocked myself unconscious," Charles answered. "I nearly drowned. Doctor, who got me out of the water? I can't recall a thing."

"Lord Fernwood, I believe."

"Ah, Henry." Charles allowed himself a small smile. "I hope Arabella is pleased with his heroics. I must thank him when I see him."

William sighed, shaking his head. "I can't leave you alone for half a day, can I, brother? I turn my back for a handful of hours and you're knocking yourself unconscious and nearly getting drowned into the bargain. I heard that Miss Waverly swam back to shore. Very heroic, I think. She must be a strong swimmer – you were a good way out."

Charles nodded. "Will, I... I lost the watch. The one Edmund gave me."

William's expression softened. "Oh, I am sorry. I know how much it meant to you."

"I can't believe I was so stupid."

William reached out and took his brother's hand. "People don't live in things, you know," he said, as kindly as he could. "Edmund was your friend, I know, and I'm sure you miss him. I know that watch meant a great deal to you, but it doesn't carry your memories of your friend. It's disappointing, but it's not as if you'll forget him."

"No," Charles murmured. "I suppose not."

In the ensuing silence, all three of them clearly heard the rattle of carriage wheels on the pavement outside. Frowning, Doctor Figg moved over to the window and peered out.

"A carriage is pulling up outside," he observed. "No visitors for you, I think, your Grace. Would you like me to go downstairs and tell them that you are well? I'm sure your friends are concerned."

William got up and moved across the room to stand beside the doctor.

"Oh, I say. It's Miss Waverly."

Charles sucked in a breath, eyes widening. "Miss Waverly? Are you sure, Will?"

"Quite sure."

Doctor Figg cast Charles a knowing look. "That's all very well, but I really can't countenance any visitors. Not today. No excitement for you, your Grace."

Charles swallowed hard, staring pleadingly at the doctor. "I really must talk to her."

"You can speak to her tomorrow."

"She'll be gone tomorrow."

William winced. "Yes, she is gong back to London tomorrow, along with her mother and friend."

Doctor Figg sighed heavily. "Very well, then. But no more than fifteen minutes, do you hear?"

Chapter Twenty-Five

Lydia was escorted down a narrow hallway by Doctor Figg himself, a severe-looking man whose pince-nez had left permanent red marks on his nose. It was clear that the good doctor was not pleased she was here but was willing to let her see Charles anyway.

"The Duke requires rest," he said peevishly, half to himself and half to Lydia. "He'll never recover if he has visitors at all hours of the day and night. Now, you're to speak in lowered voices, Miss Waverly. No excitement for him, no controversial topics. He must rest, you see?"

"I see," Lydia said. She was glad he hadn't insisted she promise to stay away from *controversial topics,* because then she would have had to lie.

The pocket watch was in her pocket, carefully cleaned and dried, and the heavy thing swung hard against her leg with every step. Nerves bubbled in Lydia's stomach.

The doctor opened a door in a pleasant, well-lit room which contained nothing more than a cupboard, a wash basin, a bed, and a nightstand.

And, of course, Charles himself.

The Duke lay in bed, covers pulled up almost to his chin. He looked pale and thin, and had a lumpy white bandage wrapped around his head. William sat on a stool at his bedside and rose to his feet as Lydia entered.

"Miss Waverly, hello," Charles managed weakly. "Forgive me for not rising when a lady enters the room."

She managed to smile back. "You're quite forgiven. How are you feeling? Are you well?"

"Sick, and I have a pounding headache. I daresay I swallowed half of the lake when I was underwater."

Lydia shivered. "You were under for a long time. Henry dived in and saved you."

"I know. He was quite the hero, I think."

"Mr Green was fairly sick with worry, you know. He wanted to come and see you, but Clara convinced him to let you rest."

"It's not Mr Green's fault. He should have told us he wasn't much good at rowing, but then, you and I should have been paying attention."

"I fear so," Lydia replied, then they sank into comfortable silence, the four of them shifting awkwardly.

Then William cleared his throat. "Doctor Figg, I wonder if I could talk with you privately, about my brother's treatment? Miss Waverly can keep him amused while we speak."

Doctor Figg frowned. "The two of them alone? Is that proper?"

"We'll only be a few moments," William said firmly, taking the doctor's arm and escorting him out. He paused at the door, glancing at first Charles and then Lydia, with an expression she could not quite read. Then he closed the door, and the two of them were left alone.

Silence fell over the room, heavy and seemingly unbreakable.

"I'm glad you're..."

"I was worried..."

They both started at once, and stopped at once, shifting uncomfortably.

Charles made an effort to pull himself into a sitting position in bed, wincing at the strain it must have put on his injured head. Lydia's heart thumped, and she wanted nothing more than to put her arms around him and hold him tight.

She didn't, of course, for a myriad of reasons. Not least of all the fact that she was here for answers.

Silently, she took out the silver pocket watch from her pocket, unwrapped the handkerchief it was carefully parceled in, and set the watch down where the Duke couldn't possibly miss it.

He stared at the watch for a long moment, then reached out gingerly, picking it up. He flipped open the lid – looking for the inscription, she thought – and closed it again with a sigh.

"Not lost, then," he said, his voice almost shaking with relief. "Not lost. I thought it was gone forever."

"My cousin, Edmund, gave you this," Lydia said, pleased at how calm and even her voice sounded. For now, at least. "I was with him when he bought it, before he left. You must have travelled together on your Tours. You came back on the ship that was to have brought him back. I found that out just today."

She wasn't sure what she'd expected. Denials, perhaps? It wasn't as if she were accusing him of cheating at cards.

Charles hung his head, nodding silently. Lydia let out a sigh.

"Why didn't you tell me? I would have loved to have known that you were Edmund's friend. We could have talked about him. This watch was what you were going to show me on the boat, wasn't it?

But you looked as though you were about to tell me bad news. I don't understand."

He closed his eyes, and his fingers tightened around the watch.

"You don't understand."

She narrowed her eyes. "Well, then, make me understand."

He drew in a few deep breaths, calming himself, preparing to speak. Lydia made herself wait patiently. He had the air of a man about to leap off a high cliff into the water below, which may or may not contain hidden rocks.

"I love you, Lydia Waverly," he said, all in a rush.

Well, she hadn't been expecting that. Lydia flinched, sucking in a surprised breath.

"I... what?"

"I love you, and I think perhaps you've guessed that already. I thought – I hoped – that you loved me, or at least cared for me. But when you find out what happened between Edmund and I..." he trailed off, and a feeling of dread settled in the pit of Lydia's stomach.

"Why, are you going to tell me you pushed him overboard?" she asked, only half joking.

He didn't smile, only shook his head.

"I'll tell you, since you deserve to know."

He began to speak. The story was one that Lydia had imagined many times, but there was more detail to it than she had expected. In her mind, she had seen Edmund standing on deck while waves crashed over the sides of the ship. She imagined him with his arms stretched wide, head tilted back, splashed with spray, laughing. It was the kind of ridiculous thing Edmund would do.

Charles talked about their Grand Tour, about how his father's failing health had summoned him back. How Edmund had agreed to accompany him, even though he could have continued his own travels. He talked about an uneventful journey, only to be broken by a sudden storm. He explained how Edmund and he had gone below decks, where it was safe, only for Edmund to peer up through the hatch to get a look at the storm.

"I should have stopped him doing that," Charles whispered. "I could have stopped it all there."

"He... he went on deck? During the storm?" Lydia asked, breathless.

Charles nodded. "A sailor was about to be washed overboard. We knew him, we'd joked with him and played cards and dice during the trip. Edmund went to save him. I should have stopped him there, too, but I didn't. We got the sailor to safety, then the wave hit."

He squeezed his eyes closed. He talked about the feeling of the wave, the power of the sea, until Lydia could almost taste the brine herself. He talked about Edmund, pulled overboard like a paper doll in a hurricane. He talked about the rope tied around his waist, how he'd gone over to get him. His eyes screwed up tighter when he described how he had almost had Edmund's hand, *almost*, then they were pulled under, and Charles was dragged back aboard. His hand fluttered up to touch his scar, almost unconsciously.

"So, you see," he said flatly, "There were many opportunities I could have taken to save Edmund. If I'd stopped him going on deck or insisted that they send me back out into the sea, I'm sure that I could have saved him. If I'd swum just a little faster…" he trailed off, voice clogged with tears.

Lydia felt like crying herself. To think that Edmund was so close to being saved. A finger's breadth away… she dashed away a tear with one knuckle.

"I'm glad… glad he wasn't alone," Lydia heard herself say. "I imagined him alone on deck, swept into the sea, with nobody noticing until it was too late. Nobody knowing exactly where he'd disappeared. I never imagined…" she faltered, shaking her head. She thought about Charles, a rough ship's rope cutting into his waist, ploughing his way determinedly through a rough, icy sea, waves so high that he could not even see the ship he'd come from.

"I'm glad you were there." She finished.

Charles' head came up. "You must resent me," he said flatly. "I should have saved him. I know I should have done it. I could have done more."

She shook her head. "I… I think that you did all you could, Charles. I miss Edmund, I miss him every day. He was like a brother to me, and I don't believe a time will ever come when I don't think of him. I wish you could have saved him, but knowing that he died saving somebody else, rather than simply standing on deck in a storm, for heaven's sake, is… well, it's more comforting than I thought it would be."

He stared at her, confused. "But you must be angry. You must…"

"I *must* be nothing, Charles," she interrupted, smiling wryly. "It seems to me that neither of us have ever come to terms with Edmund's death. I believe that you tried your best to save him. And I also believe that you *don't* believe it. I think perhaps you've spent the time since then torturing yourself with guilt, which would explain why you expected me to react so strongly."

Charles swallowed hard. "My mother said that I should not blame myself. William and Anne said that I did all I could. I didn't believe them, I thought that they were trying to console me, I thought..." he trailed off when Lydia leaned over, placing her hand on his.

"Edmund would never have blamed you," she said softly. "I know him well enough to say that with confidence. Never. And I don't blame you, either. For what it's worth, I absolve you of guilt."

He smiled weakly, and she could have sworn she saw colour rising back into his cheeks.

"Do you know, Sir Gregory tried to blackmail me over this? He threatened to tell you about it all. I already knew that you deserved the truth, but..."

Lydia snorted. "Yes, that sounds like something Sir Gregory would try. I do hope you didn't pay him."

"I certainly did not. Henry frightened him off."

"Henry, eh?" she said, thoughtfully. "Well, who would have thought he had it in him?"

"Let me tell you, I do not intend to get on the wrong side of *him* anytime soon."

She laughed softly, shaking her head. Her hand was still resting on his, and he twisted his hand around so that they were palm to palm, fingers interlaced. The warmth of his skin soaked through her, and Lydia shivered.

"I... I think I have loved you since I first saw you, Lydia," Charles said, his voice soft and almost uncertain. "But I was so afraid that once you knew I could have saved Edmund, you would reject me. I was a coward, I'm afraid."

She smiled. "I'm not sure a man who ties a rope around his waist and dives into the sea in the middle of a storm to save his friend could ever be called a *coward*. Just because you couldn't save him, doesn't mean that you didn't *try*. We can remember Edmund together, you and I. And..." she hesitated, glancing at the closed door, suddenly aware of how unladylike she was about to be, "... and for what it is worth, Charles, I love you too."

He glanced sharply up at her, eyes widening. "Truly?"

"Truly. And if Edmund were here, I think we would have found ourselves pushed together a great deal earlier."

He snorted. "Oh, yes. Edmund had *no* patience."

"No," she said, smiling, bittersweet tears stinging her eyes. "He certainly did not."

One Week Later

Welcome to the Marriage Mart! As the Season nears its height, London is crammed from top to bottom with Persons of Interest. There are half a dozen balls a day, fifty musical evenings on any given evening, countless informal visits and soirees, a hundred picnics a week regardless of the weather, and fashionable people promenade so much in the Park that their walking shoes are quite worn-out.

On this note, we can only hope that the pretty ladies and rich gentlemen who populate our world of Society can keep up their stamina until the end.

Let us spare a moment for the newcomers, the green debutantes who haven't the sense to join the Season halfway and are already flagging. Poor Miss Staple, a most promising young lady and voted the Diamond of the Season, is said to have collapsed from exhaustion at Lady Worthington's ball only last night. Let us pray for a speedy recovery, as do the three eligible gentlemen jostling for her favour.

The Season reaches its pinnacle in a flurry of engagements and marriages. The whole town is talking about the marvelous match between his Grace the Duke of Northwood and the modest Miss Lydia Waverly, who have joined the Season only a few days ago. Their engagement announcement appeared in the Gazette yesterday, to the consternation of all, and the disappointment of many suitable young ladies who had their eye on the young, unmarried Duke.

Miss Waverly, whose infamous punch-spilling incident outraged the entire Society, is every bit as outspoken an unorthodox as she was last year, to the delight of this author and the horror of various matrons and hostesses. To her, we say – good luck! Good luck, Miss Lydia Waverly, soon to be Duchess of Northwood. May your married life be as eventful as your single life. Oh, and do avoid boating trips on choppy lakes – details to follow.

***

In other news, a rather scandalous situation has sprung up between one Sir Gregory – the same Sir Gregory recently accused of cheating at cards at Mr Brummell's genteel soiree, despite Mr Brummell insisting that Sir Gregory was never given an invitation – and the recently engaged Miss Jane Tabitha. Mrs Tabitha and Sir Gregory are said to have eloped, and if word is to be believed, they are in fact *now married at Gretna Green, the scene of so many shocking marriages.*

However, further news has surfaced, unearthed by this modest author in person. Miss Jane Tabitha, although claiming to be a great heiress, is in fact in possession of no more than a thousand pounds, a large part of which has been claimed by creditors and debts of honour in London. It is said that Miss Tabitha has an extended and shockingly vulgar family attached to herself, who might ensure that she receives gallant treatment at the hands of her new husband.

We must hope that Sir Gregory did not fancy himself snatching up an heiress, as all poor Miss Tabitha is likely to inherit are debts. We suspect that London's newest and most scandalous married couple shall begin their life of wedded bliss on something of a sour note and may indeed soon come to regret their choices.

This author waits to report developments as they happen to you, our dear readers, who wait with scarcely less interest to learn about them. The Seasons come and go, but Society does not forget. Gossip might well make the world go round, and in this column, we do our best to share it with you.

Epilogue

One Month Later

Not surprisingly, the scandal sheets had followed the wedding preparations very closely with great glee, missing no detail.

Lydia had expected no less.

And now the great day was here, and she found that she didn't much care what the papers had to say about it all.

She eyed her reflection unsteadily, not sure what to make of the vision that greeted her.

The London Season was well underway and going quite well. Of course, with her engagement and upcoming marriage, Lydia didn't have to participate much. Arabella and Henry were in town, and the scandal sheets had mentioned their 'miraculously revived marriage' in incredulous tones. Lydia ignored them, and she knew that Arabella and Henry did the same.

Her bridesmaids were outside the bedroom door, making last-minute alterations to their gowns and flowers. She had chosen Arabella as Matron of Honour, with Clara and the two Misses Bolts as ordinary bridesmaids.

Lady Pemshire was in Lydia's room, making the finishing touches to her hair.

"Something old, something new," she murmured. "Something borrowed, something blue. Do you have them all, darling?"

Lydia smiled at her mother through her reflection. "My gown is new, but the jewelry is old – yours, dear Mama – and my something borrowed is the ribbon from Arabella's wedding. The something blue comes from Lady Everard, in fact. Or perhaps those are the something borrowed, too?" She reached up to touch the blue glass flowers decorating her hair.

Lady Everard had not been pleased with the engagement. Charles had told Lydia that she had earlier told him that she would not countenance the marriage and would never give her blessing.

That, of course, was before her son nearly drowned, and before her other son, William, was able to talk a little sense into her.

"Lady Everard does not like me," Lydia conceded, "But she *tolerates* me, and that is already an improvement. I have high hopes of making her like me one day."

Lady Pemshire snorted. "Fancy not liking my darling girl. You're the daughter-in-law every mother should want."

"Well, yes, Mama, you're my mother. You should think that."

Chuckling, Lady Pemshire bent down to kiss her. "You look beautiful, my darling girl."

"I feel so nervous. Should I feel nervous, Mama?"

"Of course. It's perfectly natural. Marriage is rather a serious occasion, and it marks a great chance in one's life. It shouldn't be taken lightly, and it's good to have serious thoughts about it. And don't forget, darling – the wedding is one day, but the marriage is one's whole life."

Lydia nodded, drawing in a deep breath. "I think I'm ready to go, Mama. Just... just another moment, please? Could I be by myself for a while?"

Lady Pemshire nodded, as if she knew what Lydia was thinking, and gave her one last kiss on the cheek. She left, softly closing the door behind her, and Lydia let out a long breath.

Opening her jewelry box, she drew out a plain silver necklace, decorated with a neat twist of sapphire as a pendant.

The necklace had been a gift from Edmund. He loved getting gifts, and she'd lost track of the necklaces, books, and trinkets he'd bought her over the years. It made perfect sense that he would buy his friend a beautifully engraved pocket watch as a parting gift. It touched her that Charles had treasured it so much.

This necklace, though, was her favourite. If she had to pick a favourite. She carefully tied it around her neck and smoothed her palm over the pendant.

This is my something blue, she decided. *So that Edmund is with me on my wedding day after all.*

He'd always joked that she would require an extra-wide aisle, so that both Lord Pemshire and Edmund could walk her down to the altar.

I'll think of you, dear cousin, she thought. *But then, so will Charles. You'll never be forgotten. Not ever.*

Drawing in a deep, invigorating breath, she got to her feet. It was almost time. It was a bride's right to be late on her wedding day, of course, but not *too* late.

Opening the door, she was greeted by the beaming faces of her bridesmaids and her mother, all waiting expectantly.

"I'm ready," Lydia said, somewhat breathless. "Shall we go?"

***

The church was full to the brim, of course. Aside from the usual friends and acquaintances, just about everybody wanted to see the marriage of a *real duke*. It seemed odd that Lydia would walk out of the church as a *duchess*. Almost laughable, really.

They took a few moments at the door to rearrange Lydia's skirts – why that mattered, she wasn't quite sure, but apparently it did – and then it was time.

The congregation rose to their feet, all beaming and craning their necks to see the bride. Swallowing hard, Lydia lifted her head and began to walk down the aisle. She saw a few familiar faces as she passed. Lady Deane, who was not smiling and looked a little petulant. Dowager Fernwood, who was notably *not* sitting with her daughter-in-law and her son. The Bolts family, all grinning and nodding encouragingly at her.

Arabella and Henry stood arm in arm, smiling proudly at her. For a split second, Lydia could have sworn she saw flashing green eyes and a head of chestnut hair in the crowd, eyes brimming with mischief, but then the moment passed, and Edmund was not there.

And then that did not matter anymore, because she was at the altar, and Charles was waiting for her, resplendent in a brocade suit designed to match her white-and-gold gown.

"You look beautiful," he whispered.

She smiled at him. Her heart, which had been fluttering in her ribcage like a bird trying to escape its cage, suddenly slowed. This was where she was meant to be.

"Thank you," she said.

"Ready to face the music, Duchess?"

She grinned. "I suppose I'm as ready as I'll ever be."

Hand in hand, they turned towards the priest, and Charles gave him a nod, the sign to begin.

"Dearly beloved…" the priest began.

Extended Epilogue

Three Years Later

"Edmund! Edmund, are you ready?" Lydia called up the stairs.

"Coming, Mama!" came the childish reply.

It was a fine day. Summer was here, and Lydia found herself greatly relieved that she could enjoy it out in the countryside, instead of sweltering in the heat of London.

The Season was going on, no doubt, but Lydia didn't much care to join it. Even Arabella's taste for Society had faded in recent years. Not altogether – Henry and she intended to spend a few months in London again this year, as they did every year, but Arabella was coming to love the months of peace in the countryside even more than Henry enjoyed the months spent with his friends in London.

Of course, they would all have to go to London this year, for Clara's wedding. Society had not quite forgiven Mr Green for driving his boat into Lydia and Charles, although *they* had forgiven him immediately. No doubt the scandal sheets would remark upon it even as they discussed his marriage to Clara.

Oh, well.

A smiling, chubby-cheeked two-year-old boy appeared at the top of the stairs, hand in hand with his nurse. He beamed at the sight of his mother, and Lydia held out her arms to him.

The little boy came bouncing down the stairs, and Lydia swept him up into her arms.

"Are you ready for the picnic?" she asked, smiling. He nodded furiously.

"I want to show Uncle Henry and Uncle William my pond. There are newts."

"Yes, but you must keep the newts away from Aunt Anne, yes? She doesn't much like them."

Edmund nodded obediently and began to babble on about the various beasties and creatures he would seek out in 'his pond' – which was a large, knee-deep body of water beside the hollow where they preferred to set up their picnic. Lydia uncharitably thought of 'the pond' as an oversized puddle, but in an effort to prove her wrong, Edmund constantly unearthed more and more forms of wildlife.

Carrying him in her arms, Lydia walked outside onto the terrace. It was mid-morning, and the heat of the day had not quite settled in. Even so, warmth radiated up from the paving stones beneath her feet, and the sun beat down hotly from a pure blue, cloudless sky.

It was going to be a hot day, and no mistake.

The nurse followed behind them, carrying Edmund's bucket and net. They passed footmen going to and from the picnic area, bearing hampers and various dishes. It wasn't anywhere near luncheon, but Lydia's mouth watered already.

They left the terrace and walked across the grass, heading towards distant trees and a shimmer of the lake in the distance. Once they were over a small rise, the hollow opened up in front of them, laid with blankets.

Charles was already there, deep in conversation with Henry. William was lying on his back, apparently asleep, and Anne and Arabella were talking.

When Charles saw Lydia and Edmund appear, he climbed to his feet, grinning.

"There is my sweet boy! And my sweet lady, too."

Lydia rolled her eyes at that, although she couldn't quite manage to suppress a smile.

"Here, take your son. He's been dreaming of splashing through that puddle all day."

"Ah, in search of newts and toads?" Charles crowed, taking Edmund and tossing him up into the air, making him squeal in delight.

"Just don't let him take a bucket full of frogs home again!" Lydia scolded, grinning. She found herself a spot on the blankets beside Arabella and settled herself down.

Charles was entirely in love with his little boy. The idea of parenthood had terrified Lydia – as it rightly should, in her opinion – but Edmund was perfect.

She was glad they'd had a son, so Edmund could be remembered this way. Everybody's eyes had misted over when she told them what her new baby boy was to be named. It was *right*. It was right, she knew it.

Lydia's hand drifted to her middle, where her stomach had not yet begun to swell, but it would. She was with child again. Of course, it was rather too soon to tell people – there was no rush, after all – but she had a feeling that it would be a girl. A boy would be just as nice, but still, the idea that it was a girl had lodged itself firmly in Lydia's mind.

She leaned back on her elbows, shading her eyes against the sun, and watched Edmund and Charles splash through the pond.

The two-year-old twins, Roberta and Thomasin, came squealing out of some nearby shrubs, ignoring the shouts of Arabella, their poor mother, and went diving into the pond too, splashing cheerfully around.

William and Anne's little boy, George, was three years old, and much preferred to sit quietly with his adoring parents and look at picture books.

Perfect, Lydia thought, smiling to herself. *This is perfect.*

"I hear that Clara has asked you to be her Matron of Honour," Arabella observed. "Congratulations, by the way. I'm just a regular old... what would you call me? A Brides-matron?"

"I have no idea," Lydia said, laughing. "I'm just glad that Clara had finally found someone she cares for. Mr Green and she took their time."

"I think it took him a while to recover from that boating incident," Arabella remarked, wincing. "That probably *was* an embarrassing incident for him, the poor man."

"It was funny, though," Lydia pointed out. The two women chuckled for a moment, watching their children play.

"Do... do you know what today is?" Arabella asked hesitantly, after a moment or two.

Lydia swallowed hard. "Yes, I do. Today is the day Edmund was supposed to arrive home, all those years ago. It was the day the ship docked, and we learned that he was dead. Good gracious, has it really been that long? Sometimes I can't believe it. Sometimes I..." she faltered, but pressed on. "Sometimes I can't quite believe that he's gone. I expect to look up and see him coming in through the door."

She closed her eyes, almost hearing Edmund's boot heels ring out on the stone floor. She could hear his laugh, echoing through the halls, and could see his wide, lopsided smile.

I miss him, she thought, and her heart ached miserably.

She had thought that with a marriage and a child, her grief would go away. Lydia knew better now, of course. Grief was a strange thing, and it never truly went away. Edmund had been her brother, in everything but name, and she could no more remove him from her head and heart than she could fly.

But isn't that a good thing? Lydia thought. *Why would I ever want to forget him?*

She was interrupted by squeals, and glanced over to see Edmund doing his level best to kick water onto his father. For a two-year-old boy, it was not easy, but he was certainly putting a great deal of effort into it.

Lydia smiled and laughed, shading her eyes. Soon the sun would be at its highest, and it would be too hot to picnic. They would go inside into the cool of the drawing room, talk and laugh with each other until the sun went down and the day was almost done. It was a strange, nostalgic feeling, and Lydia wasn't entirely sure where it had come from.

Did it matter, though?

Happy, she thought. *I'm happy. No more numbness, no more misery, no more wallowing in grief. Mama was right.*

The children came splashing out of the pond, laughing and squealing, and went darting off, ostensibly to make mud pies or something equally messy. A breathless Charles staggered over and dropped heavily down onto the blanket beside his wife.

"They're so energetic," he gasped. "I think perhaps I'll take a nap. William has the right idea."

She glanced over at him, and he grinned at her, taking her hand and lifting it to his lips.

"Your hand is freezing," she remarked with a soft smile. "What on earth have you been doing?"

"That pond is deceptively cold. Now, I was thinking, when we get back inside, perhaps you and I could perform a little music? You can sing, and I could play, if you like?"

A smile spread over her face. "Yes, I would like that a lot, I think."

Charles beamed and stretched up to kiss her. Lydia kissed him back, letting her fingertip trail down the familiar, ridged line of his scar, the one that made him more handsome than she could ever have thought, and the world melted away.

The End

Printed in Great Britain
by Amazon